9/14

Praise for *Ski*   P9-AQO-103

"A delightful mystery with laugh-out-loud moments, a touch of romance, and a fun, sassy style. Readers will enjoy every moment spent in Otter Lake."
—Diane Kelly, award-winning author

"A frolicking good time . . . with a heroine who challenges Stephanie Plum for the title of funniest sleuth."
—Denise Swanson, *New York Times* bestselling author

"Time spent with the folks in Otter Lake is well worthwhile, with writing that is witty, contemporary, and winning."
—*Kirkus Reviews*

"A wonderfully entertaining read!"   —*RT Book Reviews*

Also by Auralee Wallace

Skinny Dipping with Murder

Pumpkin

PICKING

With

MURDER

Auralee Wallace

St. Martin's Paperbacks

This is a work of fiction. All of the characters, organizations, and events portrayed in this novel are either products of the author's imagination or are used fictitiously.

PUMPKIN PICKING WITH MURDER

Copyright © 2016 by Auralee Wallace.

All rights reserved.

For information address St. Martin's Press, 175 Fifth Avenue, New York, NY 10010.

ISBN: 978-1-250-07778-3

Our books may be purchased in bulk for promotional, educational, or business use. Please contact your local bookseller or the Macmillan Corporate and Premium Sales Department at 1-800-221-7945, extension 5442, or by e-mail at MacmillanSpecialMarkets@macmillan.com.

Printed in the United States of America

St. Martin's Paperbacks edition / September 2016

St. Martin's Paperbacks are published by St. Martin's Press, 175 Fifth Avenue, New York, NY 10010.

10 9 8 7 6 5 4 3 2 1

For my amazing children.
You guys are the best mini-cheerleaders
a mom could have.

Acknowledgments

First, I would like to express my gratitude to my editor, Holly Ingraham, who never forgets where the bodies are buried. Your insightful comments always leave me asking, *Now, why didn't I think of that?* I'm so lucky to have your eyes on my work.

Thank you, also, to everyone at St. Martin's Press— Danielle Christopher and Monika Roe for my beautiful covers, Allison Ziegler for answering all my questions, Jennie Conway for her cheery emails that keep me on track, and Laura Jorstad for her detailed copy edits.

Many thanks, also, to my agent and dream-maker, Natalie Lakosil. Erica Bloom never would have found a home without you.

Thanks to my parents, friends, and extended family for their day-to-day support. I'm pretty sure you don't have to keep buying every book of mine you see in stock, but I appreciate it nonetheless! Special thanks to Melanie for championing Otter Lake from the beginning and for leading me out into the world of social media.

As always, I need to send my undying gratitude to Andrea—because nothing much happens without

Andrea—and to my husband and three children, who bring me coffee every morning. You guys make all the difference!

Finally, thank you to all the readers who have given me a shot to make them laugh. It would be pretty quiet without you.

Chapter One

"Okay," I said, stepping off the dock onto the cracked asphalt of the parking lot. "I'm here. Can you please tell me what's going on now?"

"Nope," the voice on the other end of my phone said. "It's a surprise. You have to see it."

I sighed and turned my face up to the warm autumn sun. "You know I don't have really great experiences with surprises. In fact, I pretty much hate them. Especially when I'm . . . here."

The voice chuckled on the other end.

Yup, here I was. Home again in Otter Lake, *Live Free or Die*, New Hampshire.

Otter Lake was a special kind of place. It had long docks stretching into lakes, nights with a billion stars, and, this time of year, crisp air tinged with ripened apples. It was also a place where everybody knew your name . . . and your family, where you lived, maybe what you had for breakfast, and most likely the reason behind you picking up that prescription the other day. And if they didn't know any of those things, it wouldn't take them long to find out. It was just that kind of town.

On my last trip home, I had dealt with a lot of the issues that had kept me away from Otter Lake for nearly eight years—most of them stemming from a bizarre prank-gone-wrong that involved me standing half naked in front of the entire town with a geriatric beaver at the annual Raspberry Social, but I had put all that behind me . . . and wanted to keep that kind of thing behind me. Hence my aversion to surprises.

"Home, Erica. It's your home. You can say it. It won't hurt you," Freddie said. "And just so you know, this surprise is awesome because it's not about you. It's about me. Although," he added, drawing out the word, "it could be about you if you played your cards right."

"Yeah . . . no." I shook my head and headed toward the crowds of people filling the street. Freddie Ng was my newly reinstated best friend from high school. We had always gotten along as the oddballs in Otter Lake. Me, because my mother ran a spiritual retreat for women that focused on veganism, yoga, and goddess power—which really sounded like a description of witchcraft to a lot of people around here. Freddie, because he had a trifecta of *otherness* going for him—gay, Asian, and mega-rich. Nobody knew what the hell to do with him. Me included. But it wasn't because of any of those things. No. It was Freddie's . . . zest for life that had me worried. Mainly because his big, big plans usually included me in some way whether I liked it or not.

Freddie and I had hung out a lot last time I was in town, and while it had been really good to reconnect, I couldn't help but think that when we did get together, in person, we got ourselves into situations that we would never normally get ourselves into. Well, at least I wouldn't. Hard to tell with Freddie. When Freddie told me a couple of days ago about his big surprise, I figured it could be anything from wanting to me to check out his new cell phone to showing off his new pet monkey. Now I was thinking that whatever this surprise was, it was definitely on the pet-monkey side of the spectrum. And I did not have time for pet monkeys this visit. Oh no, I was going to be too busy with other . . . stuff. Good stuff. Sheriff stuff.

Time to nip this thing in the bud.

"While that's very sweet of you to include me in whatever this surprise is, I'm going to preemptively have to decline taking any part," I said, skipping around a little dog on a leash making a nip for my heel. Man, the whole town was out today. "Thanks, though."

"But you're going to love it!"

"No. Nope. No, thank you. Not this week."

"Oh come on," Freddie said. "You don't even know what you're turning down."

"No," I repeated. I may have even half pointed at the phone. "You will not draw me into any of your tomfooleries this visit."

"Tomfooleries?" I could practically hear Freddie blinking his eyes on the other side of the phone. "You did not just say *tomfooleries*."

I shook my head as I picked a toy stuffie off the ground and passed it to the outstretched hands of a toddler harnessed in a stroller. The mother thanked me. I was pretty sure I went to school with her, but she was a few years ahead. I gave her a smile. She smiled back . . . like I wasn't infamous in this town. This was good.

"Besides, I'm not the one who gets us up to the *monkeyshines*," Freddie went on.

I stopped walking. "Is this like a thing? Are we doing this now?"

He ignored me and plowed on. "And, besides, you're the one who has the knack for stumbling across dead bodies."

I closed my eyes, but that only gave me a clearer vision of Dickie Morrison lying at the bottom of a well impaled

by a weenie skewer. Dickie had not been a great guy by
any stretch of the imagination, but nobody deserved that.
It had happened during my last visit and had set Freddie
and me off on a quasi-murder-investigation. I had actually
originally booked this week off—I worked as a court ste-
nographer back in Chicago—to testify at the trial, but
much to my relief the murderer had pled guilty, so I was
off the hook. "Well, I won't be finding any bodies this time
around. This is going to be a nice, normal, relaxing visit.
I'll see my mom. Eat some pumpkin pie—"

"Kiss some sheriffs," Freddie added, mocking my list-
making voice.

I stopped a moment then side-shuffled around a child
clutching a red balloon—a shade that probably matched
the color of my cheeks. "Yes, I plan to see Grady." A lot
of Grady actually. Maybe more of Grady than I had ever
seen before . . . if I was lucky. "What's wrong with that?"

"Nothing. Nothing," Freddie said quickly with a laugh.
"I mean your voice is all nervous like a teenage girl right
now, which is hilarious, but nothing."

I half sighed, half growled. Grady Forrester was the
town sheriff, my adolescent crush, and winner of Otter
Lake's most beautiful baby contest three years in a row
back in the day—he had just been that beautiful. Still was.
He also happened to have one of those man smiles that
made your knees go weak and your brain go stupid. Grady
and I had a history of, well, chemistry—the explosive kind
of chemistry—that always seemed to prevent us from getting things right. But that too was going to change this
visit. Grady had taken the entire week off to be with me,
and we were planning to spend it figuring out what was
what between us. We had never made it this far in our relationship before, and I found myself wanting *something*
to happen so badly that I was too terrified to even think
about it, let alone talk about it.

I stopped again in the middle of the sidewalk, forcing people to move around me like a stream around a boulder. "Can we just not talk about Grady. It's not like . . ." I began, then stopped to find my words. "I mean, we're not . . ." I stopped again. "Can we please just drop it?"

Freddie laughed some more.

I ignored him, instead opting to take in the sight of Otter Lake's transformed Main Street. Colorful banners fluttered from every lamppost as people milled in the streets. A few shops had set up tables outside showcasing wares—pies, tackle, and snowmobile gear were all popular items—and half-barrel planters overflowing with orange, pink, and maroon mums marked the corners of every intersection—all two of them. I looked up at the huge banner stretching across the street.

WELCOME TO OTTER LAKE'S FALL FESTIVAL!

I couldn't help but smile as the sound of calliope music reached my ears. Finally a town event that didn't have a traumatizing memory to go along with it. "Hey, so— Whoa."

"What?" Freddie asked.

I couldn't answer at first. I just shook my head for a moment. I was surprised I hadn't seen it sooner given that . . . *it* was about the size of the Ferris wheel. The bright sun had caused just the right amount of glare. But now . . . now it was impossible not to see it. "The berry. What happened to the berry?"

A few months ago MRG—colloquially known as Many Rich Guys, the development company trying to turn Otter Lake into a cottage playground for the very rich—had erected a giant wooden raspberry with a cartoon happy face over the town for Otter Lake's annual Raspberry Social. It was meant to be gesture of good faith to reassure the town that the development company's presence wouldn't change the local flavor of the town—and, of course, it did just the opposite.

Freddie chuckled. "Terrifying, isn't it?"

I nodded, then realized Freddie couldn't see me. "Yeah, *terrifying* is the right word." As if the smiling monster raspberry threatening to flatten Otter Lake hadn't been bad enough, it looked as though somebody had made some *changes* to it for the Fall Festival. "What happened?"

"Well, MRG hasn't hired a new PR person since Candace left, and no one really knew who to talk to about the berry. It was kind of Candace's berry." He paused a moment. "That sounds wrong. Anyway, someone at the high school thought it might be a good art project for the students. You know, turn it into a cute pumpkin for the fair."

I blinked a few times. The sun was making my eyes water. "That's supposed to be a pumpkin?"

"Yeah, well, I don't think they used enough coats of the orange paint, so the red just kept bleeding through."

Yes, *bleeding* would be the right word.

"We're voting on whether or not we should have an exorcism at town hall next week."

"You are not!"

Freddie laughed again. "I guess you'll have to stick around to find out."

I dragged my eyes from the monstrosity looming over the town and resumed walking toward the entrance for the fair. "I'm at the gate. Hang on a sec," I said, pulling out money from my pocket to pay an older gentleman at the entrance booth to get in. I recognized him, but I couldn't quite remember his name. The people who organized the fair were all community volunteers. I then held out the hand holding my phone for my entrance bracelet. It wasn't exactly polite in Otter Lake to be talking on the phone when real live people were in front of you. A fact that was made all the more apparent by Freddie's voice calling, "Heeelllooo? Heeelllooo?" from my hand.

"Sorry," I said to the man.

He flashed me a half-pitying, half-disdainful smile.

"Right." I walked on. "Okay, I'm in," I said bringing the phone up to my ear. "So where are you?"

"By the Ferris wheel."

"Got it." I walked past the deep-fried-everything stand, plugging my ear with my index finger. I was getting closer to the rides, and all the people screaming was making it hard to hear. "I'm almost there. Where exactly are you?"

"Keep walking."

I sidestepped around and through the throngs of people, making my way to the lineup underneath the giant wheel. Wow, a lot of people had made it to opening day. "Okay, seriously, I don't see you."

"You're getting closer."

"Stop it," I said, getting up on my toes to scan the crowd. "You sound like a serial killer."

Suddenly I felt someone move up behind me. "Boo!"

I spun around then blinked a few times.

"Well," Freddie said, spreading his arms wide, "what do you think?

I squinted. "Why are you dressed like a state trooper from . . . I want to say the 'seventies?" Actually with the aviator glasses and half-grown-in mustache I wanted to say he looked like a porn star dressed as a state trooper from the 1970s, but I didn't want to set him off.

Freddie brought his shoulders together in a self-hug of excitement. "Awesome, right? I found it in a thrift store. I had to fight a vacationing hipster for it. I hate hipsters. They try to make everything that's awesome ironic. I wanted to wear the star badge too," he said, looking down at the right breast of his shirt. You could still see the faded outline of the star that had been there. "Grady wouldn't let me, though. But this is just my daytime outfit. At night I wear one of those black pullover sweaters that zips up to the chin."

"Um," I said, squinting at him. "I think you've lost me. What exactly is going on here?"

He looped he thumbs around his belt buckle and swayed on his feet. "Erica Bloom, you are looking at the newly in-stated CEO of Otter Lake Security."

I cocked my head. "CEO of what now?"

"It's my new job," he said with a big smile.

"What? Why?" I couldn't seem to uncock my head. "What happened to Madame F?" Last time I had been in town, Freddie was telling fortunes on the Internet. He seemed to like it. Had an outfit for that job too.

"Oh, Madame F was my old life." He waved a hand at the idea. "You knew I was thinking along these lines, especially after we did such a good job solving Dickie's murder."

"Again, we didn't really solve it."

"Technicalities," he said, blowing out a puff of air. "Anyway, the next logical step was to become a private eye."

"Obviously." I squinted at him again and said, "But I thought you were going to just become an author of pri-vate eye novels?"

A satisfied smile came over his face. "Why write about it, when you can do it?"

"O-kay," I said, drawing out the word.

"Besides, there's plenty of time to write about it in my memoirs later."

"Of course."

"Sadly, it turns out there's a whole bunch of rules about becoming a private investigator." He flared his nostrils with disgust. "Like work experience."

"Right."

"But it's not like there were any private security companies around Otter Lake where I could apply for a job. Besides I don't really see myself as an *employee* per se."

I waited.

"So I started my own."

"Really?" I asked, dropping my chin to my chest.

"Really."

"You can just do that?"

"Well," Freddie said, shaking his head and looking up at the sky, "Grady had some issues with it at first—maybe still has one or two—but he can't fight the people, and the people love me."

"He . . . he didn't mention any of this on the phone, and since when do the people love you?"

"You don't have to sound so surprised."

"Sorry."

He cut me a look. "Yeah, the town was so grateful that you and I solved Dickie's murder that they thought the whole thing was a great idea."

I scratched the side of my head just as a hand clapped me on the back. "Good to have you home, Erica," said a booming male voice. I stumbled a step or two forward before I could turn to see a large man, trailing scents of nicotine and grease, walking past me with the flow of the crowd.

"See what I mean?" Freddie said.

"Was that Mr. Smith from the body shop?"

"It was. And notice how he didn't call you Boobsie Bloom?"

"I don't think he's ever spoken to me."

"That's because before you were just the daughter of the wingy mom. The girl who flashed her boobs that one time at the Raspberry Social. You, not your mom, I mean."

"Thanks. I remember."

"Not that I'd put it past ol' Summer. But she'd do it as a some sort of statement—*Free the Turtles! They've suffered too long!*" Freddie said putting a fist in the air. "I digress. The point is, now you're a hero . . . or maybe *sidekick* is a more accurate term." He waved a hand at me. "We can work all that out later." Freddie turned to walk the midway and gestured for me to follow.

I skipped a few steps after him.

"So what do you think?" he asked when I caught up to him.

It seemed harmless enough. There really wasn't much crime in Otter Lake, and it was probably good for Freddie to get out of the house—he had hermit tendencies. And yet the whole thing really did seem to have a reckless vibe to it. "I'm still trying to figure out what to say."

"Just say you're jealous. That always makes me feel good."

"Who's paying you to do all this?"

"The town! Haven't you been listening? Towns hire private security all the time." Suddenly Freddie moved quickly to step in front of a teenage boy. The kid stopped in his tracks, looking mildly concerned. Freddie pointed to an empty french fry carton lying in the dirt a few feet behind the kid. The teen held his gaze for a moment, then turned, picked it up, and threw it in the trash can. Freddie gave him a nod then walked back over to me, holding his stern face. As he got closer, I watched him close his eyes and whisper, "Power." He then flashed me a smile, and we continued walking.

"Well," I said, somewhat surprised to feel a smile spread across my face, "this is not at all what I expected, but . . . I'm happy for you, Freddie."

"You are?"

"Yeah." I really was too. This wasn't a bad surprise at all.

"You're not going to be all stressed out and concerned?"

"No." I felt my eyebrows instantly try to furrow, but I told them to stand down. "Why would I be?"

"Because it's what you do."

"Okay, I'll admit I stumbled a little when you brought up the whole surprise thing," I said, finding my smile again. "But really, since last visit, I don't worry as much as I used to. I've resolved a lot of my stuff. The Erica you're thinking of is the *old* Erica."

"I thought the old Erica was the new Erica who came back to town last time, all responsible and grown up."

I looked up to the bright-blue sky and shook my head. "We both know that wasn't sustainable. But what I can do is stay out of trouble. And maybe not expect the worst all the time. This surprise of yours proves it. I have come to realize that perhaps I have a bit of a knee-jerk reaction to stress. At times I might even have a temper when, you know, people I love are threatened."

"Yeah, your bar fight at the Salty Dawg last visit really made that clear."

I ignored him. "Last visit? I still had a lot of stuff to work out. I couldn't really be myself." I shrugged. "But this visit, I'm just going with the flow. Enjoy myself. Everything is falling into place. The trial is all wrapped up. My mother is busy with a retreat this week, and she doesn't need me to help out—Ooh, caramel apples!" I moved over to the booth and pulled some money out of my pocket to hand over to the vendor before grabbing one. "And then there's Gr—"

Suddenly Freddie slapped me on the arm.

"Ow," I said. "You almost made me drop my apple!"

"What is wrong with you?"

"What?" I asked too sharply, knitting my brow. I wasn't so much annoyed with Freddie, though. I couldn't undo the tape holding the cellophane around my apple, and the delay in my gratification was starting to get to me.

Freddie sliced the air in front of him with his hands. "Okay, from now on the number four is completely off limits."

I looked up from my puzzle apple and blinked. "I'm sorry?"

"Maybe six too."

"Again," I said, turning an ear toward him, "I'm sorry?"

Freddie grabbed my apple and ripped off the plastic. I smiled and snatched it back.

"You just can't be saying that kind of stuff like that."

I gave him a look that I hoped spoke to the fact that I still wasn't following.

"*Everything's going my way,*" he said, mock-waving his hands in the air. "*This week's going to be perfect.* I may have to call my grandmother. She knows more about this kind of thing."

"What are you going on about?"

"You can't say that stuff out loud," Freddie said, throwing his hands into the air. "You're just asking to be smacked down by whatever powers that be."

"Whatever," I said, smiling and rolling my eyes. "I'm not superstitious."

"Look," Freddie said, with a sharp point. "There's a ladder over there against that shed. Why don't you go walk under it? Or maybe we should find you a black cat you can cross paths with."

"Okay, which superstitions are we following here?"

"All of them!"

"Just settle down, you," I said, linking my arm through his. "Nothing's going to ruin this week."

"Making it worse." He yanked his arm back. "And stop it. I'm working, and we are not touching friends." He made a strange sound of disgust at the back of his throat. "Happy Erica is weird."

"Oh relax," I said. "I believe in free agency. I make my own destiny. I don't believe in bad luc—"

Suddenly a scream cut me off. A scream that stood out from all the others coming from the rides.

Freddie snapped his head around like a retriever after a gunshot. "What about now? Can you hear me now?"

Chapter Two

"The Tunnel of Love!" Freddie made off in the most un-athletic run in what seemed to be the wrong direction for the ride.

"Wait! Freddie!" I yelled. "This way is faster!"

"No! That way has pumpkin people! Come on!"

"Pumpkin people?" I muttered, before taking off after him.

A moment later we were pushing our way through the crowd to the makeshift gate. A ride operator stood in a little box by the opening collecting tickets. He didn't look particularly alarmed.

"What's going on here?" Freddie asked in a stern voice.

"Kids," the tired worker said with a dismissive shake of the head.

We looked over to the giant swan cart rolling through the draping vines of plastic flowers that covered the heart-shaped exit of the tunnel. An adolescent boy had his varsity jacket zipped and pulled up over his head. He swayed his arms around in zombie-like motions, making the girl beside him squeal.

I inhaled deeply and smiled. I had to admit for a second there everything Freddie had said about superstitions and bad luck had started to get to me. I patted him on the back. "See? What did I tell you? It's just kids."

Freddie's shoulders slumped. "Bummer. I thought we might see some real action."

"Nope. Not this week." I stepped back to let more couples through the gate to the ride. "This week, it's all smooth sailing at Otter Lake."

Just then another scream pierced the air, ringing with even more horror.

Freddie looked at me. "You just can't help yourself, can you?"

It was the teenage girl again, but she wasn't screaming at her boyfriend's antics this time. She stood on the platform beside the rickety track, pointing back at the next swan emerging from the mouth of the cave.

Uh-oh.

"Hey," I said, tapping Freddie lightly with the back of my hand against his arm a few times. "Is that guy all right?" Something was definitely wrong. There was a man . . . an older man, and I couldn't quite see through the people, but it looked like he was keeled over the giant bird's plastic wing.

Freddie huffed a quick breath and whispered, "I got this." He then scissored his legs over the metal fence and shouted, "Everybody back!"

I stood frozen a moment, then shook my head and started after him.

"Erica!" Freddie shouted. "Dr. Reynolds! There! By the ring-toss game! Go!"

I spun around and pushed my way through the crowd again, weaving around wagons and strollers before hopping a small fence to reach Dr. Reynolds. He was already on his way over. I helped him navigate the crowd.

"Let him through, people!" Freddie ordered again with surprising authority. "And the rest of you stay back!"

I ushered Dr. Reynolds ahead of me. A small group of people had gathered around the swan. I caught another glimpse of the man collapsed over the side and spotted a shock of white hair. There was also someone in the cart beside him, but Freddie was blocking my view. I couldn't see who it was.

Freddie stepped back from the group and pulled out a walkie-talkie attached to his hip belt. "Rhonda, we need some help out here at the Tunnel of Love. I repeat. We've got a Code Blue in the Tunnel of Love."

I saw Dr. Reynolds push himself up and step back from the cart. He planted his hands on his hips and shook his head. "I'm afraid we're already past Code Blue."

Within minutes the shrill *Whup! Whup!* of a cop car's siren pierced the air as the vehicle slowly parted the crowd. An ambulance followed behind. I had stepped back with everyone else to make room.

A hush fell over the fairgoers, making all the carnival noises glaringly loud. Otter Lake was a small, tight-knit community—fourteen hundred citizens total. You could see the concern mirrored across faces.

Another few minutes passed before Freddie made his way back over to me, hands in his pockets.

"Is he really . . . ?"

"Dead?" Freddie asked, raising his eyebrows. "Yup."

"Who is, I mean . . . was it?" I thought I already knew the answer to that. That white hair curled into a pompadour was pretty distinctive. There was really only one man in town with that rooster's cut. "Mr. Masterson?"

"Yup."

"Oh no. That's so sad." I didn't really know the man. But again, Otter Lake was a small town and the Mastersons were a fixture. While they didn't quite rival Freddie's family in terms of money, they owned Hemlock Estate, a beautiful historic manse slash castle built in the '20s on a private inlet. I had gone to grade school with their son, Matthew, before they sent him to a private boys' college.

"Was it a heart attack?"

Freddie sucked some air in through his teeth. "Looks like it. They should probably put an age limit on those tunnels—"

"Oh no!" I looked back to the ride but couldn't see much. "His poor wife! That's so awful. Imagine your husband of what? Forty years? Fifty? Dying on you in the Tunnel of Love? That's kind of romantic . . . and really horrible."

Freddie smacked his lips together. "Yeah, no. He wasn't with his wife."

I blinked. "What?" I felt my brow furrow again. I didn't stop it this time. "Then who was with him? And why—" I stopped talking a moment to study Freddie's face. "—why do you look so nervous?"

Freddie shoved his hands deeper into his pockets. "I'm not sure if I should say anything else—"

I swatted him.

"Hey!"

"Freddie, we both know you're going to tell me what's going on. Stop drawing out the moment."

His eyes dropped back to mine. "It was Tweety."

"Tweety?" I asked, trying to meet Freddie's eyes, which had gone back to darting. "My Tweety?"

He nodded.

Tweety and her identical twin, Kit Kat, were the only other people who lived on the almost thirty-acre island housing my mother's retreat. Built like wrestlers, they smoked, drank, and lived by the belief that if you didn't have to kill it, why would you want to eat it? They also found everything my mother did hilarious. They never got tired of it. Basically they were like that one aunt every family seems to have who shows up drunk at funerals wearing red—except in this case there were two of them.

"Okay, just slow down," I said, putting my hands up.

Freddie twisted his mouth to the side then said, "I'm not going fast."

"Well, I don't like what you're implying with the whole *It wasn't his wife with him.*"

"I didn't imply anything! Why are you getting mad at me?" Freddie said, going all wide-eyed. Then his face fell. "Although other people might be implying things, which is why Grady put me on crowd control. I think—"

"Tweety's not the other-woman type. I'm sure there's a logic—" I cut myself short. "Crowd control? What are you even talking about?"

"I was surprised, really," Freddie said, looking away, "given all our recent issues. I think he wants to impress you."

"Freddie, focus!"

"Rumor has it Tweety and Mr. Masterson may have been doing, how shall I put this?" He made a clicking sound with his tongue. "The no-pants dance."

"What?"

"I'm sorry. I—"

I put a finger up to Freddie's face. "One, never say that again."

"Geriatric sex is real," he muttered. "Get used to it."

"Stop it. No. And two, there's no way. That's just . . . no." I folded my arms across my chest. "And three, what does that have to do with crowd control?"

"We need to keep people moving before they start putting things together. You know how fast rumors spread in this town." Freddie looked suspiciously at the crowds of fairgoers now moving slowly past the Tunnel of Love. "And this is the twins we're talking about. Remember when they flipped all the tables in the bingo hall when they thought Mr. Parsons was calling out rigged numbers?"

I frowned. "I'm pretty sure it was just one table."

"And that time they started the food fight at the fish fry when the band wouldn't take requests."

I half chuckled. "Well, yeah, but that band was being pretty unreasonable."

"The police also like them for a break-in at Grady's cousin's place."

"Hey!" I swatted him again on the arm. "You know they were with me, and we didn't break in. We were taking a look-see, and—"

"Right. Sure."

I mumbled something unpleasant under my breath.

"Seriously, Erica, Grady specifically told me to keep the crowd moving, and above all else keep Kit Kat away from the scene before—and I quote—*all hell breaks loose*."

I winced. "I get it, but there's no way you're going to keep her away. I'm sure their twin powers have already activated."

Freddie looked from side to side. "You're right. She's probably near."

I held up my hands and inhaled deeply. "I think you're overreacting."

Freddie grabbed my arm. "Do you feel it?"

I rubbed my forehead with my free hand. "No. I feel nothing, Freddie, and, again, we are not doing this on this trip—"

He leaned in closer. "No, it's like the whole town's sitting on a tinder box and anyone could light the match to make it all blow."

Suddenly I felt someone walk up behind me.

"Who croaked?"

I whirled around. "Kit Kat!"

Freddie leaned in at my shoulder and whispered, "Kaboom."

Chapter Three

"You saw her coming."

"What's the matter with you?" Kit Kat asked, getting my attention back. "Your top fall off again?"

My mouth, which I hadn't realized was open, snapped shut.

"Glad you're home," she added, not overly concerned with my reactions. "Hey, have you seen Tweety? The old bat's starting to wander, and the beer tent's opening in ten minutes."

"Um." My eyes flashed to Freddie's. He shook his head in a quick no.

Kit Kat's face suddenly dropped as her eyes landed on the ambulance.

I grabbed her arm. "No. No. It's not Tweety," I said quickly, realizing what she must be thinking. "It's Mr. Masterson, but Tweety—"

"A beer! You need a beer, Erica! Go! Have fun," he said, pushing me in the direction of the tent. "If I see Tweety, I'll send her along."

"What's the matter with you, Ng?" Kit Kat jumped in.

"All that polyester you wearing getting to your brain? I don't need Erica to take me to the beer tent."

"Erica, can I speak to you for a second?" Freddie asked, scratching the side of his face. Before I could answer, he yanked me by the arm and dragged me over to a water gun racing game. "You need to do this for me."

"Freddie, I really think you're blowing this whole thing way out of proportion."

"Mrs. Masterson is going to be here any second, and Grady is going to have to tell her that not only is her husband dead, but he was on a pleasure trip with—"

"Two bucks a race," a man above us interrupted.

"We're not playing," Freddie said quickly without looking up. "We're having an official conversation. As I was saying—"

"Then do it somewhere else," the man pressed. Both Freddie and I looked up this time. The man had a really remarkable handlebar mustache on his overly tanned face, and by the fading tag on his shirt, his name was Rex. "You're scaring away the customers."

Freddie stepped back, cocked his head, and hiked his pants up by the belt. "Um," he said before licking his lips, "I don't think you understand. Do you see this uniform?"

The man sharply puffed some air out of his lips, making his body jump.

Freddie literally staggered back a step, grabbing my arm for support.

"Freddie," I said, with as much calm warning as I could muster. "Take it easy—"

"I will have you know," Freddie snapped, stepping up to the counter, "that you are speaking to the CEO of Otter Lake Security, and that I have been specially tasked by the sheriff of this town to—"

The man put up his hands and waved them out in mock-fear.

"That's it." Freddie lunged for the water pistol anchored to the game table, aimed it up at the man, and squeezed the trigger. A few drops came out the end.

"It doesn't work until I turn it on." The man picked up a pistol and pressed a pedal on the floor with his boot; a spray of water shot out directly at Freddie's chest. "See?"

Water splattered all over the front of Freddie's shirt. I gasped and jumped in front of him to take the rest of the shot. I then planted one hand on Freddie's chest to push him back while using the other hand to viciously point my candy apple at the man. "Not cool, buddy! Not cool!" I then turned my attention around. "Freddie? Freddie? Focus on me," I said, patting my chest. "Calm down now. Your eyes, they're showing too much white. You're going to hurt yourself."

His gaze moved to mine. It took everything in me not to step back from it.

"He sprayed me with his gun." Freddie said each word very carefully.

"I know. I know," I said, nodding. "But . . . you did try to spray him first."

Freddie's eyes, unbelievably, grew even wider.

"I'm sorry. You're right. You had the law on your side," I said, trying to pin his eyes with my own—they were wandering back to Rex. "But you have a job to do. You were saying something about me getting Kit Kat out of here?"

Freddie's brow furrowed. Then he blinked a few times. "I was, and don't think that I don't know you are manipulating me right now." He slid his head sideways to look at the Water Pistol Cowboy and mouthed the words, *This isn't over*, before sliding his face back in front of mine. "Just get Kit Kat out of here. Believe me, I've been really patient with Grady and his problems with sharing authority, not to mention all his jealousy issues over the boat situation—"

"Boat situation?"

"But it's all starting to get annoying. I just want to get past all that and have him accept me as a brother in uniform."

I closed my eyes. I had been home what? Half an hour? "I can't do it, Freddie. Kit Kat will kill me. She's going to find out I took her from the scene. And she will kill me. They're twins."

"Please?"

Nope. This was not at all what I had imagined coming home would be like. Just then a woman accidentally bumped my shoulder, making me drop my candy apple to the dirt.

"Sorry," she called out with a *whoopsie* face.

I waved her off and turned back to Freddie. "Fine, but you owe me."

"Whatever," Freddie said, picking up my apple and tossing it in the trash. "Just go!"

I turned on my heel back to face Kit Kat . . . when I suddenly found myself saying, "Freddie, tell me that is not Kit Kat pushing up her sleeves like she's about to fight someone."

Freddie didn't have time to answer before Kit Kat shouted, "You did not just call my sister that!"

Freddie hiked up his belt. "And here we go."

Chapter Four

We ran toward Kit Kat, who was barreling her way through the crowd toward a huddle of women—in the middle of which stood Marg Johnson. I recognized her instantly. The magenta-colored hair always gave her away. Marg was the proprietor of The Sharpest Cut and the only hairdresser in town. She was also, therefore, the town gossip. Given how things were going, that seemed about right.

We got to Kit Kat just as she reached the bunch.

"What do you think you're doing?" I asked, stepping in front of her.

She pushed her sleeves up even farther on her fleshy but still-muscular arms.

"Stop it!" I snapped. "You are not fighting Marg Johnson."

"I'm not afraid of you, Kit Kat!" Marg shouted. "Bring it!"

I whipped my head around to the other contender. "Really?"

"Step aside, Erica," Kit Kat said from behind me. "This is old business we need to settle."

"Simmer down everyone!" Freddie yelled, jumping in. "I don't want to have to take you all in."

Kit Kat never moved her eyes from Marg, but said, "You and what mall cop army, Ng?"

"Wow," Freddie said, looking to me. "Is it just me, or does this town have a real problem with authority?"

Kit Kat lunged forward, taking both Freddie and me by surprise. Thankfully, some onlookers moved to help keep the ladies apart, but the situation was deteriorating rapidly. The crowd was already on edge, and more people were pushing in to see what all the hubbub was about. If someone didn't do something soon—

"Enough!"

All heads whipped over to the Tunnel of Love.

And there he was standing on the dais of the ride . . . hands planted on hips . . . sheriff's hat darkening his eyes . . . muscles rippling everywhere. The sunlight silhouetted him from behind, casting a shadow of manliness over us all.

Grady Forrester.

Freddie leaned toward me. "I swear, he practices that in front of the mirror."

I swallowed and nodded.

Grady stepped down from the platform. People fell back to clear a path as he strode toward us.

"Everybody calm down." Grady cast a pointed look in Freddie's direction.

"I tried!" Freddie yelled. "Erica wouldn't cooperate."

"Please, let's all show a little respect." Grady inhaled deeply, causing the most mesmerizing rise of his chest. "Erica," he said, keeping his eyes on the women. "Why don't you take the twins home? We'll come by later if we have more questions." He waved Tweety toward him. She had been standing by the swan, arms crossed over her stomach, looking pale.

"Okay," I said, linking arms with Kit Kat. "Come on, Freddie."

"No," Grady said with a point at Freddie. "You stay. The town's paying you good money. This is your chance to earn it."

"Of course," Freddie said in the deepest voice I had ever heard him use, before turning to me to whisper the words, "Would it kill him to say please?"

Grady exhaled roughly and rubbed the bit of forehead showing underneath his hat. When he opened his eyes, he found mine. He gave me a small smile—a smile I couldn't help but return.

"Ew," Freddie said, a little louder this time. "Get a room."

"All right, everybody!" Grady clapped his hands together. "Let's move it along."

Tweety was already lowering herself from the ride and making her way over to us. I pulled on Kit Kat's arm to walk her away from the crowd. "Let's get out of here, okay?"

"Sure," she said, not moving. "I just need to—"

I cut her off when I grabbed the hand she had put up in the air. "Are you throwing gang signs? How do you know gang signs?"

"You don't know what I know."

"You're right. Let's just go."

I started the climb up the log steps that led up the hill to the retreat after having dropped the twins off in their boat. I had tried talking to them on the short boat ride back, but both had been stone-faced and tight-lipped. In fact, they had barely even looked at each other, but when they did . . . well, I found myself wishing we were on a bigger boat. I really did want to know what Tweety was doing on that ride with Mr. Masterson, but I also knew it was none of my business.

I sighed as I looked at the tiger lily bushes that ran up either side of the steps. Even though the flowers had long since died, the long-tongued leaves were still a pretty yellow. I felt the tension in my shoulders ease a little. I lifted my head and took in the tall cedars and pines reaching for the sky. They were magnificent. I certainly didn't have this view back in Chicago. I decided to stop midway up the stairs to really let the nature sink in. Earth, Moon, and Stars was a special place. Little had been done to the property or the cabins since it was built in the 1950s, so it gave off a sleepy sense of nature mixed with nostalgia. It also had just a hint of machete-serial-killer-ness to it to keep things interesting. I took a deep breath. Okay, things had gotten off to a rough start, but I could still do this.

I resumed my climb and didn't stop until I reached the top of the stairs. At the foot of the weedy gravel path that led up to the retreat, I dropped my bag from my shoulder. Red had offered to drop it off for me at our dock. He was that kind of guy.

The main lodge stood a couple hundred feet away. I rubbed the shoulder that had been carrying the weight of my bag as my eyes ran over the overgrown hydrangeas nestled up against the sturdy wraparound porch of the lodge. I also noticed the small display of misshapen gourds lining the steps. My mother always did plant the cucumbers too close to the pumpkins.

Behind the lodge, twelve cabins dotted the woods. As far as I knew, only five were in working order. And by *working order*, I mean, didn't leak. None of the cabins had electricity or plumbing. Just beds, curtains, and the sweet smell of cedar. They'd get cold at night this time of year, so the guests had to bring some pretty warm jammies— all part of the experience, I guess. More pebbled paths led from each cabin to a communal washroom outfitted with three composting toilets and three showers connected to tanks filled with sun-warmed water, but I hadn't been in there in years. The resident fishing spider and I had come to that agreement together.

A thin trail of smoke spiraled out of the stone chimney of the lodge, which sat in front of a backdrop of trees flashing their fall colors. It was so welcoming . . . so cute . . . so cozy. Now if I could just tell that to the part of my brain that wanted to chew off all my fingernails . . .

No. No. Things were different now. I had grown. My mother had grown. It was time to develop our new relationship. It hadn't always been easy growing up with a vegan, hippie mom in small-town New Hampshire. I mean, getting through high school is hard enough without having a mother who didn't believe in shaving her armpits. I always felt like I had to protect her from so many things: embarrassment, herbal remedies gone wrong, accusations of satanism . . . basically herself. It was a lot of pressure. But last visit, I had come to realize that Otter Lake had come a long way in accepting my mother for who she was. And I had seen firsthand that she did do a lot of good at the retreat. She really cared about people. It had all led me to believe that it was time I let go of some of my teenage stuff and forge a new adult relationship.

As if on cue, a giant mauve butterfly opened the door of the lodge and descended from the retreat steps in a flutter. My mother and I both had blue eyes and brown hair, but it was hard to spot our resemblance right away mainly because her eyes always seemed to be widened in innocence, and I was pretty sure mine were not, and her hair floated around in a cloud of curly masses, whereas mine just fell straight. She rushed toward me, arms waving in the air, making the silky folds of her caftan ruffle under her shawl. My mother loved caftans. She'd wear them until the snow fell.

"Hi, Mom," I said, a smile spreading across my face.

She stopped a few feet in front of me, clasped her hands together, and smiled back . . . not saying a word.

"Hi?" I tried again.

She smiled wider and held her arms out for a hug, still not saying anything.

I took a half step back. "What's going on here? Why aren't you talk—" Suddenly I felt my face drop. It knew what was happening before I did. "No. No. No."

Her already impossibly round blue eyes widened in question.

"Tell me it's not . . ." I closed my eyes and inhaled deeply. "Tell me you are not doing a Silence of the Soul."

I cracked open one eye to see my mother beaming with pride, like I had just won the third-grade spelling bee.

"Mom," I said, rubbing my face roughly. "When we spoke yesterday morning—*yesterday*—you said, you were doing a Hey Sister, Whole Sister." Normally, I wouldn't be looking forward to a retreat for feuding sisters, but given the alternative . . .

She smiled again and shrugged.

And that would be all the explanation I'd get for days. Because for the duration of the retreat, my mom and all her guests would be completely silent. Nature walks. Meals. Meditation. All silent. And how would my mother accomplish this feat? Answer questions? Guide the guests from one activity to another? Let's just say she could be very *theatrical*.

Those who knew my mother and me might be tempted to think I'd enjoy her silence for days at a time. But they'd be wrong. I could remember many an aggravating incident as a teenager wanting a simple answer to a simple question like, *Where are the boat keys?* or *Have I been vaccinated for measles? I have a rash,* only to have to endure a bizarre form of charades that could go on for what felt like a silent eternity. Yup, my mother felt that even writing things down was a form of cheating—because our souls should be able to commune without words.

I groaned as she brushed my bangs away from my forehead—which I took to mean that they needed a cut. I closed my eyes again. Suddenly I felt her embrace me, pinning my arms to my sides. I allowed the smell of the lemongrass and mint wafting from her mass of wavy hair to fill my senses. Despite everything, I couldn't help but allow myself a moment to enjoy her mom-ness. I sighed and opened my eyes. "It's good to see you too, Mom."

She leaned back and smiled with way too much satisfaction before moving to lead me inside.

Once we got to the foot of the porch steps, I stopped to let my mom go ahead . . . mainly because of the orange-and-white planet-sized cat who sat cleaning himself at the top of the stairs, seated amid the display of misshapen gourds.

The cat rolled onto his butt, back legs spread wide into the air to clean his enormous belly.

"Caesar," I said in tired greeting.

He slowly lifted his head from his legs, tongue still half out of his mouth.

Caesar was the closest thing I had to a sibling, and he was definitely the favorite child. He consumed at least 50 percent of my mother's waking thoughts, and house rules stated if he was sleeping, he was not to be moved—even if he happened to be sleeping on the pillow of my bed. He was also the only one in the house allowed to eat meat.

"Hey, Caesar, what do you say—just this once—you not swipe my legs as I walk by?"

He didn't answer, just stared back at me with flat eyes.

I held my breath and walked up the steps, giving him the widest berth possible. Then just as I made it to the top—

"Ow!"

Thankfully, when we got inside, the retreat was empty. I could have asked my mom where all of her retreat-goers had made off to, but I didn't think I had it in me to watch the answer. Plus, I was too busy inspecting my ankle for fatal wounds. Once I assured myself I wouldn't, in fact, die from the blood loss, I quickly hustled off to my room telling my mom I needed a nap. It was entirely possible she didn't like that idea and was arguing for me to stay, but I didn't turn to see. The whole silence thing wasn't without its advantages.

I dropped my bag on the thick-planked wood floor of my old bedroom and looked around. Yup, nothing much had changed. Same frog clock telling time with his fishing poles. Same canoe paddles crossed on the wall, although my mom must have hired someone to reattach the one I had ripped off the last time I'd been home. In fairness, I had been under attack by a murderer with a weenie skewer, so it was totally justified. Yup, everything was all the same . . . except for the pile of books left on my dresser. I gently tipped the stack with my fingers to catch a look at the titles. *My Mother Myself. Freeing Your Orgasm. The Vegan Path to Reincarnation.* Nope, nothing had changed.

I flopped on my spring bed and stared up at the ceiling.

I couldn't help but think that Mr. Masterson's death in the Tunnel of Love seemed a little like a bad omen. Grady and I had been talking a lot on the phone for the past couple of weeks. We really knew how to work a relationship when it was long distance. And over the course of many phone calls, I think we were both starting to have some hope that it might go somewhere. The obvious problem, of course, was that I lived in Chicago, and Grady, well, I don't think Grady would ever consider living anywhere but Otter Lake. But the funny thing was, once I had gone back to Chicago after my last visit, I found that I had started to miss being home. I missed the colors of the trees. I missed the smell of the lake. I missed Freddie . . . and all that came with him. I was still missing the sound of my mother's voice.

What I did not miss was all the chaos that came with being home and what it did to me as a person. I felt so out of control. Otter Lake was a strange little place with lots of characters . . . and I always seemed to turn into one of them whenever I was here.

I didn't have these problems back in Chicago. I led a quiet, normal life. I worked. I sometimes ran . . . although I was letting that slide now that I had started a very serious relationship with my online streaming TV service. Freddie had gotten me watching the British crime shows. Those detectives with their big brains always made tracking down killers look so easy. And yeah, now that I had been talking to Grady, and thinking about the possibility of . . . future possibilities, I realized that I had grown some roots there too. I liked my co-workers. Well, not Gary, he was always stealing my yogurt out of the shared office fridge, but Lisa and Kate were really cool and they had just introduced me to this new sushi place that had awesome California rolls. There wasn't much sushi in Otter Lake. Kate had also invited me to try a Zumba class with her, which, you know, I wasn't entirely sure I could see myself doing because that really seemed like something coordinated people would do, but I wasn't about to rule it out entirely. And it wasn't just my co-workers or the food, or the Zumba obviously, that had kept me living in Chicago all these years. It was the freedom. I could be whoever I wanted in Chicago . . . not just Summer Bloom's daughter. If I wanted to sign up for Zumba class in Otter Lake, well, first, that would be silly because there were no Zumba classes in Otter Lake, but if, say, I wanted to start one, there's a good chance it might become a *thing*. A *thing* that everybody would need to discuss. Maybe start a petition over. It looked like Freddie had somehow managed to break free of worrying about what people thought, given his new uniform and all, but I wasn't sure I was ready to jump back into living in a fishbowl. A fishbowl with lots of moose. And flannel. Kind of made me wonder if I ever would be.

I rubbed my forehead with the heel of my hand. Everything had seemed so possible in those conversations with Grady on the phone. I had been thinking that if things kept going as well as they had been, maybe in the not-so-distant future I could look for jobs in New Hampshire. Maybe I could live with my mom until I found a place of my own . . . maybe by the lake, where I could swim every morning before I went to work . . . maybe with Grady . . . maybe without our clothes. But now that I was here, it all just seemed so impossible.

My phone buzzed, cutting me off from my thoughts.

I lifted it up and peeked at the screen through my fingers that were still covering my face.

We still on for tonight?

Grady.

I couldn't stop the smile from spreading across my face.

Yup.

My place? Half an hour?

I'll be there.

I jumped out of bed. Yeah, no, this could all still work.

I grabbed my duffel bag and quickly zipped it open. I already had my outfit picked out. Grady had said we might be outside, so I pulled out a fresh pair of jeans and a sweater that pretended to look casual but clung to my body in all the right places. I threw off the shirt I had been wearing, and quickly smelled my armpits. Not bad . . . but not good. *Shoot!* Why had I wasted all this time feeling sorry for myself when I could have been showering? I snatched my deodorant out the bag, gave myself a few swipes, then pulled the sweater over my head. I then jumped into the new pair of jeans and hustled out my door and down the hall while trying to button the waist. Maybe my jeans were getting a little too tight, because I just couldn't seem to get the button in. I needed more running and less Scotland Yard. I pulled up the fabric of my sweater and pinned it under my chin as I pushed my pelvis forward to get a better look at the situation.

"Mom? Can I borrow your b—"

I suddenly felt a lot of eyes on me. I looked slowly up from my bare waist to see half a dozen women and a few men all seated in the lotus position, smiling at me from the floor.

"Hi," I said with a small wave, yanking down my sweater. "Sorry."

A few jolted at the sound of my voice, but one man gave me a pretty clear wink.

"Sorry," I said again, but in a whisper this time. "I'll just scoot by." I weaved through the maze of yoga mats placed randomly about the floor.

Suddenly my mom popped out of nowhere and grabbed my arm. Yet another thing I hated about Silence of the Soul was my mother's ability to take on the stealth of a ninja.

"What?" I whispered.

She held her palm out and gestured to all the faces staring at us.

I sighed. Oh, I guess introductions were in order. "I'm Erica. Summer's daught—"

Suddenly my mom's finger was on my lips silencing me. I watched her then cradle an imaginary baby in her arms, smiling the ecstatic smile of motherhood, before turning her eyes from her imaginary bundle of joy to me.

All the seated faces smiled and nodded with understanding.

I once again threw out a small wave and made for the front door when my mother grabbed my arm again.

I mimed crying, but she ignored me and gestured to the person seated closest to us on the floor. She then made an encouraging gesture with her hand, and the woman got to her feet.

What was going on here?

The woman started to pirouette and dance about the room. She then stopped suddenly and pointed a finger about as though she were giving instructions . . . like a dance teacher. Oh no. Oh no, no, no! They were going to act out their occupations! My mother was already waving a hand at the next person to get up.

"Erica," a loud voice suddenly said from the screen door. "Can I talk to you?"

"God, yes."

Chapter Five

I walked out onto the porch letting the screen door bang shut behind me. "Hey Kit Kat, I didn't expect to see you. Is everything—Whoa!"

Kit Kat grabbed my elbow, yanking me away from the door. "Listen up. This is important, and we don't need all those Marcel Marceau wannabes eavesdropping."

"Okay," I said, straightening up and adjusting my sweater. "What's going on?"

"You and me, we gotta get something straight."

I narrowed my eyes to a squint and said, "You're acting like a gangster again."

"Focus," she snapped, pointing a warning finger up toward my nose. "You know Tweety and I think of you as a daughter."

"Aw." I dropped the arms that I hadn't realized were crossed over my chest. "That's so swee—"

She snapped her fingers in my face. "So you need to promise me something."

"Oh, okay." I blinked a little. I was having trouble keeping up with this conversation.

She tilted her chin in the air. "I need to know that you and that friend of yours aren't getting any ideas."

"What?" I asked, biting off the word. "I'm not getting any ideas. I can never be too sure about Freddie." I assumed that's who she meant. "And more important, what kind of ideas?"

"Ideas about playing detective."

For the first time, I really considered the possibility that Tweety was having some sort of affair with Mr. Masterson, but I couldn't see what business that was of anyone's . . . except maybe Mrs. Masterson. Still, the idea of it left me kind of hurt? Disappointed? The twins had always been role models for me as a child. Sure, they were rough around the edges, but they were also salt-of-the-earth-type people. They had their own rough sort of integrity. I'd counted on that growing up. When my mother was off with the fairies, they had their feet firmly planted on the ground. "Why would we be playing detective?"

"Oh, come on, Erica," Kid Kat said, planting her hands on her hips. "Everybody knows about Freddie's plans to produce a pilot about your crime-fighting adventures using his rich grandma's Hong Kong money."

"What?" I blinked. "Pilot? Crime fighting? Hong Kong money?"

"And I just want you to know," she said, once again bringing her slightly crooked finger up to my face, "that Tweety is off limits."

"I have no idea what you're talk—Ow!"

Kit Kat had leaned forward to flick me hard on the breastbone before moving the finger back up to point at my face. "This is serious."

"That hurt," I said, rubbing my chest with the heel of my hand.

"Good. You'll remember it then."

"Okay, first of all," I said, pointing back at her, "I can

assure you I have no plans to go running off playing detective games. What would there even be to investigate? Mr. Masterson probably died of a heart attack, and anything else . . . well, that's nobody's business."

I was really hoping Kit Kat would take the opportunity to tell me why her sister was on that ride, and to reassure me that nothing was going on, but instead she said, "You know as well as I do how this town works, and if you and Freddie go off half-cocked asking ques—"

"We're not going to ask anyone questions! There is no pilot!" I dropped my voice and added, "That I'm aware of." It did sound like something Freddie would come up with. "I swear to you, the only plan I ever had for this visit was to meet Grady for dinner."

Kit Kat scanned my face with a wary expression. "All right. Well, good," she said with a nod. "So . . . calm down then. Your eye's doing that thing again."

I rubbed my eyelids with my fingers, trying to process the drive-by thwacking I had just received. "Can I just say, though, Kit Kat, if you don't want people asking questions, you really might want to think about not demanding they not ask questions in a *really* suspicious way."

She caught my eyes and held them. "You can be suspicious until the cows come home." She paused for a moment. "Just keep your mouth shut."

I threw my hands in the air. "Okay, now I have to ask. Is Tweety in some kind of trouble?"

"What did I just tell you!" she yelled, moving to flick me again.

Thankfully I saw her coming this time and spun to the side. "Answer that question, and I won't ask any more."

"No. Nobody's in trouble," she said firmly without meeting my eye. "I'm just worried about my sister's reputation."

"Oh for the love of—"

"What?"

I walked over to the porch railing and gripped it with my hands. I stepped back to drop my head between my arms in a stretch. "You're lying to me," I muttered, looking down at the thick planks of wood. "Since when have you or Tweety ever worried what people thought of you?"

"Since now," she said, moving closer to me. "There's a lot of history between us and the Mastersons. History that needs to stay buried."

"Don't suppose you'd like to share any of that history with me?" I craned my head to look at her, but she had already moved to the steps and was easing herself down.

"We're done here, Erica. You go have fun on your date, but don't you forget what I said."

I inhaled deeply and muttered, "Whatever."

She spun around at the bottom of the steps. "And if Tweety asks, this conversation *never* happened."

Minutes later I was edging my mom's new boat around the bend that would take me to Grady's place. It was nothing fancy, a basic bowrider, but it felt good gliding across the water. The last fingers of pink and orange light were stretching across the water as the crisp evening air cooled the sweat on the back of my neck.

Otter Lake itself was just over a thousand acres. Most people would consider it a midsized lake—nothing special—but for those who lived here, it was just right.

I killed the motor as I drifted in toward Grady's dock. I inhaled deeply, taking in the faint smell of smoke from a campfire crackling somewhere nearby. In the sudden quiet, I could hear the lonely wail of a loon cry out in the distance. After a moment, its mate answered.

This was the lake I wanted to come home to. It was the perfect night—the absolute perfect fall night to spend cuddled up under a blanket watching the stars with Grady.

Now I just needed to clear my head, so that the twins weren't under that blanket with us.

I shuddered slightly at the image that popped into my head with that thought. No. No. No. It was time to stop thinking about Tweety, and Kit Kat, and the Mastersons. Even though something more was going on—Kit Kat had said as much—it wasn't any of my business . . . probably. No! No, it wasn't. Obviously, Kit Kat felt I should stay out of it—whatever *it* was—and she was probably right. Everyone had his or her own secrets . . . and maybe Mr. Masterson should be allowed to rest with his.

I hopped out of the boat and tied it to the dock, giving it one last appreciative look. Not bad for secondhand. My mom's last boat was involved in a small explosion during Freddie's and my murder investigation. She probably could have scraped together enough money to buy a new one with the money she pulled in from the retreat, but my mother wasn't overly interested in such things.

I walked up the few stone steps to Grady's place. Huh, he had a few mini chrysanthemum plants of his own in pots lining the steps. I hadn't really thought of Grady being . . . domesticated, but I wasn't complaining.

I knocked on the heavy wood door of the modernized cabin, looking around at the trees as I waited for him to answer. It was a nice spot. He'd get the sunrise over the lake in the morning. Not a bad way to wake up . . . although I should probably try it out firsthand, just to be sure.

I turned back to the door. No answer.

I knocked louder. "Grady?"

"I'm around back," a voice called out.

I hopped down from the porch and made my way around the side of the cabin. Once I caught sight of the back, my feet stopped moving and my eyes widened.

Twinkle lights were, well, twinkling from the trees

circling the crackling fire pit, and piles of thick pillows and blankets rested on low divan-type chairs underneath. A little off to the side stood a table with some plates, a few covered dishes, an ice bucket holding a bottle of white wine, and candles.

My eyes darted around at all the wonderful . . . wonderfulness before they landed on Grady, who stood on the other side of the fire.

"Grady!"

"I know," he said rocking a little on his heels, surveying his efforts.

"This is . . ."

"I believe the word you're looking for is *awesome*." He walked over to me, smiling, but stopped a few feet away. I don't think either one of us knew how to handle this greeting. I mean we had had a lot of late-night phone conversations over the last month or so . . . covering a wide variety of . . . *adult* topics. But in real, face-to-face life, we had never even kissed. It was kind of like meeting an avatar in person.

I cleared my throat. "How did you even manage to get this done? What with Mr. Masterson?"

"I've had some time to prepare," he said, once again surveying his work. "Our phone conversations left me with some pent-up energy."

I smiled. This was a pretty *awesome* start to our reboot. Grady and I really only knew each other as teenagers. I kind of liked this new adult thing we were trying on.

"Oh my God," I said, moving toward the fire. "Is that salmon? On a plank?"

He nodded. "I got the recipe out of that magazine they give you at the liquor store. There's some good stuff in there."

"You . . . you have some surprising layers, Grady Forrester," I said, throwing him a smile. "Wait, this isn't going to attract bears, is it?" Even though I had grown up on a lake surrounded by wildlife, some aspects of nature still freaked me out. Like bears. I lived on an island after all, an island without bears, and it's not like they could swim. Wait, could bears swim?

"I don't really think bears cook their salmon," he said, giving the idea an exaggerated look of consideration, "but I'll keep an eye out."

I chuckled and planted my hands on my hips again. "This is really, really great."

Grady waved a hand to one of the piles of pillows he had placed around the fire pit. "Come sit. Let me pour you some wine."

"And wine!" I added with probably too much incredulity. "Not beer?" I picked a pillow and sat myself down.

"I have some *craft* beer if you would like. I have matured some since you last lived in Otter Lake, Ms. Bloom," he said, passing me a glass.

"Of course," I said with a serious nod. I knelt to the ground then leaned back into the pillows. "This almost makes everything else that happened today okay."

"Almost?" he said, shooting me a look. "What do I need to do to please you, woman?"

My immediate response was *Oh, you could do so many things*, but I managed to keep a lid on my libido. "I'm sorry. I'm just a little overwhelmed."

"And how is the lovely Summer Bloom?"

Truth was, I still was thinking about Kit Kat and Tweety, but I was glad for the opportunity to discuss something else. "Not talking."

He raised an eyebrow in question.

"To anybody. She's doing a vow-of-silence retreat."

Grady nodded. "And you find this to be?"

I took a long sip of wine. "Slightly frustrating." In fairness, I was wondering if my mother's new counselor had bailed on her again. The retreat's insurance required a certified professional for some types of counseling, but my mother had yet to find a good fit. My guess was you didn't need a doctor to supervise people being quiet for extended periods of time.

"Slightly frustrating?" Grady asked raising his eyebrows. "Look who else is all mature."

"Oh yeah, I'm more of a live-in-the-moment type of person these days. I'm all about mindfulness. The here and now is all that matters," I said with what I hoped looked like a Zen nod. "But before I fully immerse myself in *this* now, what was all that with you and Freddie back at the fair?"

Grady exhaled so heavily that it turned slightly into a growl. "After what happened in the summer, the town finds Freddie's presence—" He paused to roll his jaw. "—reassuring."

"Really? I mean, Freddie said something to that effect, but I wasn't sure if I should believe him." I leaned forward to eye the salmon. "And you didn't mention any of this on the phone."

Grady scratched his temple. "Yeah, I guess I thought there were better things for us to discuss. Besides, it's really all about the boat." His eyes had trailed off to some distant part of the forest. "Everybody just wants to stand on the dock and *ooh* and *ahh* over it," he mumbled more to himself than me.

"The boat?" I suddenly remembered that Freddie had made a comment about a boat. I watched the furrow between Grady's eyebrows deepen. "You know, maybe we shouldn't talk about boats," I said. "Not when we have this beautiful spread before us." I held my hands in a gameshow-model gesture across everything Grady had prepared. Boats were a sore subject between us, especially considering his last one was blown up along with my mother's.

"Agreed," he said, snapping his eyes back to mine. Wow, Grady this close, and full-on . . . was a lot of Grady. The blue eyes, the muscular jaw, the full lips; I had to catch myself from keeling over. He really was too good looking to be allowed to walk around without a warning. It was like gazing directly into the sun. "But I was thinking maybe you could talk to Freddie about toning it down a little?"

I sighed and turned away. Man, the last time I had been in town Freddie had practically become a professional hermit. He kept all of his eccentricities indoors. Now he was like some sort of local celebrity. "I know Freddie can be a little . . . out there. But let's not forget that he was raised by a team of nannies, and I think it's left him with, you know, some acceptance issues. I can't help but feel it's a good thing that he feels like he belongs."

Grady made a halfhearted *harrumph* sound.

"Besides, I not sure anyone can control Freddie."

"I'm not saying you have to control him," he said, edging closer to me. "Just talk to him. Maybe ask him to remind people that *he* is not the *law*."

Whoa, Grady's face was suddenly very close to mine. I swallowed. "He does want to work with you," I tried.

"Okay, well, the *with* might be a problem." Grady leaned closer but tilted his head a little to the side to look at the fire. I could feel the heat of him on my cheeks. I could smell his aftershave and . . . testosterone. My lips were already imagining what his would feel like even though they were still inches away. "But maybe we could talk about Freddie and his plans for world domination later," Grady said, turning back to face me.

I nodded eagerly, moving half an inch closer. "We don't

even have to. It's like I told Kit Kat . . . as far as I know, Freddie has no plans." I closed my eyes to finally close the distance between our lips—and got air.

I peeked an eye open.

Grady had moved back a few inches and had a quizzical look on his face. "Why would Kit Kat care what Freddie was up to?"

Frick! Stupid subconscious mouthing off at the worst possible time. "Oh no, it's nothing," I said, trying to move in closer again and get back the dreamy feeling we had just a moment ago. "I don't even know what I'm talking about."

Grady nodded, seeming somewhat satisfied by that answer, and he moved back in toward me.

I was almost completely lost in the sight of Grady's lips moving toward mine—which made it really bizarre that I suddenly said, "So everything all cleared up with Mr. Masterson?"

Grady pulled back again and gave me a considering look. "Wasn't much to clear up."

"Heart attack?"

Grady nodded.

"Good. Good," I said, nodding in return. "I mean, not good! Just—come here." I started to lean in again, but stopped halfway and asked, "Has Dr. Reynolds had his cataracts surgery?"

Grady threw his hands into the air.

Man, why mindfulness was so hard? "No, I just mean, his eyesight was never good, and—"

"Okay," Grady said, leaning away and taking a breath. "Let's just stop for a moment. Erica, what exactly is going on right now?"

Chapter Six

"Nothing. I'm just taking an interest in your job." Truth was, I didn't think I could concentrate on enjoying Grady . . . truly, truly enjoying Grady . . . like, luxuriating in the total enjoyment of all that was Grady . . . until I could get all this other business off my mind.

He raised an eyebrow. "Just tell me."

"It's nothing," I said, looking off to the darkened trees. "Kit Kat was just acting a little weird, and—you know what? Never mind. It's not important. I did not travel nearly twenty hours by bus to talk to you about my mother or Freddie or Tweety. In fact, I'm going to be completely honest with you. There's a big, big part of me that doesn't want to talk to you at all."

Grady inhaled sharply. "While I can't even begin to express how deeply I am in favor of that sentiment, before we get started here, *again*, I think there's something you should know about me."

I threw him a sideways look. "Okay."

"Erica, at any given time, odds are I'm thinking about one of three things." He put up a finger. "Work." Another finger popped up. "Food." Another finger. "And you."

"Aw," I said, with a smile. "Wait, is that list in any particular order?"

He ignored me. "Now, during play-off season, one of those things has to swap out, but really, for the rest of the time, that's pretty much it."

I nodded sharply. "Okay, I'm with you."

"Here's the catch," he said, cocking his head. "I can't think about more than one of those things at the same time."

"I see."

"I would really like to focus on you right now," he said. "See, even as I said that, a vision of you in that bikini top you were wearing at the dock that one time just popped in my head. But if I think of work," he went on, making a *poof* gesture with his fingers, "it's gone."

"Right."

"So I guess what I'm saying is, do you want to talk about Mr. Masterson or do you want to do"—he gestured around over our bodies—"this? 'Cause I really think I may be physically incapable of doing both."

"Oh, I definitely want to do this."

"Excellent." Grady began to move toward me again . . . then suddenly stopped.

"What's wrong?" I asked, blinking the stars out of my eyes. "I thought we were doing this?"

"I can't," he said, sounding as surprised as I was. He pushed himself back a foot or two this time and looked at me. "You said Kit Kat was acting weird? What kind of weird exactly?"

"I should never have said anything." I got up on my hands and knees and crawled toward him on the rocky ground, which really kind of hurt and made it hard to keep the sexy look on my face. "Come here, you—"

"Seriously, I can't believe I'm saying this, like really,

really can't believe I'm saying this, but—" Grady shook his head and rose to his feet. "I gotta go."

"What!"

"Well, a few people mentioned that maybe—" He cut himself off when he saw how closely I was listening. "I gotta go."

"Seriously?"

He threw his hands in the air. "I know!"

"But all this—" I said, waving my hands around the fire and food.

"Oh, I know." He tapped his temple. "A lot of thought went into it when I was on Erica thinking time."

I sighed. "And I switched you to work."

"No, no. Well, kind of. It's just now, I've got all these questions," he said, shaking his head side-to-side. "It's like I'm not sure if I turned off the stove."

"This is horrible."

"I can't believe it myself," he said, putting his hands on his chest, right where my hands should have been.

"Look, Grady," I said, getting to my feet, "about Kit Kat. I really just think that maybe she was concerned about rumors starting up about her sister and Mr. Masterson. That's all."

He nodded. "I hear you, and I don't want to put you in any kind of awkward position. I'm just going to check in with the medical examiner to make sure everything is completely straightforward." Grady stopped and planted his hands on his hips. "I've never marinated salmon before." He walked toward the side of the cabin. "Do you want to take some with you?"

"No," I said, feeling my face drop. "I think I would be sad eating it back at the retreat." I sighed. "This sucks. I suck."

He walked back toward me. "It's not your fault. I

shouldn't have tried to pull this off given all that happened today. I was just so looking forward to—" He cut himself off with a shake of his head, and then wrapped his hand around mine. "I'll walk you to your boat." He gently squeezed my fingers. "Then I had better put away that salmon."

"Bears?"

"Bears."

With nothing to do, I decided to head back to town and take another walk through the midway. I certainly didn't want to go back to the retreat and make all sorts of eye contact with silent people. Besides, I loved the fair at night. The Ferris wheel all lit up. The hordes of teenagers laughing and trying to win teddy bears. The looming giant pumpkin threatening to murder the entire town . . . plus, admission was free after nine.

I shoved my hands deep into my jean pockets. The air certainly was getting nippy.

"Hey, what are you doing here?" I turned to see Freddie walking toward me, coffee in hand. Sure enough, he was dressed in a very security-looking black sweater that zipped up at the throat. "I thought tonight was *the* night?"

"Yeah," I said, kicking the dirt, "it didn't exactly work out as planned."

Freddie nodded. "That's what happens when you're star-crossed."

"Don't start," I said. "Grady and I aren't star-crossed."

"You're right. You're too old," he said matter-of-factly. "It isn't cute anymore. Star-crossed at this age just means you need therapy."

I made a face at him.

"Well, come on. You can walk the beat with me."

I fell into step with Freddie. It was probably best that I

had run into him, seeing as everybody wanted me to try to rein him in. Thing was, I didn't exactly want to . . . and it really didn't seem all that necessary. I was glad Freddie had found a niche for himself.

We walked a bit in silence until I tried to make a left at the bumper cars.

"Not that way," Freddie said quickly.

"Why?" I asked, throwing him a look. "I want to go see the petting zoo."

"What are you, eight?" Freddie asked, frowning. "I already told you I don't like the pumpkin people. Besides, the animals are asleep."

"What pumpkin people? You mean those teenage guys by the corn maze?" I pointed back over at the high fence covered with tall stalks of corn. Standing by the entrance were two guys wearing large pumpkin-head masks leaning against the booth.

"Do you see any other pumpkin people?"

"Why are you being so snarky?"

Freddie huffed a breath through his nose. "I had a bad experience as a child. A nanny left me in the corn maze with *them*, and now they freak me out."

"Oh my God," I said, grimacing. "That sounds kind of awful."

"I know, right?" Freddie said, eyes widening. "Besides, I think they're local kids volunteering, and I've been riding the adolescents of this town pretty hard to keep them in l—"

"Wait," I said, putting my hands up. "You've been doing what now?" Suddenly Grady's concerns were looking a bit more valid.

"All right. All right. Let's not make a big deal of this. I can hear the *sheriff* in your voice." Freddie picked up speed, forcing fairgoers to clear a path for him. "Besides, I don't see how anyone could not be freaked out by those

things what with the soulless eyes peering out of the gar-
ish oversized gourds."

"Right."

He shuddered. "Like they don't have any expression . . .
except for what's cut out . . . and it's frozen."

"Sure."

"Stop judging me!"

I grabbed his arm to stop him. "Freddie, it's fine. We
don't have to go anywhere near the pumpkin people,
and—Oh my God there's one right behind you!"

Freddie jumped and pivoted in the air to face the empty
space behind him.

"You are a horrible person."

I chuckled.

"Seriously. There's no excuse for that."

We walked on through the midway of games. "So what
happened tonight? Why aren't you with Grady?"

I told Freddie about the campfire with the Moroccan-
style seating. I told him about the wine, the twinkle lights,
and the salmon plank. I still couldn't quite believe it even
though I was the one setting the scene.

"Wow," Freddie said with a nod. "Talk about overkill.
Doesn't he know you're a sure thing?"

I whacked him on the arm.

"Ow," he said, rubbing the spot. "So what happened?"

"I messed up. I told him about Kit Kat coming by
and—" I snapped my mouth shut. *Dammit!* Again. Telling Grady ruined our evening, but telling Freddie, well,
that could ruin my entire trip.

"What about Kit Kat coming by?"

"It was nothing. She was worried, I mean, upset with
how Grady was questioning Tweety."

Freddie pivoted quickly to stand in front of me, causing me to veer to the right and trip over my own feet. Luckily, I recovered before I hit the dirt. "Hey!"

"You're lying to me."

"I am not." I was suddenly very aware of my face. It happened every time I lied. It was like I no longer knew how to make a natural expression, so my face twisted up into an exaggerated version of the face I made when I smelled something bad.

"You totally are."

"Freddie," I said, sighing. "It's nothing, and you have a tendency to make little things into big things."

"Oh no, my friend. Now I know it's really something," he said with a pretty self-assured nod. "When someone works this hard to say it's nothing, it's definitely something. So what aren't you telling me?"

"Nothing," I said with a little more vigor.

"Tell me. You know you want to. That wasn't me you tripped over just there," he said with a point back. "That was Freud."

I groaned. Maybe Freddie was right. I obviously was having trouble keeping this whole business with Kit Kat in. She had behaved really strangely. "Kit Kat just came by and she, she wanted to make sure that you and I weren't planning to investigate Mr. Masterson's demise."

Freddie shook his head quickly, cocked it to the side, and leaned his ear toward me. "I'm sorry, what was that last part? You mumbled."

I threw my hands into the air and raised my voice. "She doesn't want us asking questions about Mr. Masterson! Which I told her was not a problem because—" I looked at Freddie. He had stopped walking and his eyes were closed. It also looked like he was mumbling something under his breath. "Are you okay?"

He snapped his eyes open. "I was just giving thanks."

"Why? And to whom?"

"For the case," he said with a breath. "And to Farrah Fawcett. I like to think of her as my fairy godmother."

I shook my head. "Oh Jesus."

"Now, it's good that you came to me with this," Freddie said with his eyes squinted into his most considering face. "Grady, while adorable—Salmon plank! Who knew—is out of his league." Freddie started walking again, but I don't think he was seeing any of the fair anymore. Luckily people were still moving out the way.

I scrambled to keep up with him. "No. No. No. We are not doing this. Kit Kat had a very threatening air about her and she flicked my chest," I said, pointing to the bone. "We are just going to let Grady handle this and—"

"Threatening," Freddie repeated, cocking an eyebrow. "Really? This must be very serious."

"Freddie—"

"Erica."

I growled with frustration.

"Look. I'm not saying we should go stir up trouble. Let's just ask a few questions to see if there really is anything to worry about. They might need our help."

I scoffed. "Said no one ever."

"Besides, the sooner we get to the bottom of this, the sooner you and Grady can eat your salmon," he said, his eyebrows jumping up twice in quick succession.

"That had to be the worst euphemism ever."

"Yeah, I realized it as I was saying it," Freddie said, lip curling. "But you can't tell me you're going to be able to focus on love when you're this worried about the twins." I started to say something, but Freddie cut me off. "And don't tell me you're not worried because, again, you wouldn't keep blurting it out if you weren't."

I grumbled something under my breath then said, "Part of me really thinks we should stay out of it this time."

"Oh!" Freddie suddenly hopped in the air. "You know what we're going to do?"

"I'm afraid to ask."

"Bingo!"

"I'm sorry?"

"Bingo. We're going to play bingo. If you want to know what the old-timers are up to, you got to be willing to roll the balls."

I raised my eyebrows.

"Sorry, I was just trying to make bingo sound thug," he said with a quick head shake. "But nothing's landing right." He grabbed my arm.

I didn't move. "And what's this I hear about a pilot?"

"Pilot? What? Oh . . . that's the five-year plan." He gave my arm a yank. "Let's go."

Chapter Seven

I had my doubts that the bingo hall was even open given the fair, but Freddie assured me that it would be packed.

"I've been trying to get out more," he said as we approached the hockey arena. Bingo was held on the second level. "Outreach and whatnot, now that I'm a figure in the community, and it turns out I like seniors. They get me."

"You know, I'm really only coming along because I want to put this whole thing to bed," I said, opening the heavy metal door. "And you need to promise me that we're going to play this cool. We're just going to see what people are saying. Do not bring up the twins."

"Okay, okay. Will you relax? These are my people. I know what I'm doing, Stressica. Actually that doesn't really work. Too bad you weren't named Jessica."

"Yeah, too bad," I said, grabbing the railing anchored in the concrete wall. "Let's just get this over with."

Freddie and I climbed the stairs and opened the doors to the large room. It had the same wood paneling on the walls and the same vinyl floor tiles it had back when I was a teenager. It was the only room big enough in town to hold community events, and occasionally one of the more industrious teenagers in Otter Lake would bring in a real DJ from Manchester or Nashua to throw a dance. I was pretty sure I had some hearing loss as a result. Now maybe eighty or so people filled the room, seated shoulder-to-shoulder. A man with a microphone sat on the mini stage at the back of the room with one of those giant bingo cages. Beside him sat a funeral wreath on an easel. I doubted that the Mastersons ever made it out to bingo night—they were more of the class to be donating prizes—but it was nice the town was thinking of them.

Freddie and I walked in, and even though our footsteps were echoing off the walls, not a single person turned to look at us. All eyes were glued to the cards on the table.

Suddenly a microphone screeched. "B-six! I have a B-six!"

I jolted. Hands darted around the tables—one lady had at least fifteen cards. It then occurred to me that I had never actually been inside a bingo hall before. I hadn't expected it to be quite so . . . *intense*. I leaned toward Freddie and whispered, "This is kind of creep—"

"Shush!"

My gaze shot to a woman with a ferocious-looking expression sitting in the back, near where Freddie and I were standing.

Sorry, I mouthed.

The intensity of her outrage dropped a smidge. She turned back to her game as Freddie led me into the back corner of the room.

"You have to keep it down," he said once we were safely tucked away.

"I had no idea bingo could be so creepy," I said looking over my shoulder. "They're all so quiet . . . and they all have matching markers."

"Those aren't markers," Freddie whispered with a

chuckle. "They are daubers . . . or dabbers if you're weird. Big difference."

"Oh, well, pardon me."

"This is serious business. These guys are dealing in real money."

"What kind of money are we talking here?"

"The pot is two grand."

My jaw dropped. "Shut up! Two grand? I want in."

"It's too late now," he said, dropping his voice even lower. "Now behave yourself. They'll break soon."

I muttered something under my breath and leaned back against the wall, folding my arms across my chest. Suddenly it felt like I couldn't quite stand on my own anymore. All the drama of the day was finally catching up to me. I was really tired . . . maybe if I closed my eyes just for a minute . . .

Giant swans. Giant swans flying through the air with people riding them. Kit Kat and Tweety riding them. Giant swans diving. Dive-bombing! Right above my head! No! No!

"Erica, wake up," Freddie said, jerking my elbow. "You're making that snoring sound at the back of your throat."

"Sorry," I mumbled, wiping my hand against my mouth. "What's happening?"

"They're between games. Time to go."

I pushed myself off the wall with my foot to follow.

"Oh look! There's Mr. and Mrs. Cruikshank," Freddie said with obvious affection in his voice. "They hate each other. Let's go say hello."

"What? Freddie—" But he was already on his way. All I could do was hurry to keep up. Now that the round was over, more than a few players were giving me curious looks. Everyone was probably still getting used to the idea of me coming back to town more often.

"Hi, guys!" I heard Freddie call out cheerfully to the older couple. The man must have been about six four, a little hunched in the shoulders, but in pretty good shape considering he had to be in his seventies. The woman was only maybe five foot and had a slightly bewildered look about her eyes.

"Freddie," the man said, taking his hand. "Good to see you. Keeping things running smoothly?"

"You know it."

"Are you dating anyone yet?" the woman popped in.

"Mildred," Freddie said with a chuckle. "You know I don't date."

"Well, you'd better get started," she said, shaking her whole body side-to-side. Her neck must have been frozen. "You're never going to get to adopt a baby if you don't hurry up and get married. It takes a long time to adopt a baby."

"Mildred," the larger man said with a sigh.

"Well, he's going to have to adopt unless he gets a surrogate. Are you getting a surrogate? Maybe, maybe her?" she asked, jerking a thumb in my direction.

"I would rather die," Freddie said.

I smacked him on the arm.

"What?" Freddie asked, throwing me a look.

Mildred nodded before leaning in to him to whisper, "Her eggs are getting old anyway."

I felt my mouth open to say something, but I caught it just in time.

"Mildred, really," the man said, giving me an apologetic smile that looked even more worn out than I felt.

Mildred backhanded her husband lightly on the belly without turning the rest of her body. "You never want me to talk about the important stuff."

"Leave the boy alone. He's busy keeping the town secure."

I suddenly remembered what Grady had said about his war for public perception. "Well," I said, "Freddie and the sheriff's department of course."

The older man scoffed. "That's questionable. How long was Forrester investigating the wrong suspect for Dickie Morrison's murder?"

"Yeah, but he wasn't the only one," I said. "A lot of us thought—"

"It's what all the gay couples do now," Mildred said jumping back in. "There's nothing wrong with it."

"I know there's nothing wrong with it," Mr. Cruickshank answered with a sigh, "but maybe Freddie doesn't want kids. Maybe he doesn't want to get married."

Freddie chuckled and leaned over to me to whisper, "Aren't they great?"

"Of course he does," Mildred replied. "Everybody wants to get married. It gives life meaning."

The older man was shaking his head now. "What I'd give for a little less meaning."

"Oh really?" Mildred suddenly twisted the cap off her dauber and gave three good pounds with it across her husband's white shirt, leaving three purple circles behind.

"That's the fourth shirt this month." He rubbed the spot in between his eyebrows. "And she does the laundry." He sighed again before turning back to his wife. "He's never going to want to get married if you keep behaving this way."

"Stop it. Marriage is good," she said, patting Freddie on the arm. "And you don't want to leave it until it's too late." I'm not sure if she was even making an attempt at subtlety, but her eyes most definitely slid in my direction. She then patted my arm and turned with her husband to talk to someone else.

"Well," Freddie said carefully. "We didn't find much out, but that was—"

"Can I just ask why are they all supportive of your babies, but I'm a spinster? I'm still in my twenties!"

"Well, I would say it's because babies are cute, and spinsters aren't, but—"

"I hate you."

"I'm kidding! I'm kidding," he said, laughing. "Ah, it's good to have stressy Erica back. Come on. Let's mingle."

"This is not at all how tonight was supposed to go," I said, following Freddie around a table toward the other side of the room.

He kept walking. "I know."

"If only I'd kept my mouth shut, I can't even imagine what Grady and I might be doing right now." I let my hands flop to my sides. "Okay, let's get on with this. Look, there's—" I stopped suddenly because I heard someone talking from somewhere behind me. Talking about the twins.

"Tweety always did have a reputation for being a bit loose. And then there's the Viagra he was taking."

I spun around to see who had said it.

I saw the back of a magenta-colored head of hair. Marg Johnson. The same woman talking trash about Tweety at the fair.

"Erica," Freddie said. "Where are you going?"

I couldn't answer; I was too busy walking in the opposite direction.

"Erica! Slow down," Freddie called after me. "Remember what you said about laying low?"

This woman needed a talking-to.

"This doesn't feel low, Erica!" Freddie shouted. "Not low!"

Chapter Eight

I positioned myself right behind Marg's chair and said, "I'm sorry, Marg. What was that you were saying?"

She looked up at me over her shoulder. "Erica Bloom. No surprise you'd be defending the old hussy."

I reeled back a few steps. I totally should have let Kit Kat kick this woman's ass back at the fair. "You take that back, Marg. I mean it."

Suddenly I noticed that the entire room had turned to look at me.

The man with the microphone then announced, "Quiet now! Quiet now. We need to get started."

Freddie appeared at my side, hand on my elbow. "Erica, I think maybe—"

I yanked my arm away from him. "I mean it. Take it back."

Marg pointedly ignored me and leaned over to her friend, whispering intentionally loud enough for all to hear, "Wouldn't surprise me one bit if they still had a thing going on." She flared her nose with disgust. "Flaunting it for all to see. No morals, that one."

"N-seven!" the man with the microphone announced,

with just a touch of worry in his voice. "I've got an N-seven!"

"O-two!"

Whoa. What crazy person had shouted that?

Oh right. It was me.

"I-twenty-four! N-thirteen!"

Shocked faces turned in my direction.

Freddie leaned in and whispered, "What exactly are you doing right now?"

I locked glares with Marg. "Nobody's playing this game until she takes it back."

The man at the microphone recovered himself. "That was an N—"

"Y-thirty-three!" I yelled.

"There's no *Y* in Bingo!" Freddie shouted back.

"Get her out of here!" a woman from across the room cried.

Then someone else shouted, "What did he call?"

"I don't know," a reply came. "Does anyone know? Half the damn room's got dementia!"

"Sorry!" I shouted. "But I'm not leaving until she takes it back." I kept my gaze locked on Marg. "Take it back."

"Marg! Take whatever the hell it is back!" a voice shouted. "We want to play!"

The man with the microphone politely cleared his voice and said, "Could someone please escort—"

"I'm on it!" Freddie shouted. "I'm on it." He then moved to grab my arm, but I spun on him and shouted, "*Nyet!*"

"Russian? Really? 'Cause that's going to help you with this crowd," Freddie said. "Erica, are you ok—"

I quieted him with a look. "I told her to take it back. And she's going to take it back."

Freddie put his hands up.

"For the love of God, Marg! Just take it back, so we can play," another voice called out.

I spun back on the Magenta Menace. She readjusted herself in her seat. "Fine. I take it back. Satisfied?"

I gritted my teeth. "For now. But you're done talking this filth. Are we clear?" I turned and faced Freddie. "Let's go."

"Sure. Sure," he whispered before licking his lips. "But do you think we could make it look like I was, you know, pulling you out of here . . . by force? It would be good for my image."

I sighed and stuck my wrists out like I was waiting to be cuffed.

His eyes lit up, and he mouthed the words, *I'll buy you a beer*, before announcing, "On your way, Bloom. Nobody wants your shenanigans here."

Twenty minutes later, I cut the motor to my mother's boat and let it drift toward the dock. It had been a pretty chilly ride. I could barely feel my fingers. Freddie had begged me to stop at the Dawg for beers, but I really felt we had spent enough time together for one evening. The fair had also shut down for the night, and the sound of crickets replaced the grating mechanic hum of the rides. I hopped out of the boat and tied it off on the dock just as my phone buzzed in my back pocket.

Grady.

"Hey," I said in a tired but happy voice.

"Hey," he replied, in an also tired, but a little less happy tone. "I just wanted to call and say I'm sorry about tonight, and—"

"No, I'm sorry," I said pacing the planks of the dock. "You went to all that trouble, and then I had to go and derail your one-track mind—speaking of which, is everything all worked out with Mr. Masterson?"

I heard Grady sigh on the other end of the line.

"It's not?"

"I'm waiting for a report."

"A report?" My mind flitted through the possibilities of what that could mean. "Grady, tell me this is just a formality-type thing."

He sighed again. "All I'm going to say is there's still a chance it was accidental."

"You're not saying . . . ?"

"Erica," he said, voice full of warning.

"I know. I know. You can't talk about it. But . . ." I stopped to chew the side of my thumbnail.

"What?"

Ugh, I could practically hear his brow furrowing through the phone. "Just in the spirit of us being honest and all that," I said, before taking a breath. "Did you know that Mr. Masterson was taking Viagra?"

Silence.

"I just mean, maybe the medication brought on a coronary because I thought people with heart conditions weren't supposed to take it."

Another moment of silence passed before he said, "Actually, I just learned tonight that that is no longer the case. It depends on the condition. Sometimes Viagra actually helps the heart." Ooh, he was talking in a tone that I didn't like at all. "But where did *you* get this information?"

"Nowhere," I said attempting to kick a pebble off the dock, but all I managed to do was kick the edge of an uneven plank, making me stagger forward a little.

"Erica."

"Well, after I left your place, I ran into Freddie and—"

"No. No. No. No."

I paused a beat then added, "And we went to play bingo."

Grady sighed again, only this time it sounded a little more . . . angry.

"And some people were talking—"

"So you and Freddie just randomly decided to go play bingo?" he asked, not letting me finish.

"Well . . ."

"You know, Erica," he said, "if you don't want to date me, there are easier ways to go about it. Just say, *Grady, I don't want to date you.*"

"What?" I shouted, making some creature plop into the water. "What are you talking about?"

"This elaborate plan to sabotage any chance we have by playing detective with Freddie?"

"I'm not playing detective. People talk, Grady. It's a small town."

"Uh-huh."

I smacked my lips together. "Fine, maybe we were a little bit. But this is Kit Kat and Tweety we're talking about. I'm worried about them. I've never seen Kit Kat act that way before. She was practically threatening me." I heard my voice echoing off the water.

"Really? Threatening? You failed to mention she was *threatening*, but I bet you shared that little tidbit with Freddie."

I looked up to the stars, shaking my head. "Grady, come on. I swear, we didn't do anything illegal. We were just talking to people."

"And then you'll be breaking into somebody's house, and—"

"One time!" I said putting my *one time* finger in the air as if he could see it. "I swear, you break into a house one time, and nobody wants to let it go. I thought we were past all this!" I dropped my voice. "How is Tommy doing, by the way?" I didn't wait for an answer. "And I was worried you were going to arrest me for murder!"

"And there it is. The real issue." I heard him take a breath. "You don't think I can do my job."

My head was already shaking no. "I never said that."

"You didn't have to!" he shouted. "Look, I get that there was a good six-, seven-year break in our relationship—"

"Eight."

"But I've grown up since then," Grady finished. "I no longer drive snowmobiles over ice that is too thin. I don't ride around in the back of pickup trucks, especially not with beer. And I don't phone it in to work just so I get to wear a uniform that makes the women crazy."

"Women do not get crazy." Although I nearly did the first time I saw him in it. In fact, for a second there, I think I might have mistaken him for a stripper cop.

"Whatever. The point is I have grown up! I am good at my job. It's one thing to have Freddie undermining me at every turn—"

"He doesn't mean to undermine you. He's just—" I struggled to find the right explanation. "He's just finding his place—"

"I don't need you doing it too!"

I froze for a second. "Grady . . . I'm sorry. Really. I didn't realize you felt this way. I—"

"You know what?" he said, once again sounding tired. "It's been a really long day. A day that didn't turn out at all how I expected."

"I know! I—"

"Maybe we could just talk tomorrow when we've both had some sleep."

I didn't want to do that at all. I wanted to solve it now. But I figured I was in no position to make demands. "Okay."

" 'Night Erica."

" 'Night."

I ended the call and hugged myself a little against the cold before I smacked my phone against my forehead a good three or four times.

I then turned on the dock to head up to the retreat—only

to see about fifteen silent people, looking horrified and poised to run in about fifteen different directions to hide. They must have come down the steps not realizing I was here.

My mother at least had the decency to have her face twisted in an apologetic grimace.

"Midnight meditation?" I called out in a loud voice.

She nodded.

"Good. Good." I walked toward the crowd of silent people, who quickly moved to let me through. "You know, I think you people may be onto something with this whole silence thing."

If I had been asked to guess the night before, I would have thought I'd wake up in a bad mood. But I didn't. I had left my bedroom's window—I mean, my old bedroom's window—cracked just a little, and the crisp fall air had blown in, leaving me snug under quilts and comforters. Bright sunlight also filled the room, promising me another spectacular fall day. I listened to the distant sound of a chain saw rippling across the lake and the noisy calls of geese talking about flying somewhere warm. Nope, it wasn't a bad day. Not at all. It couldn't be a bad day because it was *do over* day.

So yesterday hadn't exactly launched my trip off to a good start. And I hadn't exactly handled everything the way I would have liked. My mind suddenly tripped over the memory of me shouting out random bingo numbers the night before, but I shook it off. In fairness, a lot had been thrown my way in a short amount of time. I snuggled more deeply under the covers. And really, a good night's sleep could add a lot of perspective to a situation. So Mr. Masterson had been getting a little pharmaceutical help in the penile direction; that didn't make him a target for murder. Hell, if that were the case, half the men in America would be dead. Well, maybe not half, but I could see my point. Mr. Masterson's death had just been a shock. That's why people were acting all crazy. That's probably why Grady was getting some sort of report. And once he had that report squared away, everything could get back on track. He still had the rest of the week off, and that gave me a lot of time to convince him I thought he was a great sheriff. Because I totally did! Okay, maybe when I first came home a month or two ago I was a little surprised at his career path, but I had seen a different side of him since then. He was rapidly becoming the most responsible person I knew living in Otter Lake, which was really bizarre . . . and sexy. I think it was time for Sheriff Forester to take me in for all my crimes. Yeah, now that's how I wanted to spend the week.

I wasn't *Stressica*.

As for the Freddie–Grady situation, really, I just needed to sit the two of them down with a couple of beers to talk this whole *who is responsible for keeping Otter Lake safe* thing through. I knew that Freddie secretly looked up to Grady, and Grady needed to see Freddie for the resource that he was. Whatever that was.

Yeah, everything was going to be fine. Better than fine. I would just snooze a little longer under my warm, warm bl—

Rap! Rap! Rap!

My eyes swung to the window as I jolted straight up in bed. I peered at the figure through the sheer white fabric of my drapes, and once I recognized who it was, I flopped back down.

Chapter Nine

"No," I groaned. "Go away."

"I know you're in there, Erica ! Wake up!"

I shook my head against my pillow. Kit Kat. Or was it Tweety?

I cracked one eye open to once again look at the figure appearing and disappearing through the folds of my gauzy curtain.

Tweety. Definitely Tweety. Okay, time to go round two with Twin Two. I sighed. Had news of my scuffle with Marg Johnson at the bingo hall really spread that fast?

I groaned and shut my eyes.

Rap! Rap! Rap!

"I'm coming!"

I swiveled my legs out of bed, planting one foot on a big squishy mound of fur. Half a second later claws dug into my toes.

"Ow!" I screamed, snatching my foot back. I looked over the bed at Caesar's eyes, which spoke of dreams of my violent death. "If you don't want to get stepped on, why are you sleeping there?"

"Erica!" Tweety's voice shouted from outside. "Stop fooling around with that cat and get out here!"

I shuffled down to the bottom of my bed and stepped out, giving Caesar a wide berth. I then yanked a sweater over my head and pulled on some sweatpants.

I grumbled my way outside, gearing myself up for the earful I was about to receive, while reminding myself that Tweety had been through a trauma of sorts. She had been with someone in his final moments of life. I supposed she was owed some sort of consideration.

I walked out the front door to find that Tweety had already come around the porch and was waiting for me.

I took in her expression. She seemed mad and serious. I didn't like the twins mad and serious. The twins were supposed to be loud and obnoxious and funny and happy and oftentimes just a little drunk.

"Good morning," I said carefully. "How are you?"

"I'm fine. Why wouldn't I be?" The multiple frown lines in her forehead deepened.

I threw my hands in the air. "I don't know, maybe because you took a ride in the Tunnel of Love with a dead man yesterday—a married dead man?" I sighed and rubbed my face. *Very sensitive, Erica.* There was just something about all this business that made me feel like a little kid watching a superhero take off his mask. The twins, despite all of their foibles, were good, strong women. I didn't want to believe that Tweety had anything going on with a married man. It wasn't my business. And yet, a part of me really felt it was.

She pointed at me. "That's exactly what I'm talking about."

I folded my arms across my chest, just in case this twin had any thwacking ideas.

"You leave this alone, Erica."

"Leave what alone, Tweety?" I asked. "Maybe if you told me what was going on here, I would get why I needed to leave it alone."

"Don't sass your elders."

"Oh, okay. Well, that clears that up." I sighed. "You know people in town are talking. I'd like to shut them up, but I don't know how."

Her eyes softened into something that looked a little like worry, making my stomach turn. I mean, angry Tweety sucked, but worried, vulnerable Tweety was just wrong. "Tell me how I can help," I tried. "What is going on?"

She shook her head.

"Okay, I can't take this anymore. I need to ask you something." I inhaled deeply, trying to loosen some of the tightness in my chest. "Were you having an affair with Mr. Masterson?"

Her eyes widened. "No!"

Relief rushed over me. "Oh thank God. I mean I didn't think so, but why were you on that ride with him?"

She shook her head. "You need to leave this alone. No good can come of it."

"Man, you sound exactly like your sister."

Her eyes narrowed and she took a step closer to me. "What do you mean, *you sound exactly like your sister*? What did she say to you?"

Uh-oh. I shook my head. "I swear, it feels like the entire lake has been turned upside down," I muttered. "Because, really, since when do you two keep secrets from each other?" She didn't answer. Instead she turned on her heel and made for the stairs. "Wait! Where are you going?"

"Just do as you're told, Erica," she said looking back at me and pointing, "and stay out of it."

"You can't tell me what to do," I said, letting the words

fly before realizing just how painfully immature they would sound. "You're not my mother."

Suddenly somebody tapped me on the shoulder.

"Wah!" I spun in the air to look behind me. "But you are."

My mother rolled her index finger a few times, indicating that I was to follow her into the lodge. She led me to her private office, the room that sat in between our bedrooms. I wasn't a big fan of hanging out in there, mainly because there were so many self-help books double-stacked on the shelves, it made dying in an avalanche a real possibility. But my mother had been walking with a determination she rarely took on. It meant business.

I slumped in the worn swivel chair that faced the desk. It was the only piece of furniture in the lodge made from leather. It caused my mother no end of moral angst—she was a vegan after all—but it had belonged to my grandfather, and even though I had never met the man, I knew my mother loved him—although I suspected their relationship had been bumpy.

I stared at my mother's hands, clasped at her lower back as she looked out the window. Seriously, this was ridiculous. How was she going to give me a talking-to if she wasn't even talking? And for that matter, what had I even done? I blew some air out my lips in a noisy stream. I didn't need to play this game. I planted my hands on the slender curved armrests of my chair to push myself up. I needed to buy a certain sheriff some coffee. "Mom, I—"

Suddenly she spun, slightly crouched, hands hovering in the air, palms down.

"Whoa," I said, dropping back into my seat. "Are you okay?"

She raised her eyebrows and cocked her head as though

she were listening to a voice that was coming from far, far away.

I huffed a sound through my nose. "Oh great," I said. "Story time."

She pointed a finger in the air and made small circles that trailed up and away.

"Mom, do you think maybe this one time, you could make an exception on your vow, and—"

She slapped the top of the desk hard with both palms.

"Jeez! Fine!" Say what you want about my mother, the one quality she had in spades was her authenticity. No one would ever catch her speaking during a vow of silence, and I had to admit there was something reassuring about that.

She rolled her finger again above her head.

"All right." I blew more air through my lips, making them flap slightly. "A long, long time ago."

She waved her hand in the air for me to stop.

"Okay," I said slowly, then added, "Not that long ago?"

She smiled and waved a hand for me to continue.

"A longish time ago?"

She bobbed her head from side to side as though considering, and then nodded her approval.

"Okay, a longish time ago—"

She then squinted before sticking her finger up in the air to indicate she had an idea. She then moved to pick up what looked like a very heavy—sledgehammer? She swung it over her head, and then it slammed down on the floor.

"Oh!" I shouted and pointed. "You were working on the railroad!"

It didn't take a charades expert to figure out the look she flashed me could best be described as *withering*.

"Sorry," I grumbled, slouching back in my seat. "I guess that doesn't make much sense. I got ahead of myself."

She put up another finger then squatted into a seated

position and threw her hands up into the air as though she were going down a hill. A roller coaster!

"The fair!"

She flashed me that proud smile only parents can give their children.

"The fair from a longish time ago!"

Her smile deepened.

I smiled back, readjusting myself in my seat to a more alert position. Okay, maybe this wasn't so bad.

She paused again, then curved her arms out in front of her and started walking on the spot.

"Fat man!" I said with a point.

She furrowed her eyebrows with disappointment.

"Sorry! But you made the belly!"

She moved her curved arms from her stomach higher to her chest.

"Puffed out? A powerful man?"

She snapped her fingers then rolled her hand for me to keep going.

"A powerful man at the fair!"

She nodded. Then suddenly she was gone.

She had dropped to the floor in a noisy *clunk!*

Chapter Ten

"Mom!" I launched myself from my seat, sending it spinning into the back wall. I jumped forward, planted my hands on her desk, and looked over.

There lay my mother, limbs contorted in weird angles, eyes closed, and tongue hanging out of her mouth.

"Wow," I said. "Nice commitment."

She opened one eye to give me a wink.

I shuffled back to retrieve my chair while my mother got to her feet, brushing off her ankle-length skirt.

"So the powerful man from a longish time ago died?" I asked.

She rolled her hand.

"At the fair?"

She nodded.

"Okay, Mom, what does this have to do with anything?"

She put up one finger in a *wait* gesture.

She scrunched her face up again into a thinking expression. She then repeatedly slid her head from side to side on her shoulders.

"Okay," I said slowly. "I have no idea what that's supposed to be." I pursed my lips. "Bollywood?"

She slapped her palm against her forehead.

"I'm trying!" I shouted. "Wait! I've got it!"

She looked at me expectantly.

"The twins!"

And there was that mom smile again.

"So the twins have something to do with a man who died at the fair from a longish time ago?"

She nodded.

I swiveled side-to-side gently in my chair. "And that has something to do with why they are so upset with what happened yesterday?"

She nodded again, more quickly this time.

"But what?" I asked.

My mom held up another finger for me to wait. She seemed to be thinking for a moment. Then she snapped her fingers and brought her hands to her armpits, flapped them like wings.

"A bird!" I shouted. "No! Tweety!"

She nodded then tapped the ring finger on her left hand.

"Tweety's not married," I said slowly. "Wait. Engaged?"

My mother nodded.

"Tell me she wasn't engaged to Mr. Masterson."

My mother grimaced.

"Crap." I fell back against the chair. Well, I guess that was part of the history Kit Kat was talking about. "But what does the powerful man's death have to do with Tweety being engaged to Mr. Masterson?"

My mother just shrugged.

I waited for her to continue, but she was already moving around the desk to leave.

"Wait! Where do you think you're going?"

She tapped the spot on her wrist where a watch would have been if she ever wore one.

"No! We were just getting started!" But I too could already hear the sounds of a bunch of people not saying anything entering the retreat. I sighed. "Mom, before you go . . ."

She turned.

"You know both Kit Kat and Tweety have warned me to leave this alone."

She nodded.

"But I'm worried, and I get the feeling they might need some help with all the talk that's going on around town."

She nodded some more.

"I'm not sure how Grady's going to feel about this, though."

She screwed up her face in a *Who the hell cares what he thinks?* expression. Being the overprotective momster she could be, she had an issue or two with Grady—mainly because she blamed him for my moving to Chicago in the first place.

"You're right. The twins are family," I said firmly. "I just wish I knew how to help. I don't want to make things worse." I shook my head and got to my feet. "But you know what? I am absolutely positive that once the medical examiner has looked over everything, he'll declare that Mr. Masterson died of natural causes."

"So did you hear that Mr. Masterson may not have died of natural causes?"

I fake-cried a few breaths. "Freddie, I haven't even had my coffee." I tied my mom's boat off at one of the posts on the marina's dock and wiped my hands on my jeans. It was pretty cold. I'd need gloves soon. "Don't be messing with me."

He swayed back and forth on his heels, arms folded across the front of his uniform. "I'm not. Rumor has it the medical examiner won't sign off on anything until he runs more tests."

I groaned and rubbed my eyes. *Thanks to me.*

"Yeah, Mrs. Masterson is dead-set against—oh, bad choice of words," he said, bringing a hand to his mouth, before whispering, "an autopsy. But again—"

"Rumor has it," I filled in.

"Rumor has it that the medical examiner is going for a court order," Freddie said with a knowing nod. He then raised his eyebrows and made a clicking sound with his tongue. "So you know what I'm thinking?"

"Oh God, here we go."

"Mrs. Masterson probably offed him in a fit of jealous rage because he was having an affair with—" Freddie stopped talking to take a step away from me. "—with someone." He then took a hurried sip from his coffee, peeking up at my reaction over the rim. "So what do you think?"

I didn't say anything, just planted my fists on my hips and looked up at the sky.

"Erica?"

Still nothing.

"You're mad. I knew you'd be mad. You're doing that thing where you rub the side of your teeth with your tongue like you're cleaning them—gross habit by the way—and you only do that when you're mad." He took another step back. "But, hey, it's better that you hear it from me. I'm sure I'm not the only one thinking it."

"I heard nothing, Freddie," I said as flatly as I could.

He squinted.

"I heard nothing . . . because you said nothing," I said with a sharp nod. "And do you know why that is?"

"Um, no?"

"Because you heard nothing, and, really, that means that you have nothing to say. And that's the end of that."

I stomped past him on the dock. I really could not have this conversation until I made it to the Dawg and had a coffee in my hand. This was *do over* day. Why was everybody trying to ruin *do over* day?

I heard Freddie shuffling along the planks to keep up with me. He didn't like docks. The swaying sensation always made him feel like he was falling.

"Come on," he called out, but the sound was quieter than it should have been, given that he was probably looking down at his feet to make sure they weren't going for the edge. "I'm on your side. I'm on the twins' side."

I stopped at the end of the dock, waiting for Freddie to catch up. "It's not you," I said with a sigh. Then I remembered all of Grady's difficulties with Freddie. "Well, it's a little bit you. But it's mainly that I just can't believe any of this," I said, throwing my hands into the air.

Freddie carefully stepped over the final lip of the dock onto the ground. "Which part?" he asked with a smile at his ability to once again successfully navigate the dock danger.

"So like every time I come home I can expect a murder?" I asked, meeting his eye. "Is this the new normal?"

"Are you okay?" he asked carefully. "You sound like you're working yourself up to something here."

I put my hand on my forehead. "And the twins! I know they had nothing to do with this." Okay, that was a big ol' lie. My conversations with the twins and my charades session with my mother had told me they at least had something to do with something. "But that doesn't matter in this town! You've already probably got everyone's tongues wagging with your theories," I said loudly, sticking out my palm as though I were serving up a handful of indignation to him.

"Hey! I—"

"And you know what this means, don't you?" I asked, nodding angrily. "Grady's going to be working! Probably all week. Maybe even the weekend! I'm never going to get him on that Ferris wheel or . . . or get him to win me some teddy bear at some overpriced game!"

"Well, that's probably—"

"Which sucks! On so many levels!"

"It does, but—"

"How am I supposed to be able to figure out what's going on with me and Grady if we can't find any time to spend with each other that isn't about murder . . . or you!" I shouted with probably a little too much disgust on my face.

"Hey, I can't help it if—"

"I mean, we need some quality time together that involves more intimacy than you can get through a phone!"

"Ew."

"It's ridiculous!" I shouted, turning to make my way back in the direction of coffee.

"Hey!" Freddie called out after me. "You know what else is funny?"

"What?" I answered tiredly.

"I bet you Mr. Masterson would have thought his murder would have been a little bit more about him."

I skidded to a stop. A moment later, I glanced up from the dirt I was staring at to meet Freddie's eye. "I hate you so much right now."

He nodded. "I'm keeping you firm on the path to righteousness."

I eyed his smile. "You could look a little less pleased with yourself."

"I am grateful for the small things gifted to me by life."

I turned on my heel, headed once again for the Dawg.

"Where are you going in such a hurry? I thought you could walk my beat with me at the fair. The midway doesn't open until eleven. Do you want to get breakfast?"

"Can't. Got stuff to do."

"Like what?"

"Well," I said, slowing my pace to allow Freddie to

catch up. "I thought I'd start by buying myself and Grady a coffee to apologize—"

"Uh-oh. What did you do now?"

I spun to face him. "It's not what I did. It's what we"—I gestured back and forth between us—"did."

"Now I get why you're in such a bad mood. Guess he heard about your breakdown at the bingo hall."

"Yes, he did. From me."

"What did you go and do that for?"

"I don't know," I said, throwing my hands into the air. "Maybe because I don't want to lie to him every time we talk?"

He stopped walking. "We're fighting a lot these days. I think we need a date night to revitalize our relationship."

I turned. "Freddie, don't you see that's part of the problem? I can't do the stuff you want me to do without it upsetting Grady. And I can't do the stuff he wants to do with me because he's already busy trying to be super-awesome sheriff guy. And do you know why he's doing that? Because nobody trusts him anymore because they're all too busy trusting you!"

Freddie nodded, but his face tightened. "I see."

I instantly regretted my words. This wasn't his fault. I was just frustrated by . . . everything. "Aw, I didn't mean it like that."

"No," he said quickly. "It's fine."

"It's not fine," I said. "I didn't—"

"But," Freddie said, cutting me off. "I think you're missing something pretty important here."

I exhaled roughly. "And what's that?"

"When it comes to finding out what's happening with the twins and this whole mess, you've talked about what I want to do to get to the bottom of it. And you've talked about what Grady wants. But what is it that you want do, Erica? Do you want to do something? Or nothing?"

I felt my brow crinkle. "I, I—"

"No, don't answer," Freddie said, putting his hand up in a *stop* gesture. "I want you to think about it." He was walking backward away from me. "Because if you do— really think about it, I mean—I'm pretty certain that you'll come to the conclusion that you have never felt more alive than when you're doing what we do . . . with me." His eyes darted around a moment as though he was making sure he had that right. Then he nodded and turned to stomp away, nearly running over an older couple strolling hand in hand. He had to hop around them in a semicircle with his hands up to avoid a collision.

As the couple he nearly hit moved past me, I heard one of them mutter, "I thought he was gay?"

A few minutes later, I was attempting to pull open the door of the Dawg with two large coffees in my hands. Normally, I would have refused to do what Freddie had told me to, based on principle alone, but his words were still bouncing around in my brain. What did I want? It was a pretty deep question on a lot of levels, and it brought up a lot of other questions. Had I come home just to see Grady? Or was there a part of me that really wanted to come home? And if there was a part of me that wanted that, could I handle all that came with it? What if things between Grady and me didn't work out? Did I still want to come home? Some-where, deep down, I was starting to suspect that a part of me did feel like I belonged in Otter Lake . . . and that was terrifying.

And what about Freddie and all his detective adven-tures? If I was being, completely, *completely* honest, I did get a bit of rush out of the whole business. Freddie didn't make me go to that bingo hall. I wanted to. But it was ridiculous. Otter Lake Security was not a real option for me. It was like playing dress-up—and yet Freddie had somehow managed to find a way to get paid for it. That was the most ridiculous part of all.

Gah, I had a headache with all this merry-go-round thinking. I needed to go back to the whole living-in-the-moment thing. At least for a minute or two. I finally managed to get the door of the Dawg open so I could step outside. Yes, sunshine. I needed to *feel* the sunshine, smell the fresh air, absorb the beauty of my surroundings . . . ponder why there was a group of people standing on the sidewalk staring at something across the street with looks of horror on their faces.

Yup, that was odd.

Two men, one wearing a red flannel shirt, the other a blue, were just standing there, staring, along with a woman. There was also a younger couple huddled a little farther down the sidewalk, clutching a stroller protectively, like at any moment they might have to run. All of them were looking at the same spot across the street. I tracked their collective gaze, hearing the woman say, "That poor, poor man. He has no idea."

Hmm, she must mean that tall, blond guy in the dressy pants standing in front of Mrs. Moore's house. Strange. I mean, the pants looked good. Really good. Like I was having trouble looking away good. But definitely out of place for this town. You could wear those pants to play golf. Maybe even brunch. And he didn't look like a *poor* man to me, but Mrs. Moore, who was standing beside him, pointing at the porch, well, she looked pretty upset.

"What is he thinking?" Red-Flannel asked.

"I'm telling you he doesn't know," the man in blue answered with a pitying chuckle. "How could he?"

"But she won't send him under there after it?" the woman went on.

"That's exactly what she's thinking. She's nuts. It's like that time she called the fire department for help. They wouldn't touch it either."

"But his father just died!"

My eyes whipped back over to the man. Matthew Masterson. Well, that explained the fancy golfing pants. He was an architect in New York last I heard. He must be back in town for . . . well, of course, he was back in town. His father had just died.

"Oh no! He's going to do it!"

Matthew dropped to his knees and moved his head around as though trying to see past the latticework covering the space underneath the porch. He then edged toward a gap between the interlaced wood and a bush.

The woman slapped her hands over her face. "I can't watch."

The man chuckled again.

"Don't just stand there laughing!" The woman whacked him on his arm. "Do something!"

"Oh, I'm not going over there."

"What's going on?" I asked, edging closer to the couple.

The man in the red flannel shirt gave me a nod. "It's the fair. Got Mrs. Moore's Buttercup all upset. He tried to escape the backyard and somehow got himself stuck there under the porch."

I shot a sideways look back over to the house. "I take it Buttercup's not friendly."

The man in the blue flannel shirt, standing with the woman who appeared to be his wife, laughed heartily at that. So heartily, he had to wipe a tear from the corner of his eye.

"Get ahold of yourself," she said to him sharply before

leaning around to look at me. "Buttercup has the whole town in terror."

I looked back at the house. Yup, Matthew Masterson was half under the porch now. I pointed back at the Dawg. "Maybe if I got some meat, we could lure . . . Buttercup out?"

The man squinted at me. "Meat?"

"I thought . . ." I squinted. "Buttercup's not a dog?"

He shook his head. "A dog? Heck no. I'd go in for a dog."

I raised my hand in question. "So, Buttercup is a cat?"

He shook his head again, but this time a smile spread across his face.

"Okay," I said, dropping my hand. "You've got me. What is Buttercup? Raccoon? Fox? Beaver?"

"Worse."

When he finally told me, my face dropped.

"You can't be serious."

"Oh, I'm serious."

All three nodded. The couple with the toddler nodded too from their safe distance.

My eyes widened. "And you're just watching?"

"Hey, don't judge us," the other man sputtered. "You haven't seen what that thing can do."

I threw him my best imitation of a *You're going to need to make this right with your God* look I'd learned from a particularly harsh DA back in Chicago. "Someone has to warn him."

The blue-flanneled gentleman waved out a pathway for me with his hand.

I rushed across the street, placing my coffees on the curb before racing up the lawn. Mrs. Moore cut me off halfway. "Erica, isn't it? So glad—"

"He doesn't know," I said more as a statement than a question. "You didn't tell him."

"Buttercup is just misunderstood. He's really quite—"

I ran around her to the porch. "Matthew? You're going to need to back out of there slowly. Really slowly," I said, crouching to see into the gloom.

He looked back at me over his shoulder. "Erica? Erica Bloom?"

I nodded but didn't meet his eye. I was too busy scanning the darkness. I couldn't see anything, but I could feel the danger. "Back up now. Slowly."

"It's been years. Give me a second, I'm just helping Mrs. Moore get her . . . cat? I think she said it was a cat."

"It's not a cat."

His face crinkled in question.

"If it's not a cat, then what is . . ." His voice trailed off when he heard the noise coming from underneath the porch.

The telltale hiss.

We both tracked the sound into the shadows.

"Is . . . that what I think it is?"

"Uh-huh."

The glint of two beady eyes caught the light in the darkness.

It was so much closer than I could have imagined.

Matthew backed up a little, but then looked over to Mrs. Moore, who had her hands still clutched to her chest. I watched his shoulders sink. "Well, I have come this far . . ."

"No! Don't do it!" I shouted.

The beast's mouth opened again, pink tongue quivering in another warning hiss.

Matthew rose to his feet. "I'm not leaving, Buttercup," he said throwing his arms out. "You're going to have to come get me."

Buttercup's wings unfolded and spread impossibly wide into the enclosed space.

My head shook back and forth in horror.
"Matthew . . ."
The wings gave a single flap and—
"Run!"

Chapter Eleven

"You're bleeding a little bit."

"I am?" Matthew asked, lowering himself to the curb before touching his forehead with the tips of his fingers. "I don't remember him getting me there. Then again, all I really remember is the flapping . . . and the endless charging." His eyes widened as he shook his head. "And the screaming. I didn't know I could scream like that."

Ah, Canada geese—aside from moose in mating season, probably the most aggressive predator in New Hampshire. And yes, I say predator, because they feed on fear. Buttercup was no exception.

"Don't worry. You weren't the only one screaming," I said, planting myself on the curb beside him. It was a little strange talking to Matthew like I had just seen him the other day and not years ago, but we had just survived something together. It kind of allowed us to bypass awkward small talk.

"And the honking," Matthew went on. "I think I may have lost some hearing in one ear."

Once the bird had come charging out of the darkness, wings turning like two demented windmills, Matthew had jumped back into me and we both fell. I log-rolled toward the curb, shielding my head, but Matthew got up and faced off with the goose, pacing in a circle, like a sumo wrestler. Apparently Buttercup had a hurt wing and couldn't fly, but his ground game was still pretty tight.

"Good idea to run to the backyard, by the way," I added. Mrs. Moore had a shelter set up for Buttercup behind the house, and once Matthew had run him back, she had swung the gate shut. Of course that meant poor Matthew had been trapped with the hell beast for a few moments alone, but he had managed to jump the fence in the end.

"Yeah, there was no plan. I was just running. But don't tell Mrs. Moore that. No one's ever called me a hero before. It was kind of nice," Matthew said, nodding, looking across the street. "I swear every time I'm in Otter Lake something like this happens."

"Yaaas," I said, throwing my hands into the air. "Thank you."

"You too? Like last time I was home . . ." He cut himself short, and his features suddenly froze. He looked like he had been hit. I had forgotten about his father in all the chaos. He must have too.

"I'm really sorry for your loss," I said after a moment had passed.

"It's okay." He brushed some dirt off the knees of his pants. "It wasn't entirely unexpected." I guess he saw something like shock register on my face, so he added, "My father was not a young man."

I nodded and looked away. I didn't want to imply anything else with my expression. I guess Matthew hadn't been let in on the medical examiner's plan. Grady probably didn't want to cause him or his mother any unnecessary pain.

"I didn't think you lived in Otter Lake anymore?" he

asked in an obvious attempt to change the subject. A very powerful attempt what with his gentle smile and sad eyes. He'd always had that Ralph Lauren Polo ad look going for him . . . not that I would notice such a thing when I was dating somebody else.

"Oh, I don't," I said quickly. "I'm just visiting."

"Is that coffee for your mother? Is she here?" he asked, looking around. "I'd like to say hello, and well, *my* mother said *your* mother makes this blend of tea that—" He paused to rub his forehead then winced when he remembered the cut. "—calms her nerves, I guess? The retreat was actually my next stop. I tried calling . . . and someone picked up. I could have sworn that I heard breathing . . . but I must have been wrong because no one said anything."

"Yeah, no," I said. "You didn't hear wrong. My mom's taken a vow of silence for the week. If you do call back, just talk. Pretend she's an answering machine. It's fine."

Matthew smiled.

I raised my eyebrows. "I could get the tea from my mother and drop it by your place?" Whoa. Where the heck had that come from? I wasn't normally that considerate. "I just need to find Grady first," I added quickly, picking up and raising one of the coffees in the air.

"Grady? Grady Forrester?" There was something in his voice that I couldn't quite put a finger on. Surprise maybe? "Are you two . . . ?"

"No. Not exactly," I said without thinking. "Well, maybe. I don't—"

"Come to think of it," he said, turning his head, considering me more closely, "I seem to remember the crush you had on Grady. Devastated the rest of us boys."

"What? Well . . . that's just . . ." I said, fumbling around for the right word, "stupid."

Matthew's brow furrowed in the cutest way.

"I mean not stupid . . . just not true. I mean . . . never

mind." And suddenly I was a tongued-tied idiot. What the hell was going on?

He chuckled softly. "Well, if you're looking for Grady, I can tell you he's not here."

I cocked my head.

"He's at the estate. Along with the rest of the town." An expression of utter exhaustion crossed his face. "You're welcome to come over to find him."

"Oh, I don't know," I said, shaking my head. "The timing doesn't seem . . . appropriate."

"I could use an ally," he said, touching his cut again. "You know how this town can be."

I smiled. "That I do."

"Besides, I'd rather not walk in alone with a head wound. Everyone will freak out. There will be a million questions." His eyes darted to mine with a bit of a twinkle in them. "This way I can just blame it on you."

"That . . . would probably work."

"Oh," he said, eyes widening. "I was kidding, but . . . well, great. Good. I walked, though," he added, pointing in the direction of the road. "It was such a nice day. I forgot how far it is."

"I've got my mom's boat. Let's go by water."

It was an amazing day. Bright. Sunny. Postcard-perfect with all the colors of the trees reflected in the lake. We didn't talk much during the fifteen minutes or so it took to zip across the water to get to the estate, but I wouldn't have described it as awkward. The boat's engine was loud, and given that Matthew's father had just died, bubbly conversation didn't seem quite right.

I steered the boat in the direction of the dock.

"Wow." I leaned forward as though that would help me take even more in of the house. The lower basement level was made of stone, while the three levels above were constructed of white wood. There was even a turret at the end corner of the porch that traveled up the side of the manse. The estate somehow managed to look both rustic and moneyed at the same time. A hard combination to pull off. "This place is just full of beautiful. I've only ever seen it from a distance."

"It's why I became an architect," Matthew said, but he sounded distracted. I caught him looking at the mass of cars parked on the lawn at the top of the hill. I watched his chest heave with a sigh.

Yup, there was Mrs. Carmichael's florist van . . . no missing the bouquet airbrushed onto the side panel. Then there was the hearse. Mr. Thomson, director of the funeral home, drove that one. Oh, and there was Grady's cruiser. There were a bunch of other cars too, but I didn't recognize them.

Matthew tied off the boat to the long dock, and we walked up the slope of the lawn. We made it about halfway to the house when he said, "Well, at least, this is how my mother would have envisioned it."

"Sorry?"

"All the people paying respects. She still tends to think of herself as Otter Lake royalty."

"In fairness," I said with a click of my tongue, "she kind of is."

"Right. Well, in that case . . . you want a tour of the grounds from the crown prince?"

I looked down at the coffees I was holding. Mine was practically gone. Grady's was definitely cold.

Noticing my gaze, Matthew said, "Sorry. You want to find Grady," just as I said, "I'd love to."

He chuckled.

"I mean, I do want to find Grady, but you gotta know everybody in Otter Lake wants to snoop around here."

"Oh, believe me, I know," he said, eyes widening. "I

woke up today to see Mrs. Appleton's head peeking around my bedroom door."

"You did not!"

"Oh yeah, totally did," he said. "Claimed my mother was looking for me, but . . . I think she may have been standing there a little longer than was decent for a Sunday school teacher."

A Sunday school teacher that I was suddenly pretty jealous of. I shook my head. Again, where had that come from?

"You okay?" Matthew asked.

I coughed. "Totally fine. Not sure where my mind went there." My eyes widened a touch then flashed to Matthew's. "I didn't mean . . . not that it went to your bedroom."

"It's okay," Matthew said, laughing. "The thought of Mrs. Appleton and Sunday school makes a lot of people nervous."

I nodded. Wow. A gentleman to boot. Some girl should really take this guy off the market so the rest of us could stop embarrassing ourselves.

"Come on," he said with a jerk of his head. "I'll just show you the boathouse, then we'll go in."

We walked across the grassy slant of the grounds toward the small building designed to stay in keeping with the manse.

Matthew stepped into the cool gloom of the structure, causing the floor to rock and creak. Signs of disrepair showed everywhere. Rotting planks. Broken lights. Floor sinking on the right side. But it was still beautiful. It had that romantic feeling old buildings sometimes have. You could practically hear the ghostly laughter of some flapper hooking up with a suave man in a white jacket.

"Sorry," he said turning to face me. "I'm not sure what I was thinking. There's not much to see in here. I still don't think I'm ready to go inside."

I nodded.

"My father's death is hard enough, but it's just . . . a lot being home," he said, looking back up at me. "I mean, you know, my parents sent me to this fancy boarding school when I was a teenager, and when I was there, I was known as the kid from the Podunk town with the dwindling family fortune, but when I'm here, everybody just sees a Masterson, and thinks, I . . . I—"

"Wear golfing pants," I blurted out. Why . . . why did I say that out loud? "I mean, I like them. They're nice pants . . . *really* nice pants. They just stand out in—"

"Otter Lake."

I felt my cheeks flush. "Sometimes I wonder why I even allow myself to talk."

He smiled again. "No, don't worry. I get what you mean." He looked down at his pants, furrowing his brow. "But golfing pants? Really? Huh. I was going for more outdoor adventurer."

"That works too." It totally didn't. "I think I know what you mean, though," I said, nodding probably too vigorously. "In Chicago . . . I'm invisible. And part of that is a relief, but it's also . . . I don't know, I feel disconnected. But when I come home," I said, looking away, "I'm Boobsie Bloom, Summer's daughter, the girl who parades around topless in rubber pants with beavers named Betsy."

Matthew spluttered into a cough.

My gaze snapped back. "Are you all right?"

He waved his hand to indicate that he was, but he couldn't stop coughing.

I took a step closer and grabbed his arm. "Don't tell me you didn't hear about what happened with me at the social?" I lowered my gaze to try to see his face, which was turned to the ground.

He shook his head no, still coughing.

"Here, drink this," I said, passing him the cold coffee.

He tipped it back and took a sip.

"Better?"

He nodded and wiped his mouth with the back of his hand. "I'm sorry. Did you say topless . . . in rubber pants with Betsy? The beaver?"

I waved another hand at him. "It was one time. At the Raspberry Social. It was no big deal."

"I swear, I miss everything good that happens in this town," he said, still smiling. "All I get are the deranged geese."

Suddenly a shadow filled the doorway behind us.

A shadow wearing a sheriff's hat.

"Grady?"

Chapter Twelve

Warmth once again rushed to my cheeks. Maybe I needed to see a doctor about this blushing problem I seemed to be having.

"Erica." Surprise and some other emotion crossed Grady's face . . . some sort of emotion that I did not like the look of at all. Worry maybe? Guilt? Actually he kind of looked like he might be sick. Sure, our phone call last night had been bad . . . but it wasn't that bad.

"I came to see you," I said, "with Matthew here. I brought you coffee." I looked down at my hand, realized it wasn't there, then quickly looked over to Matthew.

"I'm sorry," Matthew piped in. "I drank it. I was coughing and—"

"It's fine," Grady said. His eyes moved to Matthew. "Someone thought they saw you out here. Your mother's looking for you. She's upset." He paused a beat. "There's been a development."

"What kind of development?"

"I'll fill you in later," Grady said. "But right now you should go see your mother."

Matthew nodded and moved to leave. Unfortunately,

because there was so little room to walk in the boathouse, he had to brush pretty close against me to get by. Our mumbled apologies, and my staring up at the ceiling, really didn't seem to help the situation.

Grady turned his gaze back to me, and suddenly I found my one free hand shoved deep into my pocket. I held up my coffee in the another hand. "There's a little left if you want it."

"Don't worry about the coffee," he said, a strange look still on his face.

"Okay," I said slowly. "You're starting to freak me out. What is going on?"

"I have to tell you something, and you're not going to like it."

My mind raced, but I didn't say anything.

"The ME's preliminary report came in."

"Okay."

"It's looking like Mr. Masterson's death wasn't an accident."

"Whoa," I said putting up my hands. "You don't mean . . . and why do you keep saying *accident*? You said it on the phone the other night. Not heart attack. Not natural causes. That makes me think you guys were thinking maybe an overdose . . . of medication?"

He didn't say anything.

"But now . . . did someone drug him?"

Grady stared at me, the muscles by his temples flexed as his jaw clenched. "You just can't stop, can you?" He then rubbed his forehead with one hand and held up the other. "Never mind . . . sorry."

My stomach dropped. "What are you trying to tell me here?" I asked, planting my hands on my hips. "Because I'm starting to think I might have an idea . . . but it had better not be what I'm thinking."

"Please, Erica. Don't make this about us," Grady said meeting my eyes. "I don't want to do this."

"Grady," I said, my voice full of warning. "Don't tell me—"

"We're bringing Tweety in."

Chapter Thirteen

"Son of a—" I turned and slapped one of the boathouse's wooden beams.

"Erica—"

"Don't!" I snapped. "Just don't. I don't believe this! Are you charging her?"

He sighed. "Rhonda's on her way over to the island right now. I don't know if the twins have a lawyer, or if your uncle—"

"You sent Rhonda?" Rhonda Cooke was a bit . . . eccentric. Even for Otter Lake. I actually considered Rhonda to be a friend, but being questioned by her was a little like being questioned by a spinning top: You could never be quite sure which direction things were gonna go. This was not good. "I need to get over there."

As I passed him, he grabbed my arm. "Erica—"

"What do you want me to say?" I shouted. "It's okay?"

"I don't have a choice here."

"Neither do I." I yanked my arm away. "She's family."

Steely clouds heavy with rain moved in to cover the lake as I sped back to the island. I saw the cop boat at the twins' place, but the officers were standing in front of the cottage, looking unsure. If the twins weren't there, I knew where they had to be.

Minutes later, I docked my mom's boat and ran up the steps to the retreat. Once I got up to the top, I saw them both, sitting in their chairs on the porch, tin mugs in hand.

"Erica, get over here," Kit Kat called out. "We want to talk to you."

I sprinted up the path leading to the lodge before jumping the steps. "We don't have much time," I blurted out before stopping to have to catch my breath. "My mother here?"

"No. They went somewhere. They mimed it, but—" Tweety cut herself off with a wave of her hand. "Here. Have a drink," she said, pressing a mug into my hand. "What have you been doing? Running a marathon?"

"No, I was at Hemlock Estate," I gasped. "And—"

"Erica, we told you—"

"I know. I know," I panted. Man, I just could not catch my breath. I brought the mug to my lips and pure alcohol exploded into my mouth. "Gah! Do you ever drink water? Take this away," I said, pushing the mug back to Tweety, who was bouncing up and down with laughter.

"This is serious," I croaked. "You need to focus."

"What is the matter with you?" she asked, watery blue eyes narrowing in on me.

"Rhonda's coming," I said. "For you."

The twins flashed each other looks before turning back to me.

"We don't have much time. You need to—"

"Fire up the boat," Kit Kat said, struggling to her feet. "If we leave now—"

"We'll get the tent," Tweety added. "Live in the wild for a while then—"

"Stop it!" I shouted, herding them back into their seats. "You're not running. That's ridiculous."

"It's not," Kit Kat snapped, looking indignant.

"What?" I said, throwing my hands wide. "You going to hunt squirrels and forage for berries?"

"We could."

"Just stop. Listen," I said, lowering my hands and taking a breath. "I'll call my uncle Jack. But I don't know when you'll make bail, so you need to give me some answers now. I need to know how to help you."

The twins twisted up their mouths in identical gestures.

"Tweety, why were you on that ride with Mr. Masterson?" I asked. "You said you weren't having an affair, but was there anything at all going on between you two?"

She opened her mouth and then shut it again.

"Oh my God!" I shouted. "Well, that's just—" I stopped myself and took a breath. "Give me that mug," I said, swiping it back from Tweety and taking another sip. "Okay, let's try something easier this time."

The twins stared back at me, waiting.

"How about you just tell me that you didn't kill anyone. Let's start there." I waited a moment, but no one spoke.

"It's easy," I said, pointing at each of them with the mug. "Just say, *Erica, we did not kill anyone.*"

The twins exchanged glances.

"What the—are you kidding me right now?"

"Erica!" a voice shouted. "Stop! Not one more word!"

Chapter Fourteen

No. No. No.

I jumped and spun around.

Behind me stood Rhonda Cooke and another police officer I didn't recognize.

My mug clunked to the wooden planks of the porch floor. For a second there, I thought I was about to put my hands up, but I caught myself.

"Rhonda, I—" I fumbled around for words, but I couldn't seem to find any that fit. I settled on, "Could we have just one more minute here? Alone?"

"Sure. Sure," she said with a nod, backing away.

The other officer cleared his throat.

Rhonda turned to look at him.

He raised his eyebrows.

"What's the matter with you?" she muttered.

He raised them even higher.

"What—oh," Rhonda said, straightening. Then she pointed a finger at him. "Wait, you don't get to scold me. You're the one who uploaded Shelley's booking photo to *Hot Jugs and Mugs*."

"She made me!" the young officer said, cheeks going

red. "She said she'd tell her father not to serve me at the Dawg anymore if I didn't do it. Where else am I going to eat? Besides . . . she was really scary that day."

"You're a cop, Amos!" Rhonda said, huffing a breath. "Now, Grady's all *professional this* and p*rofessional tha*—" She looked over her shoulder as though she had just remembered we were still there. "Right," she said, hiking her gun belt. "Sorry, Erica. He's right. This isn't a social call. We don't want to do this." I closed my eyes as she climbed the porch steps. "Twyla Williams, you're going to have to come with us."

"You arresting me?"

My eyes flew open to see the junior officer stepping forward with cuffs.

"What the hell do you think you're doing?" I shouted. "Put those away!"

Rhonda waved him down as she moved to help Tweety get out of her chair. "Nobody's getting arrested . . . yet."

"I want to come with her," Kit Kat said.

"Me too," I added.

"You can come, Kit Kat," Rhonda said. "But Erica, I'm sorry. You need to stay here. Grady specifically said . . ."

"What *specifically* did Grady say, Rhonda?"

"*Do not bring Erica back here*," she said in a mock-Grady voice. "He just radioed that in." She looked to the other officer for backup. He nodded.

I shook my head.

"But you know we could always meet up for beers later at the Dawg. The high school reunion is—" She stopped herself when she caught my expression. "Maybe now's not the time." She looked at me and pinched her lips together, making her cheeks dimple before adding, "We'll take good care of her, Erica."

I felt Kit Kat move up beside me. "Don't worry, honey,"

she said, patting me halfheartedly on the back. "I think both Tweety and I always knew it would come to this."

I felt my jaw drop. I wanted to shout, *What the hell does that mean?* but I somehow managed to keep my mouth shut.

She turned from me to follow the others down the stairs.

I stood there for a moment in shock before finally managing to pull out my phone. I pressed a number and brought it to my ear. After six rings, someone answered.

"You need to get over here right now."

The voice on the other end prattled back at me.

"Freddie, I really don't care what you do with your cotton candy. Get over here. Now." I exhaled a shaky breath. "It's an emergency."

I stood waiting on the dock for Freddie, gripping my insulated windbreaker tightly around my body. The cold was coming in. It was a damp cold too. Rain was on its way. Lots of it. Not that any of that really mattered . . .

Grady had brought Tweety in. Tweety!

But then again, given the conversation I'd had with the twins . . . maybe it was the right move.

No. No. Tweety was not a murderer. I didn't know why the twins had said what they had, but that didn't change what I knew to be true. Tweety was not a murderer.

I rubbed my arms. Where the hell was Freddie?

Then I heard it. Music. Actually, not even music. Bass. The kind of bass that could make the lake ripple. Wow, somebody had spent a pretty penny on that sound system.

Then in the distance, I saw a blur—a neon-yellow blur—tearing around the bend of land.

Holy crap.

I squinted my eyes to get a better view, but it was moving

fast. Impossibly fast. My God, I wouldn't have been surprised if that sucker could break the sound barrier.

Just then the boat swung course . . . bearing down on
the island.

"Freddie!" I screamed, holding out my hands. "Slow
down!"

There was no way he could hear me. But he didn't need
to. He was already turning in a wide loop in front of my
dock. I took a few steps back, afraid that the wake might
take me out.

The loud roar of the engine cut out, and I could finally
hear the music from the booming sound system. Yup, figured. It was the theme song from *Miami Vice*.

I sighed.

Freddie pulled up as close as he could to my dock in
neutral without grounding himself. He smiled at me from
underneath his aviator sunglasses.

"Well?" he asked. "What do you think?"

I looked at the long, sleek rod of a boat, shaking my
head. I blew air out from my lips.

"I call her *Lightning*."

"Seems fitting."

He sighed happily then dropped the smile. "Is there
something you'd like to say to me?"

I shook my head. We so didn't have time for this.

"I think it starts with an *I'm* and ends with a *sorry*," he
called out across the water. "But I'll also accept a *you were
right and I was wrong*."

A cold drop of rain hit my nose. "Grady brought Tweety
in for questioning. I think they might even be planning
on . . . arresting her."

He leaned closer to the edge of his boat and cocked his
ear in my direction. "What? I can't hear you. My boat's
really loud, and my ears are still buzzing."

I inhaled deeply and shouted, "Grady took Tweety in!"

Freddie did an almost comical double take. "What the—"

"I know."

"He can't seriously think that Tweety killed Mr. Masterson?"

I threw my hands in the air.

"I swear, Erica, he may look good in the uniform, but sometimes . . . bag of hammers. That's all I'm saying."

"Freddie," I said with as much warning as I could. "Not now."

He put his hands up in submission. "Seriously, though, Tweety a murderer? I mean, a brawler? Okay. A thug? Most definitely. But a murderer?"

More icy drops hit my cheeks. *We both always knew it would come to this.* I shook my head, trying to shake the words away . . . forever.

Freddie paused a moment then said, "So, we doing this thing?" He had his hands planted on his hips, but his face was turned to the treetops as though he was seriously considering the implications of what were we about to do. He held the pose just a moment before he had to grip the boat's edge for balance.

"We're doing this thing."

"Then let's go."

I stared at him a moment.

"Get in the boat," he prodded.

"How?" I shouted. "Fly? Freddie, that thing's a monster. Can you beam me over or something?"

"Hater."

Chapter Fifteen

After several awkward minutes of my hopping from the canoe tied to the dock to Freddie's boat, I finally managed to board the craft, and we made it across the lake at record speed.

It took me a couple of seconds to find my legs once I was back on solid ground. I couldn't help but think that humans were not designed to go as fast as Freddie's boat could take us. Thankfully, he had a pretty fancy new boathouse—better than my apartment back in Chicago—so we didn't have to fiddle around too much covering the boat from the rain, which was now falling in heavy sheets.

"So Freddie," I said once we had made it up the rock stairs to his place and inside, "I know your parents are pretty good at keeping you living in the style you're accustomed to, but I gotta ask . . ."

"Yeah, I know. It's a pretty awesome boat," he said, taking my dripping jacket then looking at it as though I had brought a bag of garbage into his house. "Can this go in the dryer?"

I shook my head no.

"Then out it goes." He tossed it outside onto a chair. At

least it was a covered porch. "It wasn't my parents, though. I asked my grandmother to invest in the business."

"And let me guess. You spent all the money on the boat."

"Well," he said, having the decency to look a little un-comfortable. "Boat power equals manpower out here. You wouldn't understand. And I didn't spend it all on the boat. You're forgetting my day uniform . . . and I got a few other things."

I nodded.

"Okay, don't just stand there." He shooed me farther into the house. "You look so cold it's making me uncom-fortable. Let's turn on the fireplace and put a towel on your head or something."

"Sounds good, but I want to call my uncle Jack first."

Minutes later, I was sitting on the stone hearth of the gas fireplace in Freddie's office slash living room. I hadn't gotten ahold of my uncle directly, but I spoke to one of his assistants and gave him the details of what had happened. He said he'd give him the message and get back to me. It was a little awkward asking my uncle for help. I didn't know him all that well, but he had been there for me dur-ing my last bout of legal difficulties, and he said I could always call him no matter what the problem. I was also guessing that if my mother hadn't heard what was going on by now, she would soon, and she'd find a way to contact her brother . . . maybe telepathically . . . or with Skype.

"You want a beer?" Freddie asked. He was standing by the little fridge that had been built into the custom book-shelf behind his desk.

"No." I shook my head. "I've decided to stop drinking when I'm home. I can barely keep up with everything when I'm sober."

He shrugged then twisted the cap off a bottle and took

a long swig. After that, he moved to his office chair and dropped into it, making a loud *whompf* sound. "You know what would go really well with this?"

I raised an eyebrow.

"Bucket chicken," he said, nodding in agreement with his own statement. "I've said it before, and I'll say it again. The biggest problem with Otter Lake is its total lack of accessibility to bucket chicken."

"You've said that before?"

"Only all the time."

"Huh." I wasn't about to argue. I didn't want to send him on a tangent.

"Okay," Freddie said, adjusting himself in his seat. "Tell me everything."

I twisted my hair behind my head. "I don't even know where to begin. I guess it started this morning when I talked to my mother about the twins' past, well, not exactly talked—it was more like charades—and I found out that . . ."

"I'm sorry," Freddie said leaning across his desk, cocking an ear in my direction. "You did what?"

Despite the gas fireplace, it felt like the temperature in the room had dropped two degrees. Maybe three.

"I talked to my mother and—"

"So you were working the case without me," Freddie said with a tight nod. "But that couldn't be right because you weren't supposed to be doing that *this week*."

"I wasn't *working the case*. It was nothing. My mother grabbed me! And then she mentioned, well, mimed actually, that the twins had some sort of connection to a death that happened at the fair years ago, and—"

Freddie gasped . . . literally, audibly gasped.

"I was going to tell you," I said dropping my eyes to the floor. "I just got distracted by Matthew . . . and then Grady . . . and then Rhonda . . . and something called *Hot*

Jugs and Mugs?" I peeked up to see his reaction. It wasn't good. He didn't even seem to want to take my *Hot Jugs and Mugs* bait.

"I don't know what to say to you right now." He then gasped again. "I saw you this morning! At the dock! You said nothing!"

"I was going to tell you. I just—"

"This is a serious violation of our friendship." Freddie took a very indignant-looking sip from his beer. "I mean, I get that relationships aren't exactly your forte . . . and maybe they're not mine either. But I do know that people in relationships have things they do together. Only together. You know like how couples have *their* TV shows? Well, this was our thing. You should have called the minute—the minute!—your mom gave you this lead."

"I didn't think much of it. I wasn't investigating per se. I was just trying to find out why the twins were acting so strangely, and I really believed Mr. Masterson died of natural causes."

Freddie was staring at the ceiling shaking his head. "I'm pretty shook up about this," he said quickly. "I'm actually surprised by how shaken up I am."

"Freddie, I'm sorry." I flashed him my most remorseful face, dropping my hands to my sides. "But could we get back to what's really important here—"

"No!"

I pinched my lips shut.

"You will not dismiss my feelings!"

I inhaled deeply and held up my hands. "Okay. I understand. How can I make this right?"

"I don't know, Erica," he said, looking away. "I don't know."

"There has to be something?" I pleaded. "We don't have time to fight. We have work to do. The twins need us."

He scoffed loudly. "Oh *us*. Now it's *us*. Because this morning I thought it was just *you*."

I felt my cheeks grow warm, and it wasn't from the fire. "Fine. You know what, Freddie? If you're going to be that way about it, let's talk truth."

He raised his eyebrows, arms crossed over his chest.

"You want to know why I didn't tell you about the twins' past?"

He held my gaze, mouth shut.

"I didn't tell you the truth," I said slowly, trying to decide if I really wanted to say this. "Because sometimes you take things a little too far. You lose sight of the people and get sucked into the drama."

"Too far! Drama!" He slapped the desktop, then cringed as he looked at his palm. Guess that had stung.

"And I didn't want to make the situation for the twins even worse."

"Well," he said, trying to control his facial expression, which only resulted in a lot of cheek quivering and bird-like mouth movements. "Thank you for showing so much faith in me."

"Aw, Freddie. Come on."

"No, you come on!" he snapped back. "You should have talked to me about this."

"I—" Suddenly my mouth snapped shut of its own accord. Grady had said something similar to me a few months back about having a little more faith in people. I thought about it a moment longer and said, "You . . . are probably right."

"I . . . I know I'm right."

We stared at each other a moment.

"I really do need your help, Freddie. And—" I stopped a moment to take a breath. "—I was wrong and I'm sorry. Will you please help? If not for me or the twins," I said quickly, putting my hand to my chest, "for the people of Otter Lake?"

He squinted and raised his chin in the air as though gauging my authenticity. "You're lucky I take the security of this town seriously." He took another sip of beer . . . and then another. "That's the only reason I'm even considering forgiving you right now." Then he downed the entire bottle and reached to get another one.

"So," I asked carefully, "does that mean I'm off the hook?"

"That depends."

"On what?"

"You need to be all-in, Erica." His expression turned stony. "No more. *Oh, I don't know if we should be doing this, Freddie*," he said putting on an affected girlie voice while waving his hands in the air. "*This is probably illegal, Freddie. My boyfriend won't like this, Freddie.*" He dropped both his hands . . . and his face. "That last one sounded dirty. But are we clear?"

"Clear."

"Good. *Now* tell me everything."

I spent the next half hour filling Freddie in on everything I had learned from my mother before moving on to my conversation with the twins. Maybe it was my earlier accusations of drama, but Freddie held a shrewd, contemplative expression throughout the entire recap. He even pyramided his fingers together at one point.

When I finished, he didn't respond right away, but looked up at the ceiling . . . then at me . . . then out the window before settling back on me. He still didn't say anything, though.

"So?" I asked. "What are we thinking here?

"So very much," he replied with a slow nod. "The twins

certainly seem to be guilty of something, but I can't quite believe it's cold-blooded murder."

"I agree."

He rubbed his chin with his thumb and forefinger. "Fetch me my violin."

"I'm sorry, your what now?"

"My violin. It helps me think."

"Freddie, you haven't played the violin since you were eight."

"I've taken it back up again."

"No violin."

"You are a terrible Watson."

I didn't bother to answer.

"Okay, let's start with what we don't know and need to find out."

"Good."

"One," he said, holding up a finger. "We need the whole story of what happened to this man who died at the fair a longish time ago . . . and what he has to do with the twins."

"Okay, but I want to be careful about stirring up old stories." I wrapped the blanket from Freddie's sofa more tightly around my shoulders. It felt like cashmere. Probably was. He did know how to live . . . and how to shop on the Internet. "It might make Tweety's situation worse."

"She's already been taken in for questioning," Freddie replied. "I guarantee you people are already talking."

I sighed. "True enough."

"Two," Freddie said, putting up the next finger. "We need to find out Mr. Masterson's cause of death."

"Oh," I said. "I think it was some kind of drug overdose. Grady kind of let that slip. I guess that's why at first they thought maybe it was—" I snapped my mouth shut, but it was too late.

"Oh my GOD!" Freddie shouted.

"Did I forget to mention that part?"

"Did you forget to mention that part? Did you forget to mention that . . . when did you find this out?"

"Just earlier today, I swear."

"All right, all right," Freddie said, holding out his hands palms down, as though he were putting a lid on all his rage. "Moving forward. We need to confirm this cause-of-death theory of yours and find out what drug we're talking about here." Freddie started typing something on his computer. "I bet the murderer thought the ME would just write it off as accidental and not investigate."

"Yeah, well," I said, making a scoffing sound, "they didn't count on me thinking about suspicious deaths when I'm just about to make out with my hot sheriff-almost-boyfriend, now, did they?"

Freddie briefly looked away from the computer to say, "No, they probably didn't." His eyes moved back to the screen. "Speaking of hot sheriff-almost-boyfriends, you didn't say how things were between Grady and you, given the whole *taking Tweety in* thing."

Please don't make this about us.

I shook my head. It's not like I wanted to make this about us. And I wasn't exactly upset with Grady for doing his job. In fact, the real question was, how upset was he going to be with me for working with Freddie? Maybe I did have trust issues. I wanted to think that I trusted Grady to do his job. No, I *did* trust him to do his job . . . at least I thought I did. But Freddie and I could do things that maybe a sheriff couldn't. And if we got in trouble for them, well, we'd deal with that. I couldn't let Tweety go to jail. "Yeah, not great."

He nodded.

"There are so many drugs that can cause death," he said, face aglow from the light of the screen. "The time frame is going to be important here. Most of these are pretty fast acting—which is probably why they are zeroing in on Tweety."

"Crap," I said with a sigh. "We don't have much to go on, do we?" I frowned as I thought of something. "Maybe we can find some witnesses who saw Mr. Masterson before he got on that ride . . . who saw what he was doing . . . who he was talking to, that kind of thing. Then we could come up with a list of potential suspects."

"Yeah, there were a lot of people at the fair that day—" Freddie suddenly cut himself off and shot up from his seat, sending his office chair spinning. "We have to go!"

"What? Where?"

"To town! Now!"

"Why?" I asked not really wanting to leave my spot at the hearth.

"No time to explain! Let's go," he said, gesturing me to get up. "We're going to run out of tape!"

"Tape! What tape?"

"Come on!" he shouted, hurtling his boat keys in my direction.

I ducked as the keys bounced off the wall, leaving a nick in the paint.

"Erica!" he shouted. "Learn how to catch!"

"I don't want to drive *Thunder*."

"It's *Lightning*, moron."

"Hey!" I shot back, bending to retrieve the keys from the bamboo floor.

"And you have to drive," Freddie shouted already headed for the door. "I've been drinking."

"This better be good, Freddie."

"Oh it's good," he shouted over his shoulder. "Maybe even Betamax good."

Chapter Sixteen

Normally I like boating, but handling *Lightning* and all her power was a little intimidating, especially at night. It didn't help that after the rain had cleared up, a strong cold wind had been left behind. I was expecting the boat to launch us over to the next county any second. To make matters worse, every time I tried to slow down, Freddie whacked my arm.

I was dying to demand that he explain himself, but the boat was too loud for actual conversation. Every time I looked over at him, I could see by the light of the dash that he was mouthing the words, *Come on. Come on. Come on.*

What felt like seconds later, we approached the outskirts of the near-empty town marina by the fill-up stations. Actually the boat had sped so fast, it was possible we had gone back in time . . . or into the future . . . however the science worked. I slowed *Lightning* a good way back from the shore, not wanting to cause a mini tsunami.

"Over there," Freddie said, pointing to the side of the main docks. "The town put in an extension just for me."

I flashed him a look then muttered, "Unbelievable."

I turned the wheel, gliding toward the dock. "Now can you tell me why we are here?"

He jumped out of the boat more nimbly than I was used to seeing him move and began tying the front end off. "I know you were being all judgmental earlier with the money I spent on *Lightning*, but it just so happens that I did invest in some town surveillance."

"You did?"

"Well, you probably don't remember this, but Coach Waters had a camera set up on the foul line pole on the old baseball diamond, so that he could tape games and give feedback. But no one has used it in forever—not since they built that new diamond at the school."

"Okay, I'm following."

"Well, they took down the cage, but not the pole, and being the surveillance expert that I am, I thought it would be a good idea to buy it from him and have it running all the time, you know, just in case." Freddie lightly smacked my arm. "I can't believe I forgot it."

Hot tingles ran up my back. "Are you being serious, right now?"

"Deadly," Freddie said before running to tie off the other end. "There was a big fight at the town hall a month ago—you know, *Live Free or Die* New Hampshire and all that—but after the shenanigans of your last visit, everybody finally agreed that it was a good idea—at least during the fair. I was planning on putting it away for the winter."

It made sense that the town was willing to get on board. It probably wasn't just the murder and attempted murders that had happened in the summer. Someone had also started a bonfire and danced around it naked in the town square last time I was home pretending to be me . . . because that kind of thing happened when I came home.

"I programmed the VCR to tape for thirty-six hours before it starts taping over itself."

I climbed out of the boat onto the dock to chase after Freddie, who was already hustling away. He wasn't even watching his steps—that's how excited he was . . . or inebriated. I caught up to him and asked, "What kind of VCR can tape for thirty-six hours?"

"A double-cassette time-lapsed one!" he said with implied obviousness. "Look, you don't need to understand! We just need to move!"

"All right!" I shouted back. "Let's go then!"

We both jogged a couple hundred feet up the slanted Main Street into town before we slowed to a walk. I obviously needed to get back into running . . . and Freddie needed to start.

I took a moment to pant before I said, "What are the odds it would have caught anything, though?"

"Did you not hear me?" Freddie gasped. "It's on that old pole right on the edge of the fairgrounds!" He jogged a few more feet before slowing to a walk again. "It's the best shot we have. Besides, it's not like Mr. Masterson was a fast walker. We should be able to see at least a little something of what he was doing before the ride . . . who he was with . . . if he was eating or drinking anything."

My heart pounded even harder in my chest at all that could mean. "I can't believe you only thought of this now!" I upped my speed-walking pace.

"Hey, I didn't know we were dealing with a murder until just a few hours ago! Then there was the whole being mad at you. And the beer," Freddie added, huffing and puffing.

I stopped dead in my tracks when another thought hit me. "I also can't believe Grady hasn't thought of this. Was he at the meeting?"

"Of course," Freddie said, waving me forward. "I'm sure he knows. Then again, it was a pretty wild meeting."

"This is going to be another one of those things that makes him look bad, and you look good, isn't it?"

"We don't have time to worry about your boyfriend's self-esteem right now!" Freddie shouted as best he could through his panting. "We'll figure that out once we have the tapes."

I jogged to catch up with him.

"Besides, how bad do you think it's going to look when everybody else figures out that there was a video of Mr. Masterson's killer and all the law enforcement figures in town let it get taped over?"

"Good point."

Finally, we made it to the crest of the small slope.

"Come on," Freddie said, waving me over to a heavy steel fence the carnival had put in place. He dropped his chest and belly onto the railing, swung one leg up . . . and fell over to the other side, landing hard on his back.

"Ow!" he yelled, rolling in the dirt.

"Wait," I said, suddenly stopping in place. "We're just breaking into the fair?"

"Um, I don't see an open ticket booth, do you?" He threw his hands into the air, looking like a flipped turtle. "Get in here."

"I don't know," I said, shaking my head. Just then a swirl of dried leaves skittered across the pavement by my feet.

"Thirty-six hours, Erica!" Freddie yelled, getting to his feet. "What time is it now?"

"Fine! You're right." If my math was correct—which was always questionable—we had only minutes left to lose. I hustled over to the fence and tried Freddie's move to get over . . . which ended just as badly. "But so help me," I said, pushing myself to my feet, "if any clowns jump out at us or . . . or your pumpkin people, you're handling it."

Freddie's face dropped as his eyes darted about.

"Freddie?"

"That was a really terrible thing to say." He met my eye. "Why? Why would you say that?"

"Wow, you might need some therapy for your trauma," I said, yanking his arm. "But not now! We've got to go!"

We started running again toward the foul line pole sticking up in the distance. Once we got past the midway, we had to turn into the concessions area. All the little booths cut the path into what felt like a maze, forcing Freddie and me to slow to a fast walk.

"This wind is driving me nuts," I said, darting a look behind. "Someone could be sneaking up on us, and we'd never hear them coming."

Freddie nodded. "Or they could be hiding in one of these tents."

Just then a flap of canvas covering a booth snapped.

We both jumped and clutched each other's arms.

"Come on," Freddie said, pulling my elbow. "We just need to get through this cluster, and we're there."

We hurried toward the opening that led to the field. The old baseball diamond had been left open for the smash-up derby. Even though it was dark, I could see the wooden pole with the bump at the top that had to be the camera.

"Quick. Let's go." I had only jogged a few steps before I realized that Freddie wasn't with me. "What are you waiting for? Come on."

Freddie's body was turned in the opposite direction, toward the cluster of RVs for the carnival workers.

"What are you doing?"

Freddie still didn't answer, but he was rolling his shoulders.

"What is your deal?" I asked, running over to him.

Just as I made it to his side, I heard him mutter, "And

here I thought all the carnies would be tucked snug in their beds."

I focused my gaze where Freddie was looking between the vehicles. "So they're having a little bonfire. What's the big deal? Come on."

"What's the big deal? What's the big deal?" Freddie's voice rose into the night wind. "Don't you think it's a little windy for a fire, Erica?"

"That's it," I said sharply. "You can't drink either anymore. Not when we're on the job."

Freddie turned and smiled. "I got tingles when you said that just now." Then he snapped his attention back to the bonfire.

"Seriously, we don't have time for this. I'm sure they need a little stress relief after dealing with people . . . and probably vomit all day. And while we're on the subject, I don't think you can call them carnies. It's—"

Freddie whipped a finger at my face. "Don't you politically correct me!"

"No booze. No more. Now come on."

Freddie turned slowly in my direction, eyes trailing behind. "You're right. We need to—" Suddenly he stopped dead in his tracks and pulled back again toward the RVs.

"Freddie!" I shouted after him. "What is your problem now?" I looked back over to the group of people gathered by the fire . . . and I saw him. "Oh Freddie, no," I pleaded. I knew it was a lost cause, though, because there standing by the fire, guitar in hand, foot on a cooler, was Rex, the man with the handlebar mustache from the water gun game.

"You go." Freddie pressed a set of keys into my palm. "Run. I've got to bust someone for an illegal bonfire."

"Freddie, no. I can't let you go over there alone."

"We don't have time to argue."

I hopped angrily on the spot for a few times. "This is nuts! Leave it. We have to—"

"Tick-tock, Erica," he said, hiking up his pants. "I would hurry. That VCR could be taping over Mr. Masterson's murderer as we speak."

"Gah! Don't get killed!" I then spun and ran for the box, yelling behind me, "This may be the stupidest thing you've ever done, Freddie."

It was hard to hear what he said in return, but if I had to guess, it was something about the curse of the lawman.

Light was coming from weird angles—streetlamps, the RVs, not-too-distant houses—so it was hard to see the grass in front of me. I moved as quickly as I could without risking an ankle break on a discarded beer can. When I finally made it over to the pole, I crouched to look at the old wooden cupboard with rusted padlock anchored at the bottom.

I fumbled through the keys Freddie had given me, trying to find one even close to the size I needed for the lock. The dark wasn't helping much. Neither was the wind. It was starting to freak me out again. I glanced up from the lock to make sure I was alone, then got right back to fiddling.

A moment later I found the right key and snapped it into place, but when I tried to turn it, the tumblers wouldn't budge. "Come on. Come on," I muttered. I jiggled the key around some more. I didn't want to snap off the body in the lock. It needed just an ounce more of press—

Click!

"Yes!" I lifted the padlock off and threw it on top of the box.

I dropped to my knees to get a better look at what was inside. Well, would you look at that. Perhaps I didn't give Freddie enough credit—or Coach Waters. Someone had jerry-rigged a Tupperware container to protect the VCR from the elements. I snapped the lid off. The glowing numbers of the timer were counting up. That was good. At least it was working. I scanned the front but couldn't read anything in the dark, so I began hitting random buttons around where I thought the eject control might be. A second later the machine made a clunk, then a whine, then spit a cassette out . . . and then another.

I inhaled deeply, looking at the tapes in my hand, sending out a mental prayer to the powers that be.

I slipped the cassettes into the inner pocket of the coat I had borrowed from Freddie. Men's jackets had way better pockets then women's. I closed the box's doors and slipped the lock back in place. I almost had it snapped shut when—

"Erica?"

"Wah!" I jumped up and spun in the air so quickly I don't think my feet touched the ground. "Matthew?"

Chapter Seventeen

"What are you doing here?" I blurted out at the exact moment he asked, "You okay?"

We both chuckled awkwardly. He then pushed his hair back from his forehead. "I was just going for a run. Couldn't sleep."

I eyed Matthew's outfit. He was wearing black running tights with a matching long-sleeved running shirt. Black, but with reflective stripes at the arms and around the thighs. Definitely running clothes. I couldn't help but notice those stripes ran exactly in the best places to accent his muscles. Those designers sure knew what they were doing. They should maybe get an award—*Focus, Erica.* "You ran all the way from your place to town? On a night like this?"

"Yeah. I decided to take a shortcut across the fairgrounds. I run at least a few days a week. Good stress relief." He shook his head. "Hobby, I guess."

Huh, a really sweaty hobby that somehow managed to look good on him. When I ran, I looked like one of those jowly dogs with the loose facial skin flapping everywhere, but Matthew looked like—looked like nothing!

Because it was a totally inappropriate line of thinking for me to take! What was going on with me? I had way too much on my mind to be thinking about what Matthew looked like when he ran. And I had way too much Grady in my life to be thinking anything about Matthew at all. It was just . . . selfish.

"So," he said, taking a look up the pole before leaning slightly to the side to see the box behind me. "What are you doing here?"

"Oh," I said, looking down at my feet. What the hell was I doing here? It didn't seem right to say, *Oh I don't know. Just looking for evidence to free my pseudo-aunt who might have already been arrested for your father's murder.* "I thought . . . it was a rabbit hutch?" I inwardly groaned. I was a terrible liar.

"Is that a VCR?" Matthew stepped back to get a better look up the pole. "And a camera?" His eyes dropped back down to mine. He paused a moment then said, "You were looking for evidence to clear Tweety."

"I'm sorry, Matthew. I—"

He halfheartedly raised one hand. "You don't need to explain. This is a really complicated situation for a lot of us." He moved forward and bent in front of the box. He slipped the lock off. He then looked inside and fiddled with the same buttons I had before saying, "No tape."

He craned his head to look up at me, causing a damp lock of hair to fall back on his forehead . . . a damp lock of hair that I suddenly had the insane urge to brush back . . . but of course I couldn't, and not because of Grady this time, but because my right hand was busy holding steady my jacket full of tape!

"I know," I said quickly. "I thought maybe—"

"Maybe the police already have it," he said, straightening up.

I blinked a few times then nodded before wrapping my

free hand across my guilty, guilty arm, still under the jacket making sure the tapes weren't sliding around. Hopefully I just looked like I was staying warm. "Totally. Yeah."

"That would be something at least." He looked up at the now starry sky. A moment passed before he said, "Erica, I'm not sure if I should ask you this, but . . ."

"Anything. Ask me anything," I said quickly. Anything to make me feel less like the horrible person I knew I was. It wasn't that I didn't want Matthew to see the tape—or even give the tape over to Grady—but as wrong as it was, I wanted to watch it first. If it was somehow incriminating, I'd turn it over to my uncle and let him decide how to handle it.

"You know Tweety as well as anyone on this island," Matthew said. "Do you really think she is capable of murder?"

"No," I said, using my free hand to push back the hair whipping around my face. "I don't."

He nodded.

"Look Matthew, she's far from perfect. And I can't say with any certainty that she didn't have something going on with your father, but she's not some calculated killer. I know people like Marg Johnson are talking—"

"Good ol' Otter Lake."

"But here's the thing. The twins, they're hot-blooded animals." I moved to touch his arm but caught myself before I actually made contact. "If Tweety was angry enough to kill someone," I said, pausing to look back toward town, "everyone would know it."

He nodded and gave me a sad smile.

"I'm really sorry you're going through this."

"I'm sorry for you too."

I jerked a little at that.

He cleared his throat. "I mean, I'm sorry for what your family is going through. I know that this can't be easy."

"Please. Don't worry about us. I can't imagine what it's like to lose your father in this way."

"Yeah," he said with a laugh. "Not really how I expected him to go."

I bit my lip, debating whether or not I should ask the next question. "Matthew?" I hated myself, but it was for Tweety. "I can't believe I'm going to ask this, but—"

"Go for it," he said. "Believe me, after all the questions Grady's asked us, I'm prepared for just about anything."

I laughed slightly, but it didn't feel very happy. "Is there anyone else you can think of who would want your father dead?"

He scoffed and kicked at the grass with his toe. "You mean besides my mother?"

I felt my eyes widen as Matthew turned to look at something behind me. "What's going on over there?"

I whipped my head around.

Freddie!

The quiet little bonfire I had seen earlier had grown to near-epic proportions, flames clawing their way up to the sky—high enough that we could see it over the tops of the RVs.

I spun on my heel. "I gotta go."

"Where are you going? Are you going to warn them about the wind?"

I didn't have time to answer him. I took off in a sprint.

"Freddie!" I called out. "Hang on! I'm coming!"

I didn't know if he could hear me. The wind had gusted and whipped the words right from my mouth.

I made it to the first break between RVs, when I heard something strange coming from the direction of the fire. It sounded like . . . like a guitar and . . . singing.

"Erica?" Matthew asked, jogging to my side. "What's going on?"

I turned the corner of the RV then stopped dead.

I had half expected to see Freddie on a spit . . . but there at the campfire—blazing a little less furiously now—stood Freddie, guitar in hand, leading a bunch of people in song.

I took a few more steps forward, enough that Freddie saw me.

"Erica!" he shouted, letting the guitar swing from his hands by the strap around his neck. "Come on! Bucket chicken!"

Chapter Eighteen

"Hey everybody," Freddie shouted. "This is my friend Erica. Actually, not just friend, soon-to-be partner. She just needs to get over this really weird obsession she has with having a *normal* job with *normal* people."

A few individuals raised their beer cans at me, including Freddie, who had bent over to pick his up. Great. Just what this situation needed. More beer.

"And this," Freddie announced, swinging his beer can over, "is the ever-gorgeous Matthew Masterson." He briefly flashed me some questioning *uh-oh* eyes before adding, "Somebody get that man a beer. He could use it."

I was fully expecting Matthew to decline, but instead he looked over at me and shrugged before reaching for the beer a man sitting on a cooler was holding out to him.

"Um, Freddie," I called out. "It's kind of late. Don't you think we should be go—"

"Boo," someone shouted, rapidly joined by about ten other people.

Freddie spread his hands out wide. "You heard the people. Can't disappoint my fans!" He harshly strummed a chord on his guitar. "Now who wants to rock?"

The small crowd cheered.

A moment later Rex, the man with the handlebar mustache, walked over to me holding out a beer. "You want one?"

A waved my free hand out in front of me. "Can't. I'm boating." My eyes darted back to Freddie. "Uh, everything cool between you two? It's Rex, right?"

He nodded. "It was the weirdest damn thing," he said, shaking his head. "Your friend came busting in here shouting something about taking us all in, and all I did was hold up some chicken saying he should chill out, and then he was all, *I love you man* . . . and here we are."

I nodded.

"Erica, come on," Freddie shouted, waving a hand at me. "We're just about to do another round."

Matthew scooted over on the giant cooler he was now sitting on and patted the spot beside him.

Oh boy.

I spent the next hour or so trying to make up excuses for why we needed to leave without tipping Matthew off—and trying to ignore the signals my body was sending me thanks to sitting so close to him. Unfortunately, Freddie wasn't having any of it. Not while there was chicken, and strangely enough there was a lot of chicken. After a while I had to admit it was actually kind of fun . . . well, it would have been if I hadn't been feeling so guilty.

Finally, after what felt like hours, some of the workers started to head off to their RVs.

"Well," Matthew said, getting to his feet, "I think it's time for me to go too."

I jumped up after him. "Let me give you a ride. You can't run home now."

"I think I'd better after all that food," he said with a pat to his belly.

"You can't seriously run in the wee hours of the morning after a meal of chicken and beer?"

He cocked his head quizzically.

"Or maybe you can."

He walked a few steps then turned. "Thanks for a good night, Erica. I think I needed that." He waved and trotted off to the road.

Freddie and I said our good-byes to the rest of the group and left for the marina. The wind had completely died, and even though the sun hadn't yet come up, the birds were already singing. Once we were out of earshot, I said, "So, don't you want to know if I got it?"

"Um, given that it looked like you were about to kill us all with a concealed weapon the entire night," he said tiredly, "I'm thinking you got it."

"Well, then, pick up the pace! Let's go watch this puppy."

"Aren't you an eager little Otter Lake beaver in the morning! But I think you're forgetting one thing."

"What?"

"I don't have a VCR." He belched quietly, but it sounded painful.

"What! What do you mean you don't have a VCR?"

"I don't have a VCR! Seriously, who does? Hoarders?" He groaned. "It broke a while back, and it wasn't like I was going to rush out and buy a new one. Now stop talking so loudly. I'm tired."

I threw my hands in the air. "Well, what are we going to do? Oh! We should go back and get the VCR from the pole!"

Freddie shook his head. "The sun's coming up. Everybody will see what we're doing, and then we'll never get the chance to view the tapes before the law comes down on us. But speaking of Grady, where the heck did Matthew come from?"

"What are you talking about?" I said, trying to sound as normal as possible. "What does Grady have to do with Matthew . . . or Matthew with Grady, for that matter?"

"Uh-huh," Freddie said knowingly. "You know exactly what I'm talking about. Seriously, though, what was Matthew doing there?"

"He said he was out for a run because he couldn't sleep."

"And you believed him?"

"Yes, I believe—" I stopped dead in my tracks. "What exactly are you implying here?"

"Implying nothing. I'm saying outright that we have a killer on our hands, Matthew is the victim's son, and he just happened to be running by the only camera that might have caught the murderer on tape."

"Come on. You're reaching. Matthew's not the type! He's too—"

"Dreamy to be the killer?" Freddie asked, cocking one eyebrow.

"He rescues geese trapped under porches!"

"Quite the elaborate cover if you ask me."

We made it back to Freddie's boat and got her started up, probably waking half the town. Seconds later we were pulling up to Freddie's place. Driving *Lightning* this time was even more difficult. Speed and sleep deprivation weren't a good mix. I tried to slow down, but it was like the boat wouldn't let me. I was starting to think *Lightning* wasn't the best name for this piece of machinery. *Demon* might have been better . . . or maybe *Christine*.

Freddie stood up shakily and grabbed the boat's edge to hand-over-hand it to the side. He only managed to get one foot over the lip before I shouted, "What would his motive even be?"

"What?" Freddie asked. I was pretty sure he was at the phase of being hung over where talking hurt. "Who?"

"Matthew!"

"I don't know," Freddie said, shaking his head before grabbing his forehead with his hand to stop it. "It's family. Maybe he didn't like the fact that his father was cheating on his mother—"

I gripped the boat's wheel and twisted it in my hands.

"Or maybe it was money. Or . . ." Freddie paused, shaking his head, "It could be a million things! Maybe he just wanted to get his hands on the manse."

I made a noise while pulling my lips down into a grimace.

"What?"

"Well, Matthew does love that house," I said slowly. "But he doesn't strike me as the type of person who couldn't wait a few years to inherit it."

"Well, maybe that's it. For all we know, his father wanted to leave it to somebody else."

"Maybe." Then I slapped the wheel. "Oh! But . . . aha! You're forgetting one thing."

Freddie rolled his bloodshot eyes over to me. "Am I now."

"Matthew only came to town after his father's death!"

"And you know that for sure how?"

I felt my face drop. "I don't. I just assumed."

"Uh-huh," Freddie said again. "You really want him to be innocent."

"I do not." In fact, maybe if he were a murderer I'd stop having all these inappropriate thoughts about him. "Okay, can we just talk about what's next? We need to find a VCR and—"

"No. No. No. Freddie must sleep now."

"But—"

"Erica, I know this is hard, but even if there is evidence on those tapes that clears Tweety, no one's going to let her out at this time of night . . . morning? Let's get some sleep, and then we'll figure everything out."

I grumbled in response.

"Do you want to crash at my place?"

"You know I can't sleep with your snoring."

"I have a deviated septum!"

"I know. I'm sorry. I'm just tired and worried."

He nodded. "Okay, well, you can take *Lightning*, but you've got to promise me you'll take care of her."

I sighed.

"Hey! Most people would consider it both an honor and a privilege to drive her."

"I know. It's just kind of like being lent a double-decker bus for a quick trip to the market."

"Are you going to be able to handle her on your own?"

"Yeah. Yeah. I'll figure out some way to dock her. It will be fine."

He nodded and turned to walk up the stairs to his house. "Oh, and don't forget to cover her in case it rains."

A few hours later, I was lying snug in my bed. I still felt ridiculously tired, which led me to question why I was awake. I was nice and warm, really toasty actually, with my arms wrapped around my pillow. My mom had replaced my mattress with some organic hemp one that was way comfortable. It was all nice and quiet . . . except for the calming pitter patter of rain outside my window.

Oh crap! Lightning*!*

I tried to jump up in bed, but my arm was pinned under my pillow. My pillow . . . that wasn't my pillow!

"Caesar?" I shouted at the cat in my arms. "Oh my God!"

He blinked his eyes into slits and looked around as though trying to figure out how he'd gotten there too. He kicked his back legs into the air then rolled off the bed with a solid *thump*. I guess not all cats land on their feet.

I leaned over the bed.

"You okay?"

He looked up at me, still on his back, and hissed.

"Back at you," I mumbled, throwing off the covers.

I yanked on Freddie's jacket over my tank top and boxer shorts, and slipped on some old flip-flops. This was going to be cold, cold, cold. But there was no time to worry about that now.

I hustled out of the lodge's front door, thankful that nobody seemed to be around. How could I have forgotten to put the rain cover on *Lightning*? I was just so tired after last night's festivities. God, had any of that even happened? It just seemed so surreal. Chicken . . . RVs . . . campfires . . . Matthew . . .

I trotted down the log steps of the hill that led to the dock, trying to watch my step on the slippery wood. When I reached the bottom and looked up to see how bad the situation was . . . I saw a police boat pulled up alongside *Lightning* . . . and a man . . . snapping the last part of the cover in place.

"Grady?"

Chapter Nineteen

He looked up at me from under his dripping sheriff's hat. "Hey."

"What are you doing?"

"Well . . . it's raining." He hopped back over to his boat, wiping his hands on his pants, before drifting forward in neutral.

"Oh, thank you." I walked the length of the dock, so we didn't have to shout. "I mean, I know, uh, how you feel about the boat."

He planted his fists into his lower spine and arched backward with a groan. "My issues are not with the boat. I like the boat a lot." He pinched his lips together, and then sighed heavily. "In fact, I think this boat and I, under the right circumstances, could have something pretty great together." He shook his head. "But people keep getting in the way."

I nodded. "We're, uh, not talking about the boat anymore, are we?"

Grady's eyes widened in question.

"Or maybe we are just talking about boats," I said

slowly. "I always manage to underestimate your love for boats."

A light came on behind Grady's eyes. "Oh, you thought I was talking about—"

I held my hands out. "Please. Stop."

He chuckled. "If it makes you feel any better, I'm not here to talk about the boat." He edged even closer to the dock. "I was hoping we could maybe figure some things out."

A few minutes later we were seated in a swing chair on the back porch of the retreat.

Neither one of us really seemed to know how to start, so I said, "How's Tweety? Kit Kat?"

"She's fine," he said with a nod. "They're both fine. Kit Kat slept on the couch in my office. Rhonda brought them breakfast this morning from the Dawg. Lumberjack special." He looked out to the trees. "Got one for herself too."

I scanned his face. He didn't look sad so much as just resigned. "Not for you, though?"

"Not for me."

A moment passed as we watched some crows peck at the ground.

I sighed and shook my head before looking over at him. When I saw the expression on his face, I couldn't help but put my hand on his shoulder. I wasn't happy about any of this. But I knew he wouldn't have arrested Tweety if he had another choice . . . which meant there had to be pretty significant evidence. The other thing I realized sitting there with him was that all the worrying I had been doing about being attracted to Matthew was just nonsense. I didn't care what stood in between us. This was where I wanted to be. This was the man I had been crazy about my entire life . . . and yet, I also knew I was pretty much guaranteed to muck it all up. My mind flashed to the tapes sitting in my bedroom. I wanted to give them to him . . . I just had to see them first. Probably had to do with my trust issues again.

He met my eyes with his. "So this trip isn't exactly turning out how we planned."

"Nope," I said, smacking my lips together.

"You know I didn't want to do it, right?"

I nodded slowly and sighed.

"And despite all the evidence, I still don't believe she did it."

"Despite all what evidence?"

"Erica." I think he meant to say it as a warning, but it really just came out kind of sad.

I let my hands drop to my sides. "I know. I know. You can't tell me."

"No, I cannot."

I brought one leg up to curl underneath me as I twisted my body to face him. "Grady, you know I don't blame you." I almost reached out to grab his hand, but I just couldn't. "I get that you're just doing your job."

He closed his eyes and sighed, his face relaxing.

"But you've got to know—"

He tensed right back up. In fact, his little jaw muscles were rippling quite a bit. "Don't say it—"

"Freddie and I are going to do everything we can to find out the truth."

He flopped back onto the swing chair, rocking us both. "Why?" he asked looking up at the ceiling of the porch.

"Why? You know why. Tweety is family—"

"No, not that," he said pulling his head back up.

"Oh, then what, why?"

His head flopped back down and shook side to side. "Why are we cursed?"

I smiled a little.

"Did your mother do some kind of moon ritual? I know she hates me—"

"She doesn't hate you," I said, looking out to the trees. "She just blames you for my leaving town all those years ago . . . well, and for the whole business at the Raspberry Social."

"I thought we sorted that all out!"

I squinted my eyes and pinched my lips together before saying, "Yeah, she's not always rational. But"—I straightened up with a smile—"the good news is . . . I like you quite a bit."

He held my eyes a moment, sending heat rushing over my body. "I'm going to tell you something," he said, voice deepening, "and I don't want you to take it the wrong way . . . because it's going to sound terrible."

"Okay," I said with a dry swallow.

His eyes tightened and he clicked his tongue a few times before he said, "Erica Bloom, I want to make you mine in about nine hundred different ways."

My breath caught, making it hard to ask, "Nine hundred . . . physical ways?"

"Oh yes," he said with a nod.

I gulped. "You're right. That's terrible. Really." I nodded. "I'm my own woman. You can't make me yours," I said, voice cracking again. "But did you say nine hundred?"

"But I can't. We can't." He rolled his head back to stare at the ceiling, and just like that all the tension between us popped. "You and Freddie are going to do something illegal, and I'm going be all like, *Roar. Roar. Roar. I'm the law. You do what I say, and*—"

Suddenly I found myself straddling Grady.

"Whoa," he said in surprise, grabbing my hips. His eyes darkened when they met mine.

I looked down at his lips, licking my own. "Do you ever think, Grady, that maybe we talk too much about our problems?"

"I'm always thinking that we talk too much. Like all the time." He leaned up toward me while sliding his hand around the back of my neck and pulling me in. Our lips came together, hard, and my brain liquefied.

For a few timeless seconds, I lost myself in all that was Grady. Things were firing in my body that I didn't know existed. In fact the only words I could form in my brain were *nine hundred . . . nine hundred different ways.*

Then I realized something else . . . this was our first kiss! The very first time our lips had ever touched. Finally—

Then it all stopped.

I felt Grady tense beneath me.

With our lips still joined, my eyes flew open. Grady's were open too, but not focused on me. They were looking off to the side.

"Grady," I mumbled, lips still unwilling to leave his, "is there a group of silent people standing behind us?"

He nodded.

I sighed then turned my head. On the back lawn stood the group of retreat-goers. My eyes darted over to my mother. Yup, the look on her face said, *I'm not sorry.* A few threw awkward waves. The man who had winked at me the first day gave us a thumbs-up. I watched the group glide away before turning back to Grady. "In fairness, they may have heard us arguing on the phone the other night. I think they're glad we made up."

He gave me that sad smile I'd had been seeing way too much of from him lately. "I've accepted that I should be prepared for anything when I come over here."

"So, have we?"

He raised an eyebrow.

"Made up?"

"I should get back to work," Grady said, putting his hands on my hips and easing out from underneath me.

"Grady?" I couldn't keep the surprise out of my voice. I mean, I wasn't surprised that Grady wasn't thrilled with the idea of Freddie and me investigating Mr. Masterson's death, but I didn't think he would be this unthrilled, like let's-not-date unthrilled. Besides, he was the one who had arrested my Tweety!

"What do you want me to say, Erica?" He got to his feet and flung a hand out toward the lake. "Go! Investigate with Freddie. Do whatever you need to do. I'm just the sheriff of this town. I don't mind."

"Grady," I said. "I can't do nothing. This is Tweety. We're just going to talk to people. Maybe find out things you can't because you're the sheriff."

"And there it is once again," he said, throwing the same hand into the air.

"I didn't mean—"

"You don't think I can do my job."

"Grady, come on," I said, jumping to my feet. "That's not fair. You know I'm not the type of person who can just sit back and do nothing. It's not in my DNA."

"You know what?" he said, rubbing a hand over his face. "I'm really tired. I need to go. Again, I don't—" He held up his hands. "I don't want to say anything." He moved toward the porch steps.

"So what? That's it?" I shouted after him. "First kiss and now we're through?"

He jerked to a stop but didn't turn around. "I didn't say that, Erica, and you know it." He inhaled deeply and held it a moment before letting go. "I said I'm tired, and I need to go. And I need to go so that I don't say something like *we're through* without meaning it."

Heat raced to my cheeks. I knew he was right. Now wasn't the time to discuss this, but my emotions felt otherwise because all I heard was that he might mean it.

"So what's the deal?" I asked, shaking my head a little too wildly. "Are we going to see each other later?"

This time he did turn around. He planted his hands on his hips and nodded. "I think that's pretty much guaranteed, don't you?"

I leaned my face forward and held my hands out, giving him a *What the hell are you talking about?* face.

"Well, whatever you and Freddie have planned today, I'm sure somebody's bound to call it in. I'll have to make sure I work it into my already jam-packed schedule." He walked down the steps and put a halfhearted fist in the air. "Roar."

"Wait. He seriously said *Roar*?"

I nodded with my lips pinched together. "He did."

"He's such a weirdo sometimes," Freddie said, grimacing. "I mean, an unfairly handsome weirdo. But still a weirdo."

I was sitting at the island in Freddie's kitchen waiting for him to pass me a coffee. It was a gorgeous room, just like every other room in the house. Definitely a chef's kitchen with its stacked ovens, ample counter space, state-of-the-art appliances—I was pretty sure the fridge gave back rubs. Freddie told me his parents had it redone a couple of years ago while they were visiting. I couldn't help but wonder if it made Freddie sad to have this kitchen built for . . . well, people, and to be always be alone in it.

I had driven *Lightning* back to Freddie's with the tapes right after Grady left, avoiding my mother completely. I could not go another round of charades having had so little sleep.

"That being said," Freddie added, tightening the belt of his robe, "he did cover my boat, so I'm going to cut him some slack."

"Seriously," I said, trying to keep the emotion from my voice. "He knew who I was before we started whatever it is that we've started. This should not be a surprise."

"In fairness, he probably wasn't counting on there being so many murders around you."

"Two. Two murders," I said, sticking up one finger before I realized I needed to add another. Hmm, I *was* pretty tired . . . and upset.

"Right." Freddie nodded, passing me a steaming mug. "Although, for most people, two is a lot."

I sighed. Our plan this morning was to head over to the library to use the VCR, but that was suddenly feeling very wrong. "We probably should just turn the tapes over to Grady."

"What?" Freddie shouted. "You can't be serious!"

"Freddie," I said with a sigh. "You know it's the right thing to do." I was getting one of those tired headaches that can only be cured with about fourteen hours of sleep.

"I do not!" Freddie scoffed. "Erica, now, more than ever, we need to focus on what is important here."

"Okay," I said. "We could try to do that. I suppose there's a first time for everything."

"The important thing here is . . . me."

"What?" I yelled, pulling the mug too quickly away from my mouth, slopping hot liquid over the side. "You were supposed to say Tweety."

"Well, of course, Tweety, that goes without saying, but stay with me here a second." He straightened up and jabbed a finger on the counter. "The last time there was a murderer in town, who tried to pin it on an innocent suspect?"

I chuckled painfully. "Well, there was me. I think I may have done that."

"And?"

I realized where Freddie was going with this, and suddenly it wasn't so funny. "Grady."

"And," Freddie said quite seriously, "who was right all along about that not being the case?"

I paused a moment before I muttered, "You."

"Exactly," Freddie said, slapping the island. "So given our respective track records, who do you really think should be the first person to see that tape?"

"Still Grady."

"What!"

I turned again to look outside. It was certainly better than looking at Freddie's overly indignant expression. "You were lucky, that's all. And while I'm not exactly thrilled with Grady at the moment, I—"

"Luck?" Freddie planted both his hands on the island and leaned forward, as though he might make a lunge for me. "Luck was never part of the equation."

"Freddie, I—"

"Now, these tapes"—he snatched them off the stone surface of the island and held them up for me to see—"are the official property of Otter Lake Security. I don't see a subpoena, do you?"

I shook my head no.

"If you understand nothing else, Erica Bloom, understand this," Freddie said. "I am your best hope to free Tweety. I know this to be true." He spun to stalk out of the kitchen. "Now hurry up and finish your coffee."

I stayed frozen watching Freddie stomp to the steps that led up to his bedroom.

"Come on," he whined. "I just realized if we hurry we can make the opening of the fair after the library. The mini donut lady always gives me a sample from the first batch."

Chapter Twenty

I trotted up the concrete steps to the refurbished red-brick Victorian building and through the door Freddie was holding open for me. I stepped inside with some renewed pep. The coffee and the crisp drive across the lake had helped lift my spirits. I took a deep breath, welcoming the comforting smell of aging books.

Ah, the library. Just being surrounded by all those books made me feel smarter . . . like I belonged at Harvard or something . . . sitting at one of those tables with the little lamps with the green shades. Of course, when I'd tried to study here back in high school, I usually ended up with my face flattened against the tabletop, cheek wet with sleep drool, but whatever.

I think the real reason for my improved mood, however, was that *this* could be it. It was time for answers. Time to prove Tweety innocent.

Freddie walked up beside me. "I love the library," he whispered, mirroring my sentiment. "It takes me back to my childhood."

"Really?"

"Oh yeah. My nannies loved to dump me here for story

time. For a five-, six-year period, I never missed a single one."

"Freddie!" I turned to see Ms. Robinson slide out from in between the stacks after placing a book back on the shelves without even looking. Not that she was careless. Just the opposite, in fact. Ms. Robinson and the library were one. She just knew what book went where, kind of like how you don't need to look to scratch the itch at the back of your head. "Where have you been? And Erica Bloom," she said warmly. "How lovely to see you."

"Thank you," I replied with a smile. "It's good to see you too."

"Were you two looking for a quiet escape from the fair?"

"No, actually we were hoping that you could help us with something."

"Of course, dear. Of course. But first, Freddie, would you like a cookie?"

Freddie's smile widened. "Yes, Ms. Robinson."

She scurried off toward the back of the library, calling out behind her, "Don't move. I'll be right back."

"She gets you snacks?" I asked, turning to give Freddie a look.

He just shrugged.

"I swear, you have the weirdest relationships with people."

"We're a natural fit. The spinster and the neglected boy. It's a fairy tale that practically writes itself," he said, walking farther in. "And it always ends with cookies."

A moment later, Ms. Robinson hurried back in with a plate of cookies and a glass of milk.

"Oh!" Freddie said, excitedly clapping his hands together. "It's the ones with the jam in the middle. I love the ones with the jam in the middle."

He then sat himself down at the children's table, folding

his legs into one of the tiny chairs. I frowned. This was starting to get really weird. I needed to take control of this situation.

"Now, what can I do for you two?" Ms. Robinson asked.

I dragged my eyes away from Freddie. "We were wondering if you have an old VCR we could use. We, uh, are doing some research." I may have been willing to watch the tape with Freddie before we turned it over to either my uncle or the police department, but I was not about to let rumor get back to Grady about its existence before that happened.

"Of course, dear. There's one already set up in the basement with a TV. I'll show you."

Suddenly the front doorbells jangled.

Ms. Robinson's face fell. "Oh dear. It's Mrs. Appleton," she said, leaning toward us. "She won't be happy. Her book isn't in yet." She met my eye. "She does like her BDSM."

Freddie and I both looked back at the former Sunday school teacher. I leaned down to whisper, "I think Mrs. Appleton is far more complex than I gave her credit for."

"I know, right?"

"Oh well," I said, turning back to Ms. Robinson, "you take care of Mrs. Appleton. I'm sure we can figure things out downstairs."

"Well," she replied, with evident disappointment, "if you don't think you'll need my help . . ."

"We'll be fine."

Freddie moved to get up from the tiny chair, grasping the plate of cookies in his hands.

"Freddie," Ms. Robinson said, turning to walk away. "Cookies at the table only. You know that, dear."

"Yes, Ms. Robinson," he mumbled, reluctantly setting the plate back down.

"Let's go."

He nodded, snatching one more from the plate and

stuffing it in his mouth. "If we hurry, we can still make the mini donuts."

I threw him a look.

"What? I'm hung over."

A minute or two later, we were seated at a desk in the gloomy basement library. Even though the room was completely finished, it still felt damp and, well, basement-like.

"By the way," I said, slipping what I hoped was the right tape into the deck. "I thought you said this whole thing might be Betamax good. These tapes are obviously VHS."

"I was joking," he said, slapping my hand away to press the REWIND button. "Of course they aren't Betamax. Betamax couldn't tape for thirty-six hours. Not even with time lapse. There's so much for you to learn."

We waited as the VCR made some clicking noises.

"It's creepy in the basement," Freddie said, looking around. Not that we could see much. The desk had privacy panels. "If I were a serial killer I'd totally hang out down here."

I shot Freddie a look.

"What?"

After a few more clicks, the VCR's gears picked up some speed. I couldn't help but wonder how often Freddie changed these tapes, because this one sounded like it had seen better days. I was about to ask him when the gears slowed again. The machine then stopped with a *clunk*.

"Here we go." Freddie pressed PLAY.

The screen suddenly came to life and . . . my heart sunk. "Oh no, it's already taped over!" The screen was black with just a few dots of light.

"What?"

I put a hand up to the screen. "It's black."

"Settle down, you." Freddie pointed to the bottom of the

screen. "There's a time stamp, and if I'm right, that's close to when you stopped the tape."

"So?"

"So . . ." Freddie pressed the FAST FORWARD button. "Bingo!"

Suddenly the screen glowed white. Daylight! People! The fair! I clapped my hands together in little happy bursts.

"This," he said, pointing to the time stamp again, "is about twenty minutes before everything went down. Good thing we stopped the tape from recording over itself."

"Yeah, good thing *we* did that."

Freddie ignored me. "The Tunnel of Love is over here." He pointed just left of the TV screen. "But Mr. Masterson most likely would have had to walk the main midway to get there."

We settled back into silence as we watched the crowd of people mill across the screen.

After about fifteen minutes of watching in silence, worry began to seep back in.

"You're oozing disappointment again."

"But look at it," I said, not taking my eyes from the video. "You can barely tell one person from an—Oh! Pompadour!"

Both Freddie and I lurched toward the TV.

"Do you see it?" I asked, pressing at the screen with my index finger.

"I see it! Move your hand!"

"That's totally Mr. Masterson."

"You know, at one time I thought about trying a pompadour, but it's a lot of work," Freddie said, angling in closer. "Bit of a dandy, isn't he? Is he walking with anyone? I can't tell."

I yanked him back at the shoulder. "I can't see! Move." We both watched a moment or two in silence. "No, I think he's alone. Wait . . . wait."

"What! What!" Freddie shouted.

"No!" I couldn't stop the smile from spreading across my face. "It can't be!"

"What! Who?"

"Look who's making a beeline through the crowd to get to Mr. Masterson."

"Who? Stop it!" Freddie said smacking me on the arm. "Just tell me."

I leaned back in my chair. "Wait for it. You'll see. Now! Right there!" I pointed at the screen.

"Oh!" Freddie yelled. He turned his eyes to meet mine. "Well, this might just change everything."

Chapter Twenty-one

"If it isn't our friendly neighborhood hairstylist."

"Shush!" I waved a hand at Freddie. "I can't watch and listen to you at the same time."

"Wow," he muttered. "You really don't know how to sell yourself to future employers, do you?"

We watched in silence as Marg Johnson steamrolled her way to Mr. Masterson. Even with the lousy film quality, her bouffant stood out just as much as Mr. Masterson's pompadour. "Why is it all jerky like that?"

"What, the film? It's the time lapse! I told you it records only every sixteen frames."

The machine's whirring sound grew in volume. "Is the tape okay?" I asked, biting my nail.

"It's fine. Focus!"

We snapped back to silence as Marg Johnson approached Mr. Masterson.

"Do you think she looks mad?" I whispered. "I think she looks kind of mad."

"Why are you whispering?" Freddie asked. "She can't hear you."

Neither one of us said anything as we watched the pair

on the screen, the crowd milling around them. From the bird's-eye angle, it was impossible to tell what they were saying, but Marg was waving her arms quite a bit. Then Mr. Masterson turned, as though he was about to leave, and Marg grabbed his arm.

Freddie gasped.

I saw from the corner of my eye that he had slapped his hand over his mouth.

"Sorry," he whispered. "This is getting a little intense."

"Hey! Look!" I said, pointing again. "Is that—is that Mrs. Masterson over there by the ring-toss game? I thought she wasn't at the fair—that Grady had someone go get her."

"Yeah, I don't know," Freddie said. "Oh my God, and there's Tweety! Or Kit Kat! I can't tell. It must be Tweety. She's heading over to Mr. Masterson too!"

"You're right—what the—what the heck just happened?"

Suddenly everything went blurry. Or not exactly blurry . . . more like something was blocking the shot.

"What the hell is going on?" I shouted. "Oh my G— Look! It's a beak! A freaking seagull landed on the camera! He's pecking the lens!"

"That son of a—where's my gun?" Freddie yelled.

"It's not live," I said, swatting him. "Besides, you don't own a gun."

"This is making me think I totally should, though."

Freddie and I watched the screen helplessly as the bobbing head of the gull moved in and out of the shot. We were taking turns pointing and shouting things like "There! Nope. Is that—I can't tell—No! Move your stupid bird head!"

A minute later, I said, "Wait! I think it's gone. Is that a man leaving? Was he talking to them?"

Freddie and I leaned in again.

"I don't know," Freddie muttered.

"Marg's still there with Mr. Masterson, but I don't see where Tweety got to . . . oh my God!" I shouted, pointing at the screen. Marg had whacked Mr. Masterson on the back, hard.

"Quiet voices, dears," Ms. Robinson called from the top of the stairs.

"Erica's sorry, Ms. Robinson!" Freddie called back without turning his face from the TV. He also yanked my arm down so he could watch Marg Johnson reaching into her purse with her free hand while still holding on to Mr. Masterson with the other.

"She's going to give him something!"

Freddie and I both pushed toward the screen.

"What is it? What is it!" I shouted watching her pass *something* over.

"I don't know!"

He reached a hand out to accept a—

The machine suddenly made a horrible flapping sound right before—

"What's happening?"

—it clunked to stop.

Chapter Twenty-two

"No! Come on!"

We both stared at the snow-filled TV screen.

Freddie clutched his hair. "Why does this keep happening to us?"

Freddie's computer had died the last time we'd had a critical moment like this.

"Because we need better equipment!" I shouted. "Not super fancy—"

"So help me," Freddie snapped, "if you bring up *Lightning* one more time!"

I slammed back into my seat. "We were so close." I rocked my head side-to-side.

"I love how when things get exciting it's all *we*."

I slapped my hands over my face and muttered, "I'm sorry. I'm sorry." I dropped my hands. "If it weren't for you, we wouldn't have had this tape in the first place. I just thought that we'd have proof that Tweety didn't do it." Despite all of my harsh feelings about Marg, I didn't really want to believe that she had murdered Mr. Masterson either. It was hard to imagine people you know doing such things, but still, better her than Tweety. "Maybe it is enough for like . . . reasonable doubt. Let's go over to the police station and—"

"Slow your roll there, missy," Freddie said gingerly trying to remove the tape from the VCR. I hissed as he pulled out the thin bit of tape the machine was clinging to. "This is a whole boatload of reasonable doubt here, and as far as the tape is concerned, we can fix this."

"No, we cannot! We might wreck it."

"It's not hard. I did it all the time as a kid. We just need a screwdriver—"

"No," I said. "This has gone far enough. You're right. This tape is reasonable doubt. At the very least, I'm calling my uncle Jack again and—"

"Good! Call him!" Freddie said, shaking the arm of my chair till I looked over at him. "I mean, I doubt you'll get him. But leave another message. In the meantime," he said, holding the tape up to my face. "This here is what we call in the business a lead. A hot one. And we are not just turning it over to Grady."

"Freddie—"

"Need I remind you that this is still *my* tape. Legally speaking."

"Legally speaking! Don't make me slap you."

He smiled. "You're so silly sometimes." Then he let his face drop. "But seriously now, can you honestly tell me that in your heart you don't want to go over to The Sharpest Cut right now and find out what the hell this is all about?"

I pinched my lips together. I knew the right thing to do would be to head straight over to the sheriff's department, but I also knew the second we did that there was no way Grady would let us anywhere near Marg, and I needed to see her face when she found out we knew she was with Mr. Masterson before he got on that ride. After a moment, I nodded and said, "Let's do it."

"Cool. Good. Finally," Freddie said with a nod. "We just have one quick stop to make first."

"We're not stopping for donuts, Freddie!"

"God, you're awful in the mornings. Remind me to buy us an espresso machine for the office."

Ten minutes later, Freddie and I walked up to The Sharpest Cut's glass door. Before Freddie opened it, I turned to him and said, "Okay, I can't believe I'm about to say this, but I think you should take the lead." Given our recent history, I couldn't see Marg opening up to me.

"Um . . . sure. And it's really cute that you thought this might go any other way." Freddie swung the door open and we stepped inside, doorbells jangling.

Marg Johnson turned from the woman's hair she had been rolling a perm curler into, planting her fist on her hip. She spared us one up and down look then said, "We're closed."

"Now, Marg—" Freddie began.

"It's Ms. Johnson to you."

Freddie held up his hands. "Sorry. Sorry. You're right. No disrespect intended."

She shifted her weight from one foot to the other. Like the twins, Marg had to be in her seventies. I had to hand it to her that she was still able to run her business single-handedly. Then again, maybe retirement would improve her disposition.

"What are you two doing here?" she said, scratching the side of her face with the curler she was still holding. The woman in the chair looked up and frowned. "Visiting hours over at the police station must be starting, or have they already transferred that murderer upstate?"

I took half a step forward, thinking that the bucket of curlers would look far better dumped over Marg's head, when Freddie put out his hand to hold me back. "Listen, we're not here to fight."

"Why are you here?"

"Well," Freddie said, looping his thumbs around his belt and rocking back and forth on his heels. "We just wanted to get your side of things before we go to the police."

"Yeah!" I shouted with a point.

Freddie turned his back to Marg and made a *zip it* gesture with his fingers over his mouth.

"What are you two even going on about?" Marg asked.

"Little birdie has it that Tweety wasn't the only person to see Mr. Masterson right before he died." Freddie walked a few steps toward her, looking at his feet. Then he stopped, tilted his head, and peered up at her from under his brow. "You can see where I'm going with this, can't you, *Marg*?"

She twisted her lips into a pinch before saying, "Yeah, I saw the old dog before he hooked up with that tramp. What of it?"

"Wow," Freddie muttered. "Tell us how you really feel." He gave himself a shake and said, "And what were you two talking about?"

Marg narrowed her eyes on me and took a step toward us. I almost raised my dukes, but caught myself at the last second. "You know, Erica, believe it or not, I was trying to save you from the hurt and embarrassment of the truth about your so-called aunts, but I think it's time you knew what everybody else in town already knows."

"Oh yeah," I said toughly, trying to cover up the sick feeling gathering in my belly. "And what's that?"

"Everybody knows Tweety, and probably Kit Kat, killed Olivia Masterson's husband—"

I raised a finger at her in warning.

"—because they already killed her father."

Chapter Twenty-three

"Whoa," Freddie said, stumbling back a step and clutching his chest. "I think I literally reeled there for a second."

I held Marg's glare. "What did you say?"

"It's okay," Freddie said. "I'm fine. Low blood sugar, I think."

I shot a hand in his direction to get him to be quiet. "You're full of it, Marg."

"What exactly *are* you talking about?" Freddie asked more diplomatically.

"What do you mean what am I talking about? The twins killed Mr. Ramsbottom," she said, shooting a smile at the customer in the chair. "Ask anyone in this town over fifty. They'll tell you what's what."

"Well, we just may have to do that," Freddie said looking at me. "And *Ramsbottom*? Really? That's a lot of last name."

"Marg," I said taking another step forward. "I'm warning you. If you are going around town spreading this—"

"No," she said, sharply, pointing the curler at me once again. "Those twins of yours have caused enough pain and suffering in that woman's life. I have gone over to Hemlock

Estate every Monday for the past forty years to do
Mrs. Masterson's hair. She is a dear woman. A real lady.
She's done more for this town than anybody else. She never
deserved all that they've done to her."

"Ladies," Freddie said, putting up his hands. "Ladies.
We're getting off topic here. We were talking about
Marg"—he pointed in her direction—"being with Mr. Mas-
terson right before he died. Not Mr. *Ramsbottom*."

Both of us shot angry looks over to Freddie. He winked
at me then said, "Marg, I just have one more question for
you."

She didn't answer.

"You see, well, there's one little thing that I'm still confused about, and if the police were to look at this one
little thing the wrong way—" He grimaced and shook his
head. "—you could be in some trouble."

The woman getting the perm clutched her apron. I guess
the tension was getting to her.

"What are you going on about now?"

Freddie took two quick steps forward. "What exactly
did you give Mr. Masterson right before he died?"

The perm lady gasped. Freddie noticed. I think he
liked it.

"Give? What? I didn't—"

"Don't you lie to me, Marg," Freddie said harshly. "That
little birdie I told you about has really good eyes."

Marg furrowed her brow. A moment passed, then she
said, "You mean the cough drop?"

Freddie said nothing, just continued to stare at her.

"He had a cough. It's been going around. I had bought
some lozenges that morning from the pharmacy. Ask Sully.
He was there."

"Really," Freddie said with a nod. "How interesting.
And you saw him coughing from across the fairgrounds
and just hurried right over to offer a drop?"

"No," she said, loudly. "I hurried right over to give him hell about Tweety. Everybody knew he was taking up with her again. Mick Masterson had everything a man could want—a dream life—and yet he still had to run around. I thought someone should tell him what we were all thinking."

"You were worked up enough—one might even say *angry* enough—to give the man a good talking-to, and yet you still felt it necessary to tend to his cough?" Freddie asked, squinting. "A regular Florence Nightingale you are."

The customer nodded suspiciously.

Marg whacked her on the shoulder. "Well, there's no joy in tearing a strip out of someone who's practically dying right in front of you."

"Dying?"

Suddenly the room went completely still.

"Well . . . I don't know," Marg said, eyes darting about as though she was trying to remember. "He didn't look well at the end there."

Practically dying right in front of her. He was already dying! Which meant whoever gave him the drug, gave it to him before he met up with Tweety!

Freddie and I flashed each other looks.

"We have to go!" Freddie said, hustling over to grab my arm. "Thank you, Marg! You've been most helpful!"

He yanked me toward the door as I yelled, "You had better tell that to the police!"

Once outside, I asked, "So where are we going now?"

"I know where we *should* go next, but whether or not we go there," Freddie said, shooting a glance in the direction of the police station, "is entirely up to you."

I didn't say anything . . . because something across the street had caught my eye, sending goose bumps running up and down my arms.

"So what's it going to be, Erica?"

"We're giving the tapes to Grady."

"What!" Freddie yelled. "But we have so much to go on—"

I couldn't help an excited smile from spreading across my face. "We're giving the tapes to Grady right after we go talk to him," I said, pointing across the street.

"Who?" Freddie asked, whipping his head around. "Oh . . . you were messing with me. I love that you were messing with me! It's a sign! Let's go."

I wasn't one to believe in signs, but it was kind of funny that when we walked out of The Sharpest Cut, Mr. Sullivan, Sully, was watering his still-blooming baskets of flowers at the front of the pharmacy. At the very least, it felt opportune.

"Okay," I whispered, leaning toward Freddie. "Not only should we ask him about the cough drops here, but maybe we can get him to tell us what medications Mr. Masterson was on."

"Agreed." Freddie skipped ahead, holding up a hand of greeting to Mr. Sullivan.

"Freddie," the pharmacist said, putting down his watering can to stretch his back. "Nice morning. And is that . . . who I think it is?" It was clear he couldn't remember my name. Hey, at least he didn't call me Boobsie Bloom.

"Erica," I filled in.

"Of course, Erica. Nice to see you back in town. I'm sorry to hear about Tweety," Mr. Sullivan said, turning his shaggy-eyebrowed gaze to mine. "I don't believe for a minute that she had anything to do with that man's death."

"Thank you," I said with a nod. "Actually, Mr. Sullivan, Freddie and I were wondering if we could ask you a few questions."

Freddie shot me a look.

"We're hoping to find something that could clear Tweety."

"Oh . . . well," Mr. Sullivan stammered. "Certainly, I guess." He waved a hand to the front door. "Why don't we go inside?"

Freddie stepped in front of me before I could follow Mr. Sullivan. "Ever hear of foreplay?" Before I could answer, he added, "I've got this, okay? Just stand back. I'm on a roll."

The pharmacy was actually a lovely old Victorian home. With the library, it was one of the few remaining in Otter Lake. The inside had been renovated, of course, and had all the modern equipment of a pharmacy, but the original woodwork of the main room itself hadn't been touched, and it was decorated with medical antiques—mainly old dispensary bottles made of colored glass.

I absentmindedly walked over to a cluster of black-and-white pictures hanging on the wall. Maybe Freddie was right . . . I should be a little more subtle. Slow down a bit. Not look so anxious. The photos were mainly portraits, probably family, but there were a few of the town too. I stopped in front of a gap in the middle of the collection where a frame had been taken down.

"I lent that picture to the fair," Mr. Sullivan offered. "They have a display of photos near the agricultural building. Mrs. Masterson lent quite a few out too. I should maybe see if she would like them back for the funeral."

"That's kind of you." I hadn't noticed the display before, so I made a mental note to take a look at it.

"The one I gave them was of the grand opening of the pharmacy. I hope they take good care of it. It's the only one I have of *her* from that day." He smiled then rubbed the front counter with an affectionate look on his face.

Freddie turned his back to Mr. Sullivan, raised his eyebrows, and mouthed what looked to be *Bow chicky bow bow*.

I shot him a warning look.

"So what did you kids want to ask me about the case?"

Freddie smiled and whispered, "I love that he said that, very Scooby-Doo." He then whirled around and said, "Well, we were just talking to Marg Johnson, and she was telling us that there's been a cough going around?"

"Oh yes, she was in for lozenges the other day."

Freddie nodded. "I don't suppose you'd know if Mr. Masterson had that same cough?"

Mr. Sullivan chuckled. "Now, Freddie, you know I can't be sharing personal medical information."

"Of course. Of course," Freddie said, nodding. "Besides, rumor has it he died of some sort of overdose?"

Mr. Sullivan pointed a finger at him with a smile. "I don't put much stock in rumors . . . but I see what you're doing here."

"You do?"

"Leading me in with information you already have, seeing if I'll let something slip. Very good, my boy. Very good. Everyone's been saying that you have a knack for the detective business."

"Do they really?" Freddie said smiling. "Tell me more."

I slapped him on the back.

"Kidding," Freddie said, shooting me a look. "But in all seriousness, I know there was some talk about it possibly being an accidental overdose of medication."

The pharmacist sniffed.

"In fact, Erica tells me her uncle, the lawyer who is representing Tweety, is still really interested in this particular possibility, but I know how thorough you are in giving your patients instructions, so I don't think that's likely."

"Giving instructions is one thing, Freddie. Having customers follow those instructions is another entirely."

"Oh," Freddie said, leaning back. "I see. I thought I heard Sheriff Forrester say they were working on the possibility that Mr. Masterson intentionally took too much of his cholesterol medication."

Mr. Sullivan's eyes flashed. "Did he really? The cholesterol medication? I told him it was the morphine patches for his arthritis . . . oh Freddie," the man said, smiling and tapping the side of his nose. "You got me."

My eyes flashed to Freddie as a rush ran over my body. *Holy crap! He's done it.* He must have known it too, but his face stayed very still.

"I apologize, Mr. Sullivan. Really. I just want to keep this town safe."

"To be honest, I'm not sure why they aren't focused more on an accidental overdose," Mr. Sullivan offered. "That man certainly did have his vices. You tell your uncle that, Erica. It wouldn't surprise me one bit if he was fooling around with his medication."

I nodded. "I will."

He sighed. "I'd like to help. Sheriff Forrester asked me about Tweety's medications. I had to tell him that she did have a prescription for morphine a while back. I think it was when she cut off that part of her big toe with the lawn mower."

The exhilaration I had been feeling just moments ago fizzled away. "What? Tweety cut off part of her big toe?"

Mr. Sullivan looked surprised. "You didn't know?"

"No," I said, looking to Freddie. He shrugged.

"I felt bad telling him. I knew what he'd think." He shook his head. "So if I can help in any way, please let me know."

"Thank you, Mr. Sullivan," Freddie said, reaching out to take his hand. "You have been really helpful."

"Sully," the man interjected, giving Freddie's hand a good shake.

I rolled my eyes slightly at the male bonding. Nobody seemed interested in shaking my hand. And if Happy Erica was weird, Grown-Up Freddie was even weirder . . . but also kind of awesome.

"I'll make sure to tip off the medical examiner about your overdose theory too—"

I made a *pfft* sound.

Freddie shot me a warning look before turning back to Sully. "Just to be thorough."

"You do that," Sully replied. "Thank goodness this town has you."

Freddie tapped two fingers to his forehead, giving the man a little salute before turning and walking away.

I nodded at Mr. Sullivan. "Thank you."

By the time I caught up to Freddie, he was already halfway across the street.

"Freddie," I called out. "Slow down."

I caught up with him just in time to hear, "Oh my God, I can't believe that worked. I saw it on *Sherlock*. I need to sit down."

"You . . . did it," I said, shaking my head. I mean part of me was worried that he had thrown Grady under the bus again, but the important thing right now was Tweety, and I couldn't deny Freddie his moment. "You really, really did it."

Freddie grunted and punched the air. "I sherlocked the hell out of that man!"

I stopped walking.

Freddie turned. "Too far?"

"Too far."

Despite Freddie being pumped beyond belief, we had to put a hold on our sleuthing. He needed to put in an appearance at the fair, and I wanted some time to think about what to do next. To say Marg's story upset me was putting it mildly. Like Tweety being suspected of one murder wasn't bad enough—Marg had to tack on another? But on the bright side, at least we knew for sure now that a number of people had access to Mr. Masterson right before he died, and we knew it was most likely morphine that killed him. It was a start. We had also decided to see what my uncle Jack had to say about the tapes before we handed them over to Grady. He would be the best judge of how to handle the situation.

I walked aimlessly around town for about an hour, trying to wrap my mind around all that had happened, but everything still seemed unreal. And why had nobody told me about Tweety's accident? Was I really so disconnected from home? Had I given my mother the impression I didn't want to know about that kind of thing? I mean, I had told her once or twice we needed boundaries . . . but not lawn mower accident boundaries! I couldn't help but wonder what else I had missed.

All the thinking I was doing made me hungry, so I decided to buy a hot dog at the fair before taking a look at the photo display Mr. Sullivan had talked about.

I walked over to the agricultural building, letting the processed meat work its soothing magic. The building was located a good distance away from the midway, so there were fewer people, and even though it smelled like manure, the sound of cows mooing was kind of relaxing.

I stopped in front of the large corkboard, popping the last bit of bun into my mouth. The pictures were covered with plastic wrap, and the board itself had an overhang, so the photos were protected from the rain. That should make Mr. Sullivan happy. I spotted the photo he had been talking about pretty quickly. The ribbon-cutting ceremony for the pharmacy. My eyes dropped to the typed strip of paper pinned underneath. MR. RAMSBOTTOM AND MR. SULLIVAN SENIOR. So that was Mr. Ramsbottom. Huh. He looked to be in his fifties when the photo had been taken, probably not all that long before he had died. There was something about him that did sort of emanate power and money. Maybe it was the suit. And my mom was right. He did have a big chest. I noticed a gawky boy standing behind him. Oh my God! Was that Mr. Sullivan Junior? Sully? My eyebrows shot up. I needed to show Freddie this. He had the same *in love* smile on his face as he'd had back at the store. Wow, that guy really loved his pharmacy.

My eyes slid to another picture. This one captured a fall fair queen standing on a stage waving to the crowd in a modest bathing suit and heels. I leaned forward to read the caption. MARG JOHNSON. Well, crap. I couldn't help but admit she was a bit of a hottie back in the day . . . and that really didn't make me like her any more. I knew she had a mean-girl vibe about her.

My eyes skimmed along the board, passing one picture after the next. There was an old shot of the library . . . lots of pictures of the fair . . . then . . . twins!

I didn't recognize them at first, but, really, how many identical twins could Otter Lake have? I huddled forward to get a closer look at the grainy photo. It was a group shot, and there were lots of people surrounding them, but the twins stood out. Not in the beauty-salon sort of way that Marg Johnson had. They had more of a buxom, badass vibe, like the pinup woman flexing her bicep in that war poster. I looked at the caption. FAIR VOLUNTEERS.

I scanned the photo again. Wait a minute . . . off in the background there was a man with a cigarette hanging from the corner of his mouth, leaning against a barn, arms folded across his chest. I knew instantly who it was. The pompadour gave him away every time.

He was looking at one of the twins . . . had to be Tweety.

And the look in his eye . . . that could make a girl's knees go weak. It was all *need*.

I shook my head and leaned back. I couldn't help but wonder what broke them up. Hard to imagine a guy who could look like that giving his love up for anything, but then again, it was just one look . . . in a photo from long ago.

Once I had given the board a good once-over, I decided to walk back to the midway to see if Freddie was done terrorizing the town's teenagers yet. I only made it about halfway through the games when I realized how thirsty I was. The sun was back out, and I was shielded from the wind by all the games, so it was getting pretty hot. I walked over to a guy seated in a giant lemon and bought myself a drink.

Just as I took the first sip, something caught my eye . . . actually *someone*. Grady, back in full sheriff's gear, walking the midway with Rhonda.

My heart clenched at the sight, and I couldn't help but think again how much this trip sucked. Sure, Tweety was the important thing here. Oh God, and Mr. Masterson. I really needed to stop forgetting about him. But I couldn't help but grieve just a little bit for the week that could have been.

Just then I saw Rhonda smack Grady a few times on the arm before pointing at the Strong Man Game.

I walked a few steps closer just in time to hear the vendor call out, "Oh ho ho, it's the Strong Arm of the Law, folks! Come on, Sheriff. Step right up and give it a whack!"

Grady held up a hand to wave him off.

"What?" the man asked. "Are all those pretty muscles just for show?"

Grady arched an eyebrow at the vendor but kept on walking.

"Come on, Sheriff. Show the people of Otter Lake why they can sleep well at night."

Grady shook his head again, but Rhonda elbowed him in the side then pointed to me. Grady looked over. When he spotted me, he brought a hand up to rub his forehead, but a small smile broke over his face.

I walked a few steps closer to the edge of the gathering crowd.

"Nobody's won yet, big man," the vendor yelled, "but I got a feeling you could be the first."

Grady looked at me again, indecision still on his face, but the smile was getting bigger.

I smiled back and mouthed the words, *Do it*. Maybe I would get my overpriced teddy bear after all.

He shot me a look with his eyes under his hat that said, *Really?*

Oh yeah.

I couldn't help myself. Grady and I needed this moment . . . a moment that wasn't all serious and complicated by murder. We needed a moment full of fun, flirtation, and . . . oh yes, him unbuttoning his sleeves at the wrist and rolling the fabric up his rippling forearms.

"Woo! Sheriff!" a woman shouted from the other side of the crowd. My eyes snapped over. Hmm, Kelly Green. She was at least fifteen years Grady's senior and worked at the post office. She was also my new mortal enemy. My eyes darted back to Grady. He was gripping the sledge-hammer and finding his stance . . . which made me forgive Kelly just a little bit. Really, who could blame her? Grady in his uniform, showcasing his muscles, was a lot to take. Besides, it sounded like she had visited the beer tent.

Grady shot me one more look, definitely flirtatious this time. Then he swung the hammer.

"Oh, Sheriff!" the man at the game shouted. "You can do better than that! Good thing you've got two more tries."

Grady frowned at the man but then glanced back over at me. I fanned my hand in front of my face to let him know it was getting hot out here. Grady's smile widened at the sight, and my heart skipped a beat.

He adjusted his stance and grip, then took another swing.

"Oh no!" the man shouted. "That was worse than the first one. Are you sure those pecks are real?"

"I'll check," Kelly shouted. "Let me check. I'll be real thorough."

Okay, Kelly was getting on my nerves again.

Grady stepped back from the game and wiped his brow with the back of his hand. He looked at me, and I took a long sip from my straw before mouthing, *Thirsty?* with a quick double pop of my eyebrows.

Grady chuckled this time and nodded.

I stepped over to the lemonade guy and passed him some money without taking my eyes off Grady.

He split his legs a bit farther apart to anchor his stance . . . and my God did the man make a good stance.

Grady swung this time in a big, big wide arc.

Bam!

Ding! Ding! Ding!

"We have a winner, folks!"

The crowd cheered while I mumbled under my breath, "Wow. Nailed me."

Someone coughed at my side.

"Matthew?"

He had one fist at his mouth; the other was waving me off. His eyes looked half shocked, half amused. What was so funny? Then it hit me. "I mean *it*! He nailed *it*! Not me! He's never nailed me."

Matthew laugh-coughed harder, unable to catch his breath.

"Are you okay?" I said, trying to whack him on the

back, but my hands were full of lemonade. "Here. Drink this." I passed him one of the cups just as Grady and Rhonda walked by . . .

Aw . . . crap.

Grady took a look at the drink. Then at Matthew. Then at me.

"No. No. No," I said, waving my free hand in the air. "I gave him mine this time. This one's yours." I held out the full lemonade.

But they kept walking. Grady tossed the teddy bear he had won to Rhonda . . . who looked over her shoulder at me, head slowly shaking with disgust.

"Oh, man," Matthew said. "First I drank his coffee, and now this. Did you want me to go explain what happened? Give him his lemonade?"

"I really doubt that will help," I said, watching Grady walk away. "Besides, I don't think he's thirsty anymore."

"Funny," Matthew said. "I'm always thirsty." His expression stayed completely still, straw in his mouth . . . before his eyes widened just a touch in feigned innocence.

I couldn't help my drop my chin to my chest and laugh a little.

It was either that or cry.

Chapter Twenty-four

"So why is Mrs. Masterson our next step again?" Freddie shouted over *Lightning*'s engine. "What about following up on this thing with Tweety and Mr. Ramsbottom?"

"Not yet," I shouted back. "For all we know, Marg is the only one who thinks there's a connection between the twins and Mr. Ramsbottom. I don't want to stir up more gossip." I pushed some hair from my face. "Besides, we need to know what Mrs. Masterson thought was going on between her husband and Tweety."

Freddie nodded and eased off the gas. "Good plan. Besides, you know what they say about murderers."

"I do?"

"It's usually the wife."

"I don't think they say that."

"Well, it's the person closest to the victim."

I sighed.

"Oh stop. You were the one who told me Matthew pinned his mother as a suspect."

"I don't think he meant it, though." I was kind of regretting telling Freddie what Matthew had said the night before at the fairgrounds. "It was just a flip comment."

"Uh-huh."

Freddie had made me wait until end of the day to leave the fair. Luckily, there was a concert tonight, a small country band, and Matthew had mentioned that he was thinking of sticking around to watch, so we knew there was a good chance we could talk to his mother alone. We were headed there next. We just needed to make a quick stop at the retreat first.

"Don't take too long, okay?" Freddie said, gliding toward the dock. "I hate waiting."

"You're always welcome to come up with me."

"And have all those silent people stare at me?" He shuddered. "They're almost as bad as the pumpkin people. Besides, I hate watching you and your mom do charades. It's like watching monkeys on typewriters . . . but less funny. I can't take it."

After hopping once again from *Lightning* to the canoe to the dock, I hurried my way up the steps. I didn't particularly want to go another silent round with my mother either, but we needed a pretext to go over to Hemlock Estate, and she had the perfect one.

I searched the lodge but couldn't find anyone, so I decided to check out back. The sun now hung low in the sky, but it was still a pretty nice night. Maybe they were on another walk or doing an outdoor meditation. I turned the corner of the porch and—

Thwack!

"Ow! Frick!" I shouted bringing my fingers to my brow bone. "What the—" My watery eyes dropped to the ground.

Birdie.

I looked up through my fingers. Yup, there they were. Playing silent badminton. I spotted a horrified-looking woman mouthing, *Sorry!* over and over. I put up my *It's okay!* hand and muttered, "This is what happens when you can't shout, *Look out!*"

My mother hurried over, eyes wide.

"I'm fine. I'm fine."

She smiled.

"And before you try to ask," I said, holding up a hand, "I don't have any news on Tweety."

She nodded, the worried crease between her eyebrows deepening.

"Um, listen. I'm not staying long," I said, not quite able to meet her gaze. "I just came by because I ran into Matthew Masterson, and apparently you make some tea for his mother that calms her nerves?"

My mother nodded . . . suspiciously. This was going to be tricky. I really didn't want to tell her I was going over to interrogate Mrs. Masterson. She might have feelings about that . . . and her silent feelings took so long to communicate.

"Well, I'm headed over there, and I thought I could bring it with me? It might help with the . . . grieving."

My mother scanned my face. A moment later she nodded and went inside.

That had gone better than I'd thought. I shoved my hands into my pockets, turning back toward the game right when—

"Wah!" I ducked down as another birdie zoomed by my head.

Same woman.

I wagged a friendly finger at her as the screen door slammed shut. My mom walked back out with a small bag in her hands.

"Thanks, Mom, I'll just take that and be on—"

She folded the bag underneath her arms.

"—on my way?"

She arched an eyebrow.

"What?"

She arched it even higher. Wow. She must be doing face yoga now.

"Fine," I said, planting my hands on my hips. "I'm not just going over to Hemlock Estate to deliver tea. I'm going over to see if I can find out anything that might help Tweety."

My mom's expression didn't change.

"Hey, you were the one who told me about Mr. Rams-bottom," I said. "And thank you for not acting out that name, by the way."

A smile touched the corner of her mouth, but she still didn't release the bag.

This was ridiculous. "Look, I'm just going to see if, you know, Mrs. Masterson has any thoughts she'd like to share on who she thinks might be behind . . . everything that's going on."

She regarded me closely for a moment then nodded . . . but still didn't give me the bag!

"So . . . ?" I asked, holding out my hand.

She put up a *hang on a second* finger.

I groaned.

She pointed at my chest.

"Me?"

She then started flying around the porch. Like a bird. Flapping its little hand wings. Dipping its head down every now and then.

"Tweety again?"

Her shoulders slumped before she caught a glimpse of all the guests watching her. She straightened back up then held up three fingers.

"Third word?"

She got up on her tiptoes and walked in a line like . . .

"A sobriety test!"

She gave me yet another look that did not need interpreting. She really had those down.

"Mom, I don't kn—"

"For the love of vegan balls!" I whipped around to see Freddie walking toward my back. "She's saying, You." He pointed at my chest. "Bee." This time he flapped his arms like wings. "Careful!"

My mother jumped up and down, air-clapping.

"Oh," I said loudly drawing out the word. "Yeah, of course, I will. No problem."

Suddenly my mom's arm were wrapped around me.

"She loves you too, Ms. Bloom," Freddie said quickly, then muttered, "Give me the monkeys any day. Let's go!"

Ten, fifteen minutes later we were pulling up to the Mastersons' long dock. It was nice not to have to make a jump for shore from Freddie's boat for a change.

We tied off *Lightning* then headed up the slope to the manse just as the sun dipped into the water.

"So," Freddie said, pointing to the small paper bag I was holding. "You must have been talking to Matthew for quite a bit to get all the way to his mother's beverage choices."

I cut Freddie a look. "What are you doing right now?"

"I'm not doing anything," he said with a shrug. "But seriously, what's going on with you and Mr. Architect?"

"Nothing."

Freddie stopping walking.

"What?" I asked, stopping too.

"Your face," he said, pointing directly at it.

I resisted the urge to touch my cheeks. They felt warm. "What about my face?"

Freddie shook his head. "I thought I saw it last night at the bonfire with the carnies . . . but you were all *No, no, no. Grady. Grady. Grady.* But now . . . I'm not so sure."

"What are you talking about?"

"It's written all over your face, Ms. Smitten Kitten." He swirled his finger. "And by the way you're blushing, well, let's just say I'm guessing there's a pretty steamy scene in chapter five of your Erica–Matthew novel."

I batted his hand away. "Stop it. You know Grady and I are on the cusp of . . . well, something! Matthew's just nice, and . . . and why are we always talking about me? Let's talk about you for a change!"

"Easy now," Freddie said. "I didn't mean to pick a fight. It's only natural you'd find Matthew attractive. We've all wondered what it would be like to be Lady of the Manse."

I exhaled a breath. "It is a pretty awesome manse."

"Oh yeah. Would you look at those porches?" Freddie said, finally turning away. "You could totally wander around those puppies at night thinking mournful thoughts."

I shot him a sideways look. "You have put some thought into this."

"He's handsome too. Almost as good looking as Grady."

"Nobody's as good looking as Grady."

"He's close, though, and in a weird way that almost makes him more attractive. You know what I mean?" Freddie looked to me for agreement. "Grady's perfection can be off-putting."

I huffed a breath. "You're just jealous."

"I am," he said, nodding. "Oh! And I bet Matthew wouldn't have any issues with our crime-fighting partnership."

"Seriously, just stop it," I said. "And Matthew might have some issues with our *investigation* if he knew you kept naming him as a suspect."

"Oh right. I forgot that part." Freddie tapped his finger in the air. "You know, we need a flow chart or something to keep everything straight. Ooh! Or a whiteboard!"

I headed back up the lawn. "Let's just go."

Freddie and I walked around to the front of the house.

Both of us were slightly out of breath by the time we got to the door. We really needed to work on our cardio if we were going to—I gave my head a shake before I finished the thought. I reached forward, grabbed the heavy door knocker, and gave it a good rap.

We waited half a minute or so before I said, "Maybe she's not home."

Freddie screwed up his face. "Let's give her a little more time. It's a big place."

We waited another minute or two before I reached forward to give the door another rap. Just as my fingers touched the knocker, the door jerked. I snatched my hand back. Freddie snickered.

The door swung open, bringing a woman into view. "Peter, we've been over this. I—" She stopped abruptly when she saw us.

It took everything in me to prevent my jaw from hitting my chest. I shot a quick look to Freddie. I could tell he was having the same problem. Mrs. Masterson was . . . stunning. I mean, growing up, I had seen her at a number of community events giving speeches and stuff—she was on a lot of committees—but never actually up close. She kind of reminded me of Audrey Hepburn in the way she held herself, but a little more . . . hard?

"I'm sorry. I thought you were my gardener," she said. "I do not patronize solicitors." She moved to close the door.

"Wait," I said stepping forward. "Mrs. Masterson?"

She blinked and turned her large green eyes to mine.

"My name is Erica Bloom. Summer Bloom's daughter?" I held up the brown paper bag. For a brief moment, I was worried it might be pot. "I brought you some of my mother's tea."

"Oh! Forgive me," she said, pushing the door back open. "Come in. Come in. And bring your handsome friend."

My eyes darted over to Freddie. His eyes rounded as he mouthed the words, *Handsome friend? I love her.*

We both stepped into the palatial foyer then stopped dead.

"Oh great Gatsby," Freddie whispered, taking in the sight. "It's better than I thought."

The floor was a classic white-and-black tile design, and two wrought-iron staircases curved up either side of the large room leading to the top floor. Dropped down in between was an enormous mirrored glass chandelier.

"I can't. It's just too much," Freddie whispered, taking in the silver geometric print of the wallpaper. "You have to marry Matthew. We need to hang out here. Oh! We can drink sidecars . . . or . . . or bee's knees-es," Freddie said, having some trouble making the word plural. "And I'll have someone set off fireworks over the lake in the summer."

"Freddie, calm down," I said under my breath. "You already live in a beautiful house."

"Not like this."

"Please try to stay focused."

"I don't think I can. Oh, look through to the back living room. She has floaty white curtains. Can you just imagine them in the summer . . . in the breeze?"

I looked the gauzy curtains over. They were beautiful. Everything was beautiful. I couldn't imagine the amount of work involved in keeping up a house like this.

"Mrs. Masterson," Freddie said, trotting to catch up to her. "Your house is spectacular."

She smiled. "You are very kind." Her eyes swept the room. "This house was my father's dream. It needs a great deal of love and attention, but I think it's worth it."

"Indeed," Freddie answered eagerly.

I struggled to keep my face friendly as Mrs. Masterson's gaze swept in my direction. I was trying to figure out whether or not I was looking at a woman who was capable of killing both her father and husband . . . and my suspicions kept creeping up into my face.

"Please, come in," she said, gently waving us forward once again, her long jeweled fingers swirling in the air. "I don't have the help I used to, but I'm sure I can find us some iced tea or lemonade."

Freddie waited for me to catch up before he whispered, "Don't you just love her eyes!"

"Her eyes?"

"She's got those big doe eyes. You know, like Mia Farrow in the early days."

"I think maybe it's just a thyroid problem."

He swatted my arm.

"Sorry. You're right. They're great eyes," I whispered hurriedly, "but before you get completely swept away, let's remember why we're here."

"Right. Right," Freddie muttered. "But I don't know if I can! I feel swept away."

"Obviously, I don't need to marry Matthew," I said. "You can just marry Mrs. Masterson."

"Don't joke. There is a part of me that would really love that."

"You are so weird."

I walked into the grand sitting room after Mrs. Masterson. The view was spectacular. Even better than Freddie's. I really could see fireworks going off above the lake. This manse certainly knew how to sell a dream.

"Now what can I get for the two of you?"

"Nothing . . . please," I said. "We really just wanted to express our condolences about Mr. Masterson's passing." Not going to lie, I felt a pretty bad twinge of conscience, but it was for the greater good. Besides, we really weren't doing anything other than making conversation. It wasn't like we were about to try out some advanced interrogation techniques.

"Thank you, dear. I'm not quite sure how I will get on without Mick, but I suppose it is all God's plan."

Huh. Somebody's plan. Not sure if I'd blame it on God. I couldn't help but notice she wasn't exactly beside herself with grief, but then again, in fairness, if Mr. Masterson had been unfaithful, could I blame her? Plus, she kind of had the air of a woman who had practice wearing a public face. Hard to say if we were seeing the *real* her.

"How long were you two married?" Freddie asked.

"Nearly fifty years," she said with another smile.

"That's amazing. What was your secret?"

For the briefest moment, Mrs. Masterson's face hardened. "Determination."

Freddie chuckled . . . nervously.

Her smile snapped back into place. "I think young people give up too easily these days." She looked out the windows, twisting the wedding band still on her finger. "I knew at a young age the life I wanted—the legacy I was gifted to carry on—I never wavered from that vision."

Freddie and I exchanged looks. I wondered how Mr. Masterson's infidelity fit into that vision. Then almost as if she could read my thoughts she said, "Mick was the same way. He certainly wasn't a perfect man, but he was devoted to me"—her eyes snapped to mine—"to the very end."

I froze. I suddenly felt very guilty by my association with Tweety.

"Well . . . that's just lovely," Freddie said, clapping his hands together and flashing an overly big smile. "Mrs. Masterson, could I trouble you for a glass of water?"

"Of course. Make yourselves comfortable."

Freddie waited until she had left the room then said, "Okay, the wedding's off. She may be a little . . ." He grimaced and shook his head back and forth.

"You think?" I whispered. "But it could just be the infidelity that has her so worked up."

"Maybe," he said. "But she stays at the top of the suspect list for now."

"Agreed."

"Would you look at these photographs, though." Freddie moved to the piano. A number of framed pictures sat on the top. "She should have been in the movies." He held up a black-and-white glamour shot. Mrs. Masterson with her classic high cheekbones and big eyes really was something else. I moved beside Freddie and picked up another photo. A wedding photo. They certainly were a gorgeous couple, but there was something about Mr. Masterson's expression that left me cold. It wasn't fair to judge—it was a posed shot—but all of the hunger he'd had in that other photo with Tweety . . . well, it was all gone.

A moment later Mrs. Masterson walked back in the room holding out a cut-crystal glass for Freddie. "I took the liberty of adding some mint and lem—"

Suddenly a loud bang tore through the house.

"Mother? Where are you?"

Mrs. Masterson's hand flew to her chest as Freddie and I jumped to our feet.

"What were you thinking?"

I looked nervously to the front of the house. I recognized Matthew's voice, but I had never heard him sound quite so upset.

"Tell me. Tell me that you didn't—" Matthew stopped abruptly when he got to the mouth of the room. "I'm sorry. I didn't realize . . ."

"Is everything all right?" I asked.

Matthew's fists, balled at his side, suddenly released. He brought one hand up to push his hair back. "Erica," he said before taking a breath. "I'm glad you're here. And no, everything is not all right."

Chapter Twenty-five

"What's going on?"

"Kit Kat is outside."

"What?" I looked back out the window to the lake. I didn't see her boat.

"She drove here," Matthew said. "She *borrowed* a police cruiser."

I groaned. "Why? Why would she—"

"Apparently, my mother invited her."

We all turned to Mrs. Masterson.

"I have questions that require answers," she said, not shrinking from our gaze.

"Maybe you could go talk to her?" Matthew suggested. "Given everything that's happened, I really think it's best that they don't mingle."

"Right. Of course."

I hurried toward the door, just catching Freddie say, "So, Matthew . . .'sup?"

The sun was nearly gone now, and the temperature had dropped with it. My eyes scanned the large driveway. Yup, right there, around the last bend, sat a police cruiser.

I jogged toward the car. What the hell was she thinking?

Borrowing a cruiser? Grady would just love that. It would do wonders for his reputation.

I slowed the last few feet. I could see she wasn't in the car. Her white hair and dentures had a tendency to glow in the dark.

"Kit Kat?"

Nothing.

I turned back toward the house and called her name again.

A cold wind spun a pile of dried leaves by my feet.

"Kit Kat! Seriously, where are you?"

The gloom settling over the trees played tricks with my eyes, melding shadows together.

I turned in a slow circle as a bad feeling tiptoed its way up my spine.

Then, in the corner of my eye—something moved. Just by the footpath leading into the trees.

I ran toward it, muttering, "So help me, you had better not be messing around."

The trees closed in atop me as I entered the trail. I still had the light seeping in from the lake side of the path, but in minutes I wouldn't be able to see my hand in front of my face.

I walked with slow, deliberate steps, not wanting to trip over any branches or tree roots. Worn bits of gravel crunched underneath my feet. I didn't like this at all. I should probably just head back and get Matthew and Freddie . . . and maybe a flashlight.

I balled my fists against the cold. "Kit Kat?"

Nothing.

Yeah, this was getting ridiculous. It was really dark now, and I couldn't even be sure that I had seen anything. She could have snuck around to the back of the house for all I knew. She could be inside. The path slanted upward. Where the hell did this thing lead? I took a breath and thought, *Just to the top of the hill.* I'd get to the top, look around, and if there was nothing—which I was positive was the case—I'd go back down and get help. I opened my mouth to call Kit Kat's name again but quickly snapped it shut. Maybe it was the dark, or the rustling wind—or maybe the fact that there was a murderer on the loose—but suddenly I had the distinct feeling I was being watched.

Just to the top.

I took another step but a sudden scurrying to my left made me jolt so hard I nearly cracked my spine. "Freaking squirrels," I muttered, wrapping my jacket more tightly around me. *Almost there.*

I crested the hill. My shoulders dropped in relief as my eyes darted over a clearing with a little stone bench overlooking the lake. It was kind of pretty actually. I walked toward the small seat, looking up at the first few stars darting the sky . . . then froze.

Something lay on the ground right in front of the bench. *No. No. No.*

It wasn't something . . . it was *someone*. Someone with white hair.

"No!"

I launched into a sprint.

My feet skidded to a stop a foot or so back from the bench. It took me a second to figure out what I was seeing. It wasn't Kit Kat. It was a man covered in blood from a head wound . . . a fatal head wound by the look of it. My eyes darted to the shovel lying on the ground a few feet away.

My head started to shake of its own accord as my feet moved back.

This couldn't be happening . . . not another murder.

I was just about to turn and run when—

"Kit Kat! Oh God, no!"

Chapter Twenty-six

"You just always seem to be turning up dead bodies, Erica," Rhonda Cooke, deputy at large, said. She leaned back in her chair and plopped her feet up on the corner of her desk. "How do you do it?"

A couple of hours had passed since I had found grounds-keeper Peter Clarke and Kit Kat. Kit Kat was still alive when I had found her—I could still feel the small bump of her pulse under my fingertips—but the ambulance had taken her away, and we had yet to be given an update.

Now I was seated in Otter Lake's sheriff's department being questioned by Rhonda.

"Well? Erica? How do you do it?"

"Rhonda, I'm really sorry," I said, rubbing my face with both hands. "But I don't have time for this, so could we please skip the thinly veiled questions? Just say what you want to say."

Her face dropped into something pretty earnest. "No, I really want to know how you keep turning up dead bodies." She dropped her feet off the desk and leaned toward me to whisper, "It could help my career."

I gripped the arms of my chair. "I can't do this right now. I have to find out what's going on with Kit Kat."

She nodded but waved me down. "Erica, I know you're worried, but I promise, as soon as we know something, you will. In the meantime, you have to help us find whoever did this."

I slumped back in the chair, resting my head against its hard wooden back.

"Erica? That you?" a voice called out.

I shot up, giving Rhonda a quizzical look. She just closed her eyes and shook her head.

"Tweety?" I shouted, leaning back to look down a hallway. I couldn't see anything . . . well, except a hand waving into the open space.

"What are you doing here?" the hand asked with a point.

"Ms. Bloom," Rhonda said. "Please ignor—"

I lunged across the desk toward her and hissed, "Don't you tell her about Kit Kat until we know if—" I couldn't finish the sentence. "Not unless you're going to let her go to the hospital."

"I can't authorize that," Rhonda whispered back.

"Then don't you say anything," I said, slowly sitting back in my chair.

Rhonda considered me for a moment then said, "Erica, don't take this the wrong way . . . but you're kind of freaking me out right now."

"I'm done playing."

She looked at me sideways. "Okay, what does that mean? And before you answer, I feel I should remind you that you're talking to a police officer."

"Nobody," I said, jabbing a finger on top of the desk, "messes with my family, Rhonda." I watched her eyes widen with concern. "I'm gonna find whoever did this and—"

"What's this about finding a body?" Tweety shouted from the hall. "I told you to stay out of it!"

I struggled to figure out what to say. Probably sticking as close to the truth as possible was the best bet. "Yeah, I found a body."

"Another one?"

I didn't answer.

"At least they can't pin that one on me," the voice cackled from the back. "Are they trying to pin it on you?"

I looked to Rhonda for the answer. She shrugged. I kept my eyes on her but turned my face to the hallway. "Too soon to tell."

"Okay, okay," Rhonda said. "Could we please get back to—"

"So who was it?"

"Peter Clarke," I shouted. "Do you know—"

"Erica! Stop it!" Rhonda yelled. "You just can't go telling her police stuff until we're ready to tell her police stuff!"

My eyes whipped back to hers. She popped her hands up.

"Don't listen to her," Tweety shouted. "Now, who did you say got offed?"

"Erica," Rhonda said, setting her jaw. "Don't answer that."

I considered Rhonda for a moment and took a breath. I wasn't upset with her. She was just trying to do her job. Besides, the less I said to Tweety the better. I really didn't want to let anything slip about Kit Kat until we had news. It would kill her. "You'll hear the whole story soon."

"What kind of answer is that?" Tweety shouted. "Erica? Rhonda?"

Rhonda clunked her head against the desk. "All day it's like this. Yap, yap, yap." She flung her head up. "Okay," she said, dropping her voice. "Let's ignore Tweety and get back to the questioning. Why don't you tell me again why you were at Hemlock Estate."

"Hemlock Estate!" the voice screeched from down the hall. "What were you doing at Hemlock Estate?"

Rhonda jumped to her feet and leaned across her desk, shouting down the hall, "Tweety, I've told you about a thousand times already, I ask the questions."

"Ah, you're just jealous," Tweety shouted back, her hand giving a dismissive flop in the air.

"Jealous?" I asked Rhonda, who was lowering herself back in her seat.

"She questions everyone who comes in," Rhonda said tiredly. "Okay, so fine, she was right about Mr. McCloud's stolen wallet being in his *other* back pocket, but for the most part she's just a real pain in the—"

"I get it," I said, holding my hands up. "All the more reason for us to work together to get her out of here. But I can't do this right now. I gotta go."

"You can't just go, Erica."

I dropped my chin and raised my eyebrows, "You arresting me?"

"No, but Grady, he said to keep you here until he got back."

Suddenly the door swung open just as I was saying, "I don't care what Grady told you—"

—and Grady was saying, "No handcuffs, but I want a guard on her room."

Chapter Twenty-seven

I slowly rose to my feet as Grady and I locked eyes.

"Is Kit Kat . . . ?"

"Stable. I got a call from the hospital," he said quietly, shooting a look down the hall. "They've got her in a medically induced coma to reduce swelling."

"I've got to tell Tweety," I said, turning on my heel.

"No. I can't let you do that."

I froze, every muscle clenched. "I'm sorry?"

"I can't let you do that."

"You can't be serious."

"Erica, I've got a job to do here, and I'm going to make sure it's done properly. Lives are at stake." He shook his head. "I thought tonight would have made that pretty clear to you."

I walked toward him. "And what's this about a guard? You don't think Kit Kat had anything to do with Mr. Clarke—"

"Erica," he said tightly, eyes boring into mine. "I've got two dead bodies. Two."

"I know, but—"

"This cannot keep happening in my town."

"Grady—"

"No, Erica," he said. "There will be no more bending the rules. No more taking it easy. No more personal favors." His eyes darted around my face. "That includes you and Freddie. This isn't a game anymore."

He turned to walk away from me, but I grabbed his arm. "Grady, come on. She's not even conscious."

His face softened. "I know, and I'm sorry for that, but—"

"So what? You thinking she's going to skip town? Where's she going to go? Who are you trying to impress with all this?"

He spun back around and pointed his finger close to my face. "You may not care what I say," he said in a low voice, "but the people of this town are counting on me. I'm not taking any chances." He walked a few steps toward his office again. "Now go home, Erica."

"Grady, could we please talk about this?"

"No."

"Grady!"

He closed the glass door behind him.

I let out a scream of frustration. Then before I even realized what I was doing, my foot shot out and connected with the corner leg of Rhonda's desk. "Ow!" I grabbed my toes. "Son of a—"

Grady's door swung open. He took three quick steps out, looked at my foot, and then up to my eyes. For a brief second, his face softened, and I thought he was going to ask me if I was okay, but then he pinched his lips and stomped back into his office, slamming the door behind him.

"What was all that yelling about?" Tweety shouted from down the hall. "I couldn't hear everything. Was that something about Kit Kat?"

My eyes flashed to Rhonda. She shot me a warning look.

"Nothing!" I shouted back before dropping my voice. "At least nothing I'm allowed to tell you."

"So I guess this means you're not going to be seducing the keys to my cell out of him, huh?"

"Yeah, no. You might have better luck with that than I would."

She laughed.

"'Night, Tweety."

"Yeah, 'night," I heard her call out as I headed toward the door. "And Erica? You know, you might want to consider laying off on finding the dead bodies. You're going to get a reputation."

I straight-armed the door and stamped outside right into—

"Matthew?"

Chapter Twenty-eight

"Oh boy," Matthew said, brushing his hair back. "By the look on your face, I'd say I'm too late."

"What are you doing here?"

"Freddie thought you might need a ride," he said. "Actually he wanted you to drive him home, and I thought maybe while I was here, I could calm Grady down."

"That's really considerate of you," I said, throwing him a sideways look. "But . . . why would you need to calm Grady down?"

Matthew shoved his hands in his pockets. "Well, after you left with Rhonda, Freddie decided to make some sidecars to settle everyone's nerves." He paused, looking as though he was considering his next words carefully. "He maybe said a thing or two he shouldn't have when Grady was questioning him."

"Of course." I threw my hands into the air. "What did he say?"

"Are you sure you want to know?"

"Oh, I'm sure."

Matthew grimaced. "Well, there was lots of yelling

about who keeps this town safe, a subpoena for something . . . Freddie said it was Otter Lake Security property, but Grady disagreed . . . then there was you," he said with an apologetic tip of the head, "and something about *Lightning*?"

I pinched my lips together and nodded. "Sounds about right. Go on."

"Well, they were both pretty mad, and then Freddie may have made a sound . . ."

"What kind of sound?"

He didn't answer.

"Matthew?"

He looked up to the stars and said, "A sound a pig might make?"

"Oh come on," I yelled, looking back at the station house. I clutched my forehead. No wonder Grady was so upset.

"You could tell he didn't mean it," Matthew added quickly. "He apologized right away."

"Did he really?" I asked, dropping my hand.

"Well . . . not in so many words."

I groaned.

"By the look on his face, though, you could tell he knew that he had gone too far."

"I don't believe this," I said, throwing my hands into the air again. "I really don't freaking believe this."

He nodded.

"Listen. It's sweet that you want to talk to Grady on Freddie's behalf, but it probably won't help." Definitely not after the lemonade. "Could you just give me that ride back to your place?"

"Sure."

"Freddie and I need to have a little talk."

* * *

Trees whipped by the window of Matthew's car, but I wasn't really seeing them. I tried to hold on to the feeling of being angry at Freddie, but even that was seeping away. Nope, now that I had stopped moving and everything was quiet, all I could focus on was the snapshot of Mr. Clarke lying on the grass . . . and Kit Kat . . .

Who could do that? Why?

Right now, the twins should be sitting on my mother's porch, clinking their mugs of gin together . . . not lying in a hospital bed, or locked up in a jail cell.

I looked over at Matthew. A pang of guilt shot through me. He was going through so much, and yet he seemed so concerned about everybody else. It made what I was about to do so much worse. And yet I couldn't stop myself. I needed answers. We all needed answers.

"Matthew?"

He turned his head from the road to look at me.

"I need to ask you something."

His jaw clenched, like he knew what was coming. "Go for it."

"The other night at fair? By the VCR?"

He met my eye again.

"You said something about your mother."

He nodded and looked away.

"I'm sure you were just joking around, but I have to ask . . ."

"You can just say it," he said tightly. "It's fine."

He did not seem fine. I swallowed. "Are you sure?"

"Go ahead. Say what you really want to ask me."

"I—"

"You want to know if I think my mother is a murderer."

Chapter Twenty-nine

"Matthew, I—"

He waved me off. "It's okay, Erica. I know you're worried about Tweety . . . and now Kit Kat. And it's not like Grady hasn't asked me the same thing." He rolled his grip over the steering wheel. "You'd think with all the people asking me, I'd have a better answer by now."

I waited, giving him a moment to work through whatever it was he was feeling.

"Truth is, I don't know the answer to that question." He looked off again at the road. "I don't know if my mother killed my father. How crazy is that?" He pulled the car into the winding drive of the manse. "I was kidding—if you can call it that—the other night at the fairgrounds, but I've found out a few things since then."

"What things?"

"You mentioned Marg Johnson the other day. Don't listen to anything she says."

"Why?"

"You've probably heard that my father was less than faithful." He took a shaky breath. "Well, turns out, they had a *relationship*."

"What?"

"For years." He shook his head. "My mother just turned a blind eye to it."

"Wow. I—"

"This thing with Tweety, though? Apparently that was something she couldn't ignore."

Matthew drove the car to the side of the house and cut the engine. He didn't say anything or move to get out. I didn't either. I couldn't. Not with him sitting there, staring out the window . . . looking so sad.

Before I even realized what I was doing, I reached out and grabbed his hand. I had only meant it to be a gesture of sympathy, but when our fingers touched . . . something passed between us.

"I can't imagine what this has been like for you. All of it. I've been so focused on the twins," I said, shaking my head. "I haven't even asked if you knew Mr. Clarke well."

He nodded, hand still on mine. "I didn't. Not really. I mean, from what I knew he was a good man, but—" He cut himself off with a shake of the head then looked up at me.

I could barely breathe with the intensity of his gaze. Actually, I didn't want to breathe if it broke whatever it was that was happening between us, and that was . . . not good. I gently pulled my hand from his. "I think maybe I should say something here. I don't want to give you the wrong impression. I—"

Suddenly someone's hands crashed against the windshield.

I screamed, and Matthew's elbow knocked the horn.

The person on the other side of the glass laughed.

"Jesus, Freddie."

"You two," he said, voice muffled by the glass. "You should have seen your faces."

I swung the car door open, sending Freddie scuttling

back. Yup, there was all that nice anger back. "You and I need to have a talk."

"Oh no." He waved out some jazz hands. "Is Dad still mad at me?"

"You know what? Go to the boat," I said with a point. "I'll meet you there."

"Yeah, no," he said, backing up two steps. "I'll just wait over here. Seeing as there's a *killer* on the loose!"

I took a breath and turned back to Matthew. "So . . ."

"Erica, really you don't have to say anything. It's been a crazy day for the both of us." He opened his door, but kept his eyes on me. "I know you and Grady have something. I can respect that."

"Thanks. I—"

"But," he said, cutting me off with a smile, "if that *something*, turns out to be *nothing* . . . I'd like to be the first to know."

"Understood. I feel the same." I winced and made a fist with my hand. "I mean, *feel* is probably not the best word." I jumped out of the car. "I should go now." I hustled over to Freddie, throwing a quick wave over my shoulder. "Thanks for the ride."

I didn't wait for a response. "Let's go," I said, yanking Freddie's arm.

"You're mad."

"Little bit."

"But you also seemed kind of . . . fired up."

"Kit Kat is in the hospital," I said tightly. "Someone put her there. That someone is going to pay."

"Okay," Freddie said, stumbling while trying to keep up with me. "But what exactly does that mean?"

"It means no holding back anymore."

"Right. Well, I gotta say, part of me loves this side of you, but . . ."

"But what?"

"I'm also a little afraid."

"You should be."

Freddie stopped walking, but I didn't wait for him. It wasn't until I had almost made it to the boat that I turned back around and shouted, "What are you doing now?"

"Just writing YOU SHOULD BE on my hand," he shouted back. "I want to remember this moment. For the pilot."

"You know what else you write on your hand?"

"What?"

"Freddie pushes Erica too far, and she drowns him in the lake. I like that episode."

"What? Oh . . . good one. Coming!"

Chapter Thirty

Once we got back to Freddie's, I decided to crash at his place—not to talk, he was in no condition—but because the lake was getting a little choppy, and I couldn't face taking *Lightning* back to the retreat. I chose the bedroom farthest from Freddie's to put some distance between me and his snoring, and then made a call to my uncle Jack. Not surprisingly, given the hour, he didn't answer, so I left another message.

I then grabbed some sheets from the linen closet, made the bed, and crawled in. Before I closed my eyes, though, I reached once again for my phone. There was just one more call I had to make. I tapped the first number in my contacts and lay back against the pillows.

The phone rang five times before someone picked up.

"Hello?" I asked after a moment. "Mom?"

Silence.

"Oh right," I said more to myself than her. "Hey, Mom. It's me." I rubbed my forehead. Talking on the phone without someone answering was pretty awkward. "Sorry if I woke you. I know I should have called earlier to tell you I wouldn't be home." I bit the corner of my thumbnail. "Listen. A lot happened tonight, but I want you to know, in case you hear anything, I'm fine." I could practically feel my mother's eyes widen on the other end. "I, uh, found another body. Peter Clarke. I don't know if you knew him. It's a long story."

While I was talking, I heard something clatter, like she dropped . . . a mug?

"I'm fine. Really." I took another breath before continuing. "But you should also know that Kit Kat's in the hospital. She's stable, but—" My voice cracked. I had to take a breath before I could keep going. "She's in a medically induced coma. I'm not sure what happened. I'm still trying to get ahold of uncle Jack. Maybe you could help in that regard?"

I sighed again. "Okay, so, I'm going to spend the night at Freddie's. We're working on finding out who's behind all this. I'll probably see you sometime tomorrow." I almost hung up, but the conversation I'd had with Matthew put a lot of things into perspective. My relationship with my mom had never been easy . . . but the sadness I had seen in Matthew's eyes . . . well, I had a lot to be grateful for.

"Mom?" I asked, not expecting her to answer. "I also wanted to say . . . I love you." I looked up to the ceiling and shook my head. "Okay, so good night. Bye."

Just as I moved to press END CALL, I heard, "Erica! I love you too!" then a click.

I stared at my phone in disbelief.

She had broken her vow . . . to tell me she loved me.

Whoa.

I clicked off the light and collapsed into bed. A moment later, I was asleep, and when I woke the next morning, I couldn't remember having a single dream.

* * *

"So, I was thinking," Freddie said before making a popping sound with his lips. "I should probably apologize to Grady."

"You think?" I dropped down on one of the stools at the island in Freddie's kitchen.

"Can you do it for me?"

"No!" I shouted, cringing at the volume of my voice. It was too early for yelling. "Besides, Grady and I aren't exactly talking."

Freddie shot me a quick look before flicking on the coffeemaker. Guess the tone of my voice stopped him from probing that one too deeply. "Fine. I'll do it." He reached to take some mugs from the cupboard. "He's pretty mad about the tapes."

I nodded slowly. "I can imagine."

"And for the record, I only told him to get a subpoena because he was so upset. I was afraid it might kill him if he found out we broke the tape." Freddie grabbed a spoon from the drawer. "And really, by the time he had even gotten around to remembering the tape, it would have already been—" Freddie cut himself off when he saw the look I was giving him. "Okay," he said slowly. "You know what? Fine." He planted his hands on the counter. "Let's just get to it, shall we?"

I rolled my eyes up to his.

"You'll be happy to hear that I've come to the conclusion that I probably shouldn't drink when we are on the job."

I squinted. "Why have you been drinking so much lately?"

He tapped the counter and shrugged.

"Freddie?"

"I don't know," he said quickly. "I've been putting myself out there more . . . and I'm not entirely sure people can be trusted to see how awesome I am. It makes me nervous."

I considered him a moment—then a lightbulb exploded in my head. "Oh my God!" I felt my eyes widen. "Now I get it."

Freddie's brow furrowed. "Get what?"

"The uniform? *Lightning*? You're afraid people might really see you," I said, nodding, "like the real you. So you're causing all this"—I threw my hands in the air—"distraction. You've always done it a little bit, but—"

"You shut up, Erica Bloom. You just shut up right now."

"And here I was thinking you were so much more evolved than me for finding a way to be yourself, like really be yourself in Otter Lake, without worrying what people would think. But you're just as bad as me!"

"You take that back!"

"Freddie, it's not a bad thing. In fact, now that I know what's going on—"

"No," he said with a snap and a point at my face. "I psychoanalyze you. Not the other way around. It's a one-way street."

"But Freddie, I think—"

He yelled—really loudly—making me freeze.

"This conversation is over."

I opened my mouth to speak, but he snapped and pointed at me again.

"Look. I've said what I needed to say. I'll apologize to Grady, and no more drinking on the job. Let's move on. What's the plan for today?"

I looked at him a moment longer before finally saying, "The hospital."

"And then?"

I shook my head. "I don't know. Maybe we should go back and talk to Mrs. Masterson, or—"

"Okay, just stop. It was a rhetorical question. And I'm too hung over to wait for you to finish," Freddie said, dumping a bunch of sugar into one of the mugs. "I've already got our next step all planned out."

I scrunched my face in question.

"Two steps ahead, Erica." He tapped the side of his head.

A moment of silence passed as Freddie handed me my coffee.

"Well, are you going to tell me?"

He shook his head. "Not yet. Right now, I want you to tell me about what happened with Matthew last night."

I rubbed my face. "He doesn't know if his mother's guilty or not."

"And what about him?"

I raised an eyebrow.

"Does he know if *he's* guilty?"

I sighed and took a long sip from my mug. "He's not the murderer, Freddie. I now know for sure."

"And how exactly do you now know for sure?"

"Because the universe just wouldn't make it that easy for me."

We tried to get in to see Kit Kat, but the nurse informed us that she wasn't allowed visitors, and seeing as I wasn't officially family, she wouldn't even give me an update.

I waited until we got back to the parking lot before asking, "So now will you tell me where we're going?"

"We're following up on a lead."

"What lead?" I asked getting into Freddie's old GMC, Jimmy. It was the same one he'd had back in high school. He was a little sentimental about it.

"Well, remember how Marg said we just had to ask anyone in town over fifty what the deal was with Mrs. Masterson's father, Mr. *Ramsbottom*?"

"You can stop saying it like that," I said. "I get it. It's a weird name. *Ramsbottom*."

"See? You can't resist it either."

I half smiled. "Before you continue, I forgot to tell you. Matthew told me last night that there was something going on between his dad and Marg."

"No way!" Freddie shouted, hitting the wheel with his palm. "Shut up!"

"For years."

"Well, I guess that explains why she hates Tweety," Freddie said, tapping his finger in the air. "Okay, but anyway, I called Ms. Robinson last night—"

"That late?" I asked. "Do you often call librarians in the wee hours of the morning?"

"Stop trying make something weird of me and Ms. Robinson."

I almost fully smiled this time, but my face couldn't quite remember how to go all the way.

"And while she didn't know what the whole story was," he said, turning down a small dirt road, "she pointed me in the direction of someone who would."

"Who?" I asked as Freddie pulled into the parking lot of a building tucked away in the trees. I read the sign. DOGWOOD GLEN. "Isn't this a nursing home?"

"Yup."

Something in the tone of his voice made me look at him.

"Nursing homes kind of make me nervous," he said, taking a deep breath. "But Mr. Carver lives here now."

"The old librarian?" I asked from a memory I didn't know existed.

"He's over a hundred and apparently knows everything that has ever happened in Otter Lake."

Freddie and I walked up to the locked front doors and pressed the button underneath a keypad. I guess they didn't want any residents wandering.

I peered through the glass to see if anyone was coming.

"So why are you nervous? I thought you were all about the seniors these days."

"Spritely active seniors. This is different."

"Don't be silly," I said. "It's fine."

"Then why are you picking at the skin around your thumbnail?"

"I am not—" I started to answer before I realized I totally was. I dropped my hands. "Okay, fine. I'm a little uncomfortable. But that's normal, right? I mean, it's kind of hard not to confront your own mortality in nursing homes. It doesn't make us bad people."

"It doesn't make us good people either," Freddie replied matter-of-factly.

I spotted a woman in scrubs walking down the hall toward us. She opened the door.

"Hello," Freddie and I said in unison.

"Hi," the nurse replied with a quizzical look on her face. "Can I help you?"

"We're here to visit our grandf—"

I elbowed Freddie in the side and gave him a *What are you doing?* face before turning back to the nurse. "Sorry. We're here to visit with Mr. Carver if we could?"

"Of course. Come in," she said, holding the door open. "He said he might be having visitors. I'll take you to him. He's in the sunroom."

Freddie and I followed the nurse down the brightly lit hallway.

"Hey," he whispered, a moment later, leaning toward me. "I'm not sure what I was expecting, but"—he stopped to inhale deeply through his nose—"it kind of smells like banana bread in here."

"I know." I looked around the hallways. It was a sort of cheerful place. I heard a TV cooking show playing in the distance and what sounded like a piano accompanied sing-along from a far-off room.

"Here you are," the nurse said, gesturing us into a room filled with tables. "He's over there by the windows."

"Thanks. I recognize him." Freddie led the way toward a man in a wheelchair with a blanket on his knees.

"Mr. Carver, I don't know if you remember me, but—"

"Of course, Freddie," he replied. "How could I forget? Please sit down. You too, Erica."

We made ourselves comfortable around the little table.

"Renata told me you might be coming by."

"Renata? Oh, Ms. Robinson," I said answering my own question. "Sorry."

"It's quite all right. What can I help you with?"

"Mr. Carver," I began, "we wanted to ask you a few questions about something that happened at the Fall Festival years ago."

He nodded. "You mean the death of Mr. Ramsbottom. Renata filled me in."

"I do."

"What can I tell you, my dear?"

"Everything," I said with a sigh. "I'm not sure what might help."

He smiled, eyes curving in sympathy. "You're trying to help Katherine and Twyla, of course."

"We are."

"Well, before I begin the story," Mr. Carver said, turning his head, "there's something you need to understand. About one person in particular."

"Okay," I said slowly.

"Olivia Ramsbottom."

Freddie clapped his hands a little and whispered, "I think I'm going to like this story."

My heart thudded in my chest. "Mrs. Masterson," I said for clarity's sake.

Mr. Carver nodded and folded his hands on the table.

"You see, Olivia Ramsbottom was always the type of girl who knew exactly what she wanted, but . . ."

"But what?"

"Well, unfortunately for everyone involved, she was also the type of girl who would stop at nothing to get it."

Chapter Thirty-one

"Would you all like some tea or coffee?"

Freddie and I jolted.

"God, yes," he replied to the woman standing behind us. "But make mine decaffeinated."

Mr. Carver and I declined. We waited for the woman to leave before we resumed our huddle.

"Now, as far as I'm aware, there was never trouble between Olivia Ramsbottom and the twins before Mick came to town." Mr. Carver tapped the table with a shaky finger. "Everybody knew he was trouble. Worked at the mill for Olivia's father. Good looking. Had all the girls in a tizzy."

Freddie turned and gave me an excited shrug.

"But Twyla, your Tweety, was the only one who could keep him on his toes," he said, looking back and forth between us. "Mick was shameless in his pursuit of her. Mainly, I think, because she wanted nothing to do with him at first. But that didn't stop him. Oh no. He'd be yanking flowers from people's gardens to give her. Reciting terrible poetry in the town square. Flashy stuff. More about him than her if you ask me."

"But he won her over, though, right? We were told they were engaged."

"Oh yes, they got engaged. Too quickly in my opinion. He had only been in town a couple of months." Mr. Carver dabbed at his nose again with his hankie.

"So what happened?"

"Olivia Ramsbottom happened," he said, leaning to tuck his hankie back into his pocket. "She saw herself as the lady of that house her daddy built . . . and in that vision, she saw Mick at her side."

"But Mick wanted Tweety."

He nodded. "They both wanted the person they couldn't really have," he said, shaking his head. "You see, ever since she was a little girl, Olivia Ramsbottom could charm the pants off a snake. People were just bedazzled by the idea of this perfect little girl sitting on her big pile of money. And I swear . . . butter wouldn't melt in her mouth. Never an unkind word. Never a misstep. So everyone just did things for her. Gave her anything she wanted . . . except for Mick. He was just so blinded by Twyla's vigor that he never gave Olivia a second look."

"So," Freddie said, leaning in closer. "What did Olivia do?"

Mr. Carver shrugged. "Nobody knows. One minute Mick was head over heels for Twyla, the next he was engaged to Olivia. Didn't seem overly happy about it, though. Lost his zest. A man like that doesn't appreciate a woman who's willing to fawn all over him, and Olivia did that. Although he did seem to enjoy driving that fancy convertible around town."

"Wait, wait, wait," I said, closing my eyes and waving my hands out in front of me. "You think he dumped Tweety for a car?"

"Well, maybe not just the car. The lifestyle." Mr. Carver moved his head side-to-side as though weighing all the possibilities. "Certainly didn't have to work in the textiles mill after he took up with her."

"Wow," I said under my breath. "Poor Tweety. She must have been ticked! I mean, not ticked enough to murder him fifty years later, but, you know what I mean."

Mr. Carver nodded. "Well, again, everybody in town tried to warn her what kind of man he was. Katherine—Kit Kat—hated him. That woman couldn't hide an emotion if her life depended on it."

"Okay," I said, straightening up. "So I get what happened with Tweety and Mr. Masterson, but—" I stopped to take a breath. I didn't even want to say the words. "Marg Johnson implied that Kit Kat and Mr. Ramsbottom had—" I stopped, searching for the right words. "That there was something going on between the two of them."

"Marg Johnson is a nasty busybody of the highest order. She wanted to be Olivia Ramsbottom so badly, she didn't know what to do with herself . . . other than lick that woman's boots every chance she got."

"That's not the only thing she licked of Olivia's," Freddie muttered under his breath.

I slapped his arm then asked, "So there was nothing going on between Kit Kat and Mr. Ramsbottom, Olivia's father?"

"Well, no. I didn't say that."

I ran a hand over my face. "Really?"

"Well, now, I don't know the truth," Mr. Carver said, waving a hand of deniability at us. "But there were rumors. In the man's defense, his wife was long dead."

"What kind of rumors?" Freddie asked.

Mr. Carver looked at us both in turn. "A few people claimed to have spotted them having *private* meetings." He sighed. "Couldn't quite see it myself. Although Mr. Ramsbottom was not a bad-looking man, and, of course, there was the obvious attraction."

"You can't mean the money," I said already shaking my head. "Kit Kat's not like that."

"I tend to agree with you, but she never did give a good explanation for what she was doing with Mr. Ramsbottom in that tent right before he died."

"She was with him? Right before he died?"

He nodded.

Freddie cleared his throat and shot me a nervous glance before he said, "Marg also insinuated that at the time, people suspected Mr. Ramsbottom didn't die of natural causes, and that maybe Kit Kat had something to do with . . ." Freddie's sentence withered under my glare.

"A few people did," Mr. Carver said, nodding. "But Mr. Ramsbottom was not a young man, or a thin one for that matter. Most people just figured the simplest explanation was a heart attack."

"And the others who didn't?" I asked more sharply than I intended.

"It wasn't just the fact that Kit Kat wasn't talking that made her look so suspicious."

"Okay."

"It was the speculation about her motive."

"What motive?" I couldn't stop myself from cringing a little. "Lovers' spat?"

"Nope." Mr. Carver frowned, face nearly disappearing into the folds of his wrinkles. "Not exactly."

"Then what?"

He scratched his chin for a moment considering me. "There was another rumor going around. It was a little crazy, though. The scandal would have been terrible."

"What?"

"Well, rumor had it, Mr. Ramsbottom was intending to marry Kit Kat, and he was none too pleased with his daughter's infatuation with Mick, so some say he called his lawyer in."

"Lawyer?" I asked trying to sort it all through. "Why?"

"To change his will."

Freddie gasped. "You don't mean . . . ?"

"He was planning to leave everything—Hemlock Estate and all the money—to Kit Kat."

Chapter Thirty-two

"Shut up!" Freddie clutched his head. "Oh my God! Kit Kat? The Lady of Hemlock Estate! Come on!"

"But obviously that was just rumor, right?" I said, trying to control my own reaction. "Because Kit Kat did not inherit Hemlock Estate when Mr. Ramsbottom died."

"Well," Mr. Carver said, frowning a little, "that's where things get a little bit sketchy."

"*That's* where things get a little bit sketchy!" Freddie shouted, half getting up out of his chair before dropping back down. "That's where—you're blowing my mind today, Mr. Carver. Like seriously, mind blown." Freddie made an explosion gesture with his fingers.

I grabbed Freddie's arm to quiet him down, maybe a little too tightly by the *ow* sound he made. "What do you mean, Mr. Carver?"

"The lawyer's secretary claimed that Mr. Ramsbottom sent her boss a letter about changing his will, and, well, this next part, it's almost too ridiculous to even say," he said.

"Please say it," Freddie moaned.

"First, I need to explain—and this part is absolutely

true—Mr. Ramsbottom wanted to be buried on the property of Hemlock Estate." He straightened up in his wheelchair. "But the town had an issue with that. They didn't want everyone to think they could start burying their dead on their own properties. So they denied the application."

"Okay," I said. "I don't see what this—"

"You will," Mr. Carver said with enough warning that Freddie was practically squirming in his seat. "So Olivia decided the next best thing was to fill the coffin she had picked out with memorabilia of her father and bury it on the estate at the clearing on that peak overlooking the water."

"I know the one," I said, feeling my stomach roll as Peter Clarke's body flashed through my mind.

He nodded. "I'm told she put up a little plaque and a bench," he continued. I couldn't remember seeing the plaque, but then again it had probably been under the body. "But none of that matters. The important part is that the lawyer's secretary claimed that her boss took that letter to the memorial."

"No," Freddie gasped.

"Yes," Mr. Carver replied. "And, well, a few people say that, after the service was over, the lawyer and Olivia had a conversation up on that peak." Mr. Carver stopped to take a breath. "That she was pretty upset. Crying. Some say they embraced."

Freddie and I both leaned forward. "And then?"

Mr. Carver leaned in too. "He dropped the letter into the coffin."

"No!"

"Closed it up. Then tossed the first shovel of dirt himself."

Chapter Thirty-three

"Erica? Slow down," Freddie called out, jogging to keep up with me as I made a beeline for his Jimmy.

I wasn't sure why I was walking so quickly. It might have been to get away from all that Mr. Carver had told us . . . but I suspected it had a little more to do with trying to get away from what I was thinking we needed to do next.

"Erica!"

I stopped in the middle of an empty parking space, waiting for Freddie to catch up.

He stopped beside me, his hands on his belly. "Wow. Okay," he said. "That back there? My ears are still ringing."

I didn't answer.

"But seriously, we need to talk about what all this means before we even *consider* thinking about our next move."

I still didn't answer.

"All that stuff he said about some mysterious letter to a lawyer being hidden in some grave?" Freddie chuckled. "It's a pretty crazy story, right? I mean, no sane person would think there's any truth to that."

I turned and looked at him.

"No, no, no!" Freddie shouted. "I know that look. That there is Crazy Erica! She's way worse than Happy Erica!"

I didn't change my expression.

"You can't be thinking . . ." Freddie trailed off, shaking his head. "You know—*you know*, Erica—that I'm down with doing a lot of *things* the average person wouldn't. In fact I normally encourage those *things*, but you can't be thinking what I think you're thinking."

"You heard him, Freddie," I said in a voice that didn't quite sound like my own. "It's not an actual grave."

Freddie grabbed my shoulders. "Erica, I want you to take a moment to think about what you just said."

"What about what you said?" I asked. "You said in the beginning you wanted me *all-in*, Freddie. This is what *all-in* looks like."

"What!" Freddie held up a finger to my face and said, "No. You just stop it! Right now."

I started walking again to the SUV. "Whatever it takes, Freddie."

He ran in front of me, forcing me to stop. "No. Sorry." He cut the air with his hands. "As CEO of Otter Lake Security, I have to veto this plan. This crosses a line."

I moved past him, cranked the door to the SUV open, and hopped in the seat. Freddie followed suit on the other side.

We sat for a moment in silence, both of us looking out the windshield.

"You're still thinking it. I can feel you still thinking it."

I leaned back against my seat. "Freddie, when I saw Kit Kat lying in the grass like that . . . it changed everything."

"Look, I get it," he said. "But this is too far. Causing a ruckus at the bingo hall? No problem. It was kind of cute. Getting in the occasional bar fight? Why not? It's Otter Lake. But what you're thinking right now? No."

"What if it were your grandmother in that hospital bed?"

Freddie's eyes flashed over to mine. "You talk about my poppo again, and I'll stab you in the ribs."

"Exactly," I said, throwing my hands in the air. "Listen, if Mrs. Masterson killed her father to stop him from giving the house to Kit Kat, that really makes it a lot more plausible that she killed her husband and her caretaker. Especially if Mr. Clarke somehow found out the truth. I find it highly suspicious that the second murder took place right at the memorial plaque thingy for her father. What if the caretaker knew and was going to dig it up?" I scanned Freddie's face to see if any of this was registering.

He was biting his lip. Oh yeah, he was thinking about it.

"What other option do we have?" I asked. "Do you have any other leads? Because, really, I'm open to suggestions."

"I . . . not really."

"Well then?"

"Erica! Think it through," Freddie pleaded. "You and I both know that Grady's not playing anymore."

I buckled my seat belt. "So what do we do with all this then? Nothing? Tell Grady? I don't think he's exactly listening to what we have to say right now."

Freddie chuckled and held his arms out to the side like his lat muscles were too big. "Nah, he'd be all like, *I'm Grady Forrester. And nobody is digging up anything. There was no evidence of a murder, and your witness is a hundred years old. I wish I had Freddie's boat. Maybe then I wouldn't be so angry all the time.*"

"Not helping, Freddie."

He exhaled all his fake muscles with a *whoosh*. "Erica, I'm pretty sure what you're suggesting is a felony."

"It's not a felony."

"And you know that how?"

"Work," I said. "I transcribe these kinds of cases all the time."

"Really? Just like all the time?"

"Yup."

"Erica, you're lying! And you're terrible at it."

Suddenly my phone buzzed. I fiddled around in my jacket pocket to retrieve it. "Just a second," I said. "It's my uncle. I have to take this." I swiped the screen. "Hello?"

"Erica, it's Uncle Jack."

"Hi," I said quickly. "It's really good to hear from you. I take it you got all of my messages?"

"I did. I did. And your mother sent me quite the email. I apologize for not getting back to you sooner. It's been a busy week." His voice sounded as though he meant it. "Listen, I've looked into the case, but Erica . . . I'm not sure how much we can do for Twyla."

"What do you mean?" I asked, not at all liking the seriousness of his tone. "Is the evidence against her really that bad?"

"Not at all. Well, the ME hasn't handed over the report yet, but all things considered—frankly, I wouldn't expect them to get past discovery. So I don't know why—"

"Why what?" I asked. "What's the problem?"

A moment passed. "You don't know."

"Know what?"

"Erica, I don't how to tell you this . . . but Twyla has decided to plead guilty."

Chapter Thirty-four

"What?" I yelled, ignoring Freddie, who was yanking on my arm.

"Well, yes. They're typing up a confession for her to sign as we speak," he said. "I've let them know that nothing, *nothing*, is to be signed until I get there, which should buy us some time, but you need to talk to her. I can't delay this forever, especially if she suddenly decides to waive her right to an attorney too."

"She wouldn't," I replied quickly, before I realized that I never would have thought she'd have pled guilty either. "This is crazy."

"Erica, I know you and your mother love this woman, but, I have to ask, is there any possibility she could have—"

"No!"

"Okay, then you know what you have to do. My assistant's booking me a flight, but I won't get there until tomorrow at the earliest."

"Got it. Thank you. So much."

"Talk to her, Erica," he said with a sigh. "Your mother will kill me if this thing goes sideways."

"Understood." I ended the call and looked up at Freddie. "What's happen—"

"She's pleading guilty. Tweety is pleading guilty to murder."

Freddie's eyes widened, "Why?"

I shook my head. "I don't know."

"How long do we have?"

"My uncle Jack's trying to delay, but soon. We're running out of time."

"Oh man," he moaned. "Oh man."

"Freddie, please. We need to do this."

He nodded. "All right. Okay. Yes," he hissed, slapping the steering wheel. "I can't believe I'm saying this, but . . . I'm in. Let's do it!"

"You mean it?"

"Well," Freddie said, pulling us out of the parking lot. "If we're going down—and let's face it, sooner or later we were going to go down—I say let's do it in a blaze of glory." He reached his fist over to me.

I stared at his knuckles, not moving.

"Fist bump, Erica," he said, with his eyes on the road. "Don't leave me hanging."

I sighed.

"Come on! Balls to the wall!"

And before I even realized it, my knuckles collided with Freddie's.

"Yeah! We're digging up a grave!" he screamed, before adding, "We're so going to jail."

Unfortunately after we got ourselves all psyched up, we realized it was probably best to wait until well after dark to do that actual . . . deed. Grave digging wasn't exactly a broad-daylight type of activity. I decided to head back home for a shower and a change of clothes before meeting up with Freddie later. He wanted to stop in at the fair, so I dropped him off with *Lightning* then took her to the retreat. I had to admit *Lightning* was growing on me now that I was figuring out how to handle her. Sure, she was loud and obnoxious, but she was also really, really fast.

When I got inside the lodge, I found the guests meditating in front of a photo of Kit Kat. For a moment, I thought the worst, then realized they were just doing a prayer slash meditation session. My mother was a great believer in the healing power of positive thoughts. Thankfully, when I excused myself, she didn't try to stop me. I couldn't sit and be calm. I just couldn't. I'd rather pace the floor any day.

As soon as I had shut the door to my room, I pulled out my phone. The red message light was blinking. Huh. Missed call.

I scrolled past my uncle's number to see who had called before him. Grady.

For a moment I debated whether I wanted to listen to the message. If Freddie and I really went through with digging up the—what? memorial coffin?—it might just be the last nail in my relationship with Grady.

How had everything gotten so out of control so fast?

I had been thinking, like my uncle, that the case wouldn't even make it to trial, especially with the VHS tape that showed all the other people who had access to Mr. Masterson right before he died—of course, we still had to turn those tapes over—but now with Tweety confessing, well, there *still* wouldn't be a trial. They'd go right to sentencing.

No, there was no way around it. I could tell myself I was torn about digging up this coffin. I could hem and haw and feel terrible about Grady. But I knew in my heart, I was going to do whatever it took to help the twins. I really was all-in.

I swiped my phone and brought it to my ear.

Hey, Erica. It's me. I could hear him inhale deeply. *If you haven't heard, you will soon. Tweety's decided to plead guilty. I just want you to know I tried talking to her. I know this isn't—but it doesn't mean you should go off and—*He paused a moment longer and then said, *Never mind. I just wanted you to know.*

I dropped the phone away from my face.

Well, I guess it was official. Grady wasn't even trying to warn me off anymore . . . and that had to mean he had given up on us. For good.

"Frick!" I shouted, throwing my phone onto the bed.

A startled scream sounded from outside my room.

"Sorry!" I shouted back. "Sorry."

After a couple of really miserable hours of chewing off my fingernails, I picked up Freddie from town and took him back to his house for what could be our last meal on the outside. Frozen fish sticks and fries I had wanted to eat at the fair, but Freddie looked a little green at the thought. Guess he had overdone it with all the fried food.

Once we had cleared up the dishes, Freddie disappeared into another room. He came back a minute later with a pile of clothes and passed it to me. A black track suit, toque, and gloves.

I flipped through the stack, checking the labels. "Um, Freddie," I said, picking up one of the gloves and trying it on. "Why do you have a breaking-and-entering outfit ready to go in my size?"

He shrugged. "I've been surfing the 'Net a lot for the business . . . and I may have a bit of an online shopping problem. A problem that is totally paying off for us right now."

I nodded, pinching my lips together. "Do I want to know how many other outfits, in my size, you just happen to have lying around?"

"I don't think knowing the number will contribute anything to what we're trying to accomplish this evening," he replied. "But you should know, I have an awesome maid's outfit if we ever have any business in a hotel. It's beige and totally shapeless. You'll love it."

I blinked. "Right."

I shoved the toque on my head. Couldn't deny it. Good elasticity. "So, I don't suppose you've given any thought to how we are going to accomplish . . . what it is we are planning to do tonight?"

"Dig up the bodiless coffin, you mean?"

I shot him a look.

"Hey, this is your baby. You need to own it," he said matter-of-factly. "But what about it?"

"Well, the logistics," I said. "I don't exactly have much upper-body strength . . . or a shovel. Do you own a shovel?"

Freddie smiled slyly in return. "I've got something way better than a shovel."

"Does it require strength, because, as I say, I'm not exactly . . ." I trailed off, flexing my biceps. "And you're not exactly . . ." I gestured a weak hand in his direction.

"What, Erica?" he replied, raising an eyebrow. "What am I not exactly?"

I threw the same hand in the air. "You're not exactly in grave-digging shape. There. I said it."

Freddie brought his fingertips to his chest. "How dare you."

I closed my eyes and shook my head. "Please. I can't take the normal theatrics. Not tonight. Just answer the question."

"Erica. Erica. Erica," Freddie began.

"I said *please*."

"Of course I've given it some thought," Freddie said. "As always I'm way ahead of you. Always thinking, I am."

I cracked one eye open.

"Unlike you, who just decides to dig up a grave willy-nilly, I *have* thought about the logistics of your insane plan. In fact, I'm fairly certain, I have thought of everything."

"Really," I said, dropping my chin to my chest. "Then do share. How exactly are you and I going to dig up six feet of dirt?"

"I have one word for you."

I closed my eyes again.

"Backhoe."

Chapter Thirty-five

"Okay," I said, planting my hands on my hips. "I'll bite. Why do you have a backhoe?"

Freddie and I were standing in his three-car garage, staring at what indeed appeared to be a backhoe.

"It's a recreational backhoe for, you know—"

I smacked his arm with the back of my hand.

"All right. All right. Jeez," he said rubbing the spot. "A couple of years ago, I thought I might try digging out my own pool."

"Seriously?"

He nodded. "It was a hot summer. I wanted a place to cool off, but the last time I went into the lake, I got this leech stuck between my toes, and, well, that doesn't really matter," Freddie said, dismissing the story with a hand. "I kind of lost interest, though, when I started digging and there was all this water—"

"Imagine that," I muttered. "You know, living by the lake and all."

Freddie ignored me. "And then the city was all, *Permit this. Permit that.*"

"Of course."

"And here we are."

I stared at the dirty yellow piece of machinery parked under the naked bulb hanging from the ceiling.

"I don't know, Freddie."

"What now?"

"Well, what are we going to do? Drive this thing over to the Mastersons' property, off-road it up to the burial site—which let's not forget is still a crime scene—dig up the grave, check out what's inside, then replace all the dirt and grass? Without anyone noticing?"

"Where's your sense of adventure?"

I sighed. "It just jumped off a cliff, headfirst, into a pile of rocks. It's dead now."

"Oh come on," Freddie said, bumping me with his shoulder. "Stop looking so sad. It will be fine. You'll see. Everyone owns a backhoe out here. We'll probably pass at least two or three on the way over."

"That is not true," I said. "You are saying things that just aren't true."

"It *is* true," he went on. "But how about this? Because it's not like anyone's forcing us to dig up this grave—"

Somewhat crazy-sounding laughter burbled out of my mouth.

"—if at any point either of us feels uncomfortable and wants to bail, we bail. No pressure."

I looked over at Freddie, trying to see if he meant it.

"Good?"

I nodded. "But we're not bailing."

"Excellent." He slapped his hands together.

"You're being awfully accommodating," I said, catching his gaze in mine. "Almost like you really want to do this . . . and you're worried I might call it off."

"The idea's grown on me. That's all. Team twins!" He raised a fist in the air. "Now let's get the rest of our stuff from inside and be on our way." He turned to leave then stopped with a jerk. "Oh! I know what will make you feel better!"

"What?"

"A safe word!"

"No," I said shaking my head. "That will not make me feel better."

"Sure it will."

"No, it won't."

"Come on."

"No."

"What about banana?"

"Banana!" I shouted. "Banana!"

"Oh calm down," Freddie yelled over the noise of the engine. "I'm not going that fast."

I wrapped my fingers in the holes of the driver's cage. "You are going to flip this thing. It is not meant to go this speed!"

"It's fine," he said, hands gripped to the wheel, forearms shaking. "Look. We have a small window here, and I'm not sure how long it's going to take us to—oh my God! Look!"

I followed his gaze. Another vehicle was coming toward us on the dirt road. Another backhoe.

Freddie laughed hysterically. "Wave. We want to be friendly. It's like when the bikers do it."

"Yeah, let's draw more attention to ourselves," I said, halfheartedly throwing a hand up when I saw the other driver do it.

Freddie laughed even harder.

"Sometimes I hate you."

He shrugged happily.

A few minutes later, Freddie pulled the mini digger into the mouth of a snowmobile trail. It had grown over a bit in the summer, but not enough to give the backhoe any trouble. We had looked online, and supposedly the trail went all the way up to the escarpment of Hemlock Estate.

"So what do you think," he said, cutting the engine. "Do we just start driving up there? Or do you want to do some recon first?"

"Recon," I said firmly.

"We'll lose some time."

"It's probably still a crime scene." I was pretty sure the police would have been all through the site by now, but I couldn't be certain. "They might even have a police officer up there . . . or Matthew and his mom might have hired some sort of security."

Freddie shot me an incredulous look. "Um, Otter Lake Security is the only game in town, my friend."

"Whatever. You know what I mean."

He mumbled something under his breath that sounded quite unpleasant.

"Look. Given Mr. Clarke's unfortunate demise, I think it's clear that somebody wants what is buried in that grave site to stay buried. We need to be careful."

An almost sick look came over Freddie's face. "I see your point." I don't think he'd realized up until now that *we* might actually be in danger. "Okay, well, off you go." He shooed me with his fingers. "I'll wait here with the hoe," he said, jerking a thumb. "Ha! I'll wait with the *ho*."

"Yeah, nice try," I said, yanking at his jacket. "You're coming with me."

A good fifteen minutes later, we were creeping up to the tree line just before the clearing. Well, I was creeping; Freddie was flapping his arms in the air.

"Why are there so many bugs?" he whispered. "It's fall!"

"We haven't had a frost yet, and it's been wet."

"Why aren't you dead? You should be dead," Freddie whispered again. Obviously not to me. Probably to some mosquito. I heard a smack. "Now you're dead."

"It's okay," I whispered as he moved to my side. "I'm a little freaked out too."

"Who said anything about being freaked out?" Freddie snapped. "I'm not freaked out!"

"Really? Because you're giving off a whole lot of nervous energy right now."

"No, I'm not. We are so doing this, and it's going to be awesome. It's just . . . I mean Halloween is right around the corn—" Suddenly he grabbed my arm and dropped to the ground. "There's someone there!"

I tried to get up, but Freddie was stronger than I had given him credit for. "Let go," I whispered through my teeth. "I can't see."

Freddie released his grip, and I straightened up to get a look over the bottom branches of an evergreen.

"Oh, you're right. It's Matthew!"

"Is it?" Freddie asked, pushing the branch down a little farther.

"What do you think he's doing sitting there all by himself?"

"Thinking lonely romantic thoughts about you?" Freddie offered. "Or plotting his next kill?" He moved his head to get a better viewing angle. "Oh look! He has a shovel! Oh no . . . it's a stick."

"So are those my only two options? Romance or murder?"

"I don't know," Freddie said, planting his hand on my back. "But you're about to find out."

I whipped my face around to his. "What are you doing?"

"He needs to go," Freddie said. "And you need to get rid of him."

"No. No. Forget it," I said. "This wasn't the plan. It destroys any kind of alibi we might have had—"

Freddie threw me a questioning look. "Was this really a crime you thought we'd get away with? 'Cause I was thinking it was more of an *I'd rather ask for forgiveness than permission* kind of deal." He pushed me a little harder.

I dug my feet into the ground. "Okay. How is it that you are so on board now? Back at the nursing home—"

"That was forever ago."

"What about Otter Lake Security?"

Freddie dropped some of the pressure. "What about it?"

"If you get arrested for this, it's going to destroy your business model."

Freddie chuckled. "Oh Erica, I've been thinking about it, and this here is a misdemeanor—a misdemeanor that could solve a murder that happened fifty years ago— that could solve a murder that happened a few days ago—that could—"

"Live in the house that Jack built? What the hell are you going on about?"

"This here is *news*. Maybe even national news. I can afford the legal costs, but you can't buy this kind of publicity. Freddie Ng is going to be the new face of security." He pushed at me again.

"Oh my God!" I nearly shouted. "That's why you're so eager now. You could have—"

"This is a conversation for later," Freddie said with a solid push. "Love you."

Chapter Thirty-six

I crashed through the tree branches.

"Erica?" Matthew asked, jumping to his feet.

"Hey," I said with a small wave.

He cocked his head, eyes wide. "What are you doing here?"

Oh boy. My gaze jumped around. "I was just, uh—"

"Don't tell me." He looked me up and down. "I think the outfit says it all."

"It does?"

"You're back looking for clues," he said with a faint smile. "That . . . or you're working on becoming a professional mime?"

I felt my shoulders drop. "The first one."

He held out his hands. "I didn't find anything, but you're welcome to look around."

"Oh," I said. "That's really . . . nice."

"Well, consider it my apology for dumping all that stuff about my parents on you last night," he said. "It got a little intense. I'm really sorry. I wasn't myself."

"Given what you've been through, I think you're entitled."

"Thanks." He sat back down on the bench.

I walked around randomly for a couple of minutes pretending to look for clues, but really I was trying to think of way to get rid of Matthew without it looking suspicious. Shockingly, I didn't come up with anything. This plan had disaster written all over it. After a few unpleasant flashbacks of the night before, I decided to just sit down—on the side of the bench where the body hadn't been—and play it by ear.

Matthew smiled as I sidled in beside him.

I smiled back, nodding.

Nope, this wasn't weird or suspicious at all.

"So," I said, lightly clapping my hands together. "What are *you* doing out here?"

"Me?" he asked, taking a deep breath. "Just thinking."

I nodded some more. "What about?" I mentally slapped myself upside the head. What the heck did I think he was thinking about? How awesome it was to be alive? Smooth, Erica.

Surprisingly, though, Matthew said, "A bunch of different stuff. Work. Crab fishing in Alaska. I like that show. Oh! And my choice of pants. I've been thinking a lot about that lately."

I felt my eyes widen.

He laughed and bumped me with his shoulder.

I hit him lightly back on the arm.

"To be honest, though," he said, looking out at the water. "I was also thinking about you and Grady."

"I'm sorry?"

He shot me a quick smile. "Well, it's easier than thinking about all this." He gestured around. "I talked to Peter's family today. It . . . was not easy."

"Oh, Matthew," I said. "That sucks. I can't imagine."

He patted my leg. "It's okay."

"It's not," I answered, wanting to pat him back, but that

would probably just lead to more patting. "Me and Grady, though?"

"It's just—" He paused, biting his lip. "—you two remind me of the relationship I had with my first girlfriend."

"Oh," I said, not really sure where this was going . . . or how I was going to get out of it. If I even wanted to get out of it. Suddenly an owl hooted from the trees, an owl that sounded an awful lot like Freddie.

"I won't bore you with the details," Matthew said. "You probably have plans after . . ." He looked me over again. "This."

I laughed awkwardly. "Not really."

"Well, I mean, it's not like there was anything special about us." He sighed. "Her maybe. She was smart. Funny. I mean, she still is. I'm making it sound like she's dead." Matthew froze. "*And* that was a really poor choice of words given . . . everything."

"It's fine."

He ran a hand over his face then threw me a sidelong look. "I must be nervous for some reason."

I darted my eyes away from his crazy magnetic gaze. A big part of me so wanted to ask him ever-so-innocently why he might be nervous, but I knew there was a pretty good chance he would say it was because of me . . . and I also knew there was a *really* good chance I would enjoy him saying that . . . and that would just be . . . wrong. Truth was, I was starting to worry that I liked Matthew. Like really liked *him* . . . as a person. Not his looks. Or his job. Or his . . . enormous manse . . . which somehow now sounded dirty in my head. But him.

"It's fine," I finally mumbled again, looking away. This was so not fine. And it wasn't just the whole feelings things either. Here was this sweet, sweet man, flirting with me, sharing all this personal information—and what was I doing? Oh yeah. That's right. I had almost forgotten. I was trying to get rid of him, so that I could dig up his grand-father's pseudo-grave.

The owl hooted again. Matthew looked over his shoulder to the trees.

"So what happened between you two?" I asked quickly, drawing his attention back.

He shrugged. "We tried to make it work. We lived together for a while. But no matter how hard we tried, things just kept getting in the way."

"Things?"

"Stupid things. At first it seemed like it was out of our control. Outside forces." He sighed. "But it became a pattern. Fight. Break up. Make up. Fight. Break up—" He waved a hand. "You get the idea."

I inhaled deeply. That wasn't Grady and me. At least not yet.

"Finally, we just had to accept that if it had been right, it wouldn't have been so hard. Love shouldn't be hard." He looked at me sideways. "Not sure if you can relate to that part."

I shook my head. "No comment."

He half smiled again, making a dimple at the corner of his mouth. "Sorry. It's none of my business."

I waved a hand, feeling my cheeks burn.

"Believe me, though, I get it," he said, looking up again at the stars. "Those first loves . . . they're the real killers." He jolted slightly. "What the hell is the matter with m—"

"Freddie and I are here to dig up your grandfather's memorial site." I slapped my hand over my mouth.

"I'm sorry . . . what did you say?"

Chapter Thirty-seven

"Matthew," I said, looking at his very wide eyes. "You've been so nice to me . . . and honest . . . and sharing all that about your first love? I don't want to lie to you."

"Erica!" a voice shouted from the trees. "What are we doing here?"

Matthew whipped his head around. "Is that Freddie back there?" he asked, jerking a thumb to the woods.

I nodded. "It is."

Matthew turned back to me. "Why would you want to dig up my grandfather's memorial site?"

"We got some information today," I said. "Do you remember Mr. Carver the librarian?"

Matthew just stared back at me, looking confused.

"He knows all of Otter Lake's past, and he seems to think that in the empty coffin, which they buried at this site, there may be a clue as to who killed your father." My eyes darted over Matthew's face, trying to gauge his reaction.

"He what?" Matthew asked, but before I could answer, he added, "How are you even going to—" He looked me over again. "Do you have a shovel?

"Freddie has a backhoe," I answered quickly. "It's parked on the road. But we brought some shovels too, for the, uh, detailed work." I closed my eyes at that last part.

I opened them just in time to see Matthew's chin drop nearly to his chest. "A backhoe? Freddie owns a backhoe."

"Well, he was going to dig a pool—" I cut myself off. "It's not important."

"I have no idea what to say right now," Matthew said, shaking his head, mouth hanging slightly open. "This Mr. Carver, is he reliable? And why aren't you going to Grady with this?"

"Because he won't look into it. Not if it comes from us."

"How do you know he won't? Have you asked him?"

"I think in his mind . . . the case may be over." I felt the tears begin to well. One spilled down my cheek. It had been a long day. "Tweety has decided to confess."

"What?" Matthew raised his hand to brush the tear from my cheek with his thumb, but I waved him off. "But you still don't think she did it?"

"I know she didn't," I said, wiping my eyes. "But I'm running out of time. Do you think your mother would agree to—"

Matthew leaned back and his eyes went wide. "Oh yeah, no. She'd never agree. Digging up graves would not be something Mastersons would do."

"Freddie and I thought—" I let out half a groan, half a shout of frustration. "I don't know what we thought."

We sat in silence a moment looking out at the water before Matthew said, "Do it."

My head snapped around. "What?"

"Do it," Matthew said, getting to his feet. "I'll make sure my mother's distracted and doesn't hear the noise." He walked backward a few feet. "I'd better go. She'll be out looking for me soon if I don't get back in there."

"Matthew, I—"

"I want to know who killed my father, Erica," he said, pointing down to the ground. "And for whatever reason, I trust you when you say this source is legit." He shook his head. "Besides, the town seems to think that Freddie is more reliable than Grady."

"Oh, I don't know if that's tr—"

"It's true! Totally true," the voice called out from the trees again.

"Give me your phone," Matthew said, walking back toward me.

I rifled it out from my pocket and passed it to him.

"There. You've got my number. You call me the minute—the minute—you know what's in there."

I nodded.

Matthew turned and headed back down the slope before stopping and swirling around again. "You might want to get started before any of us give this more thought."

"Right. Got it."

"Okay. Good luck." Matthew shook his head as though confused about whether that had been the right thing to say. He then headed to the trail as Freddie popped out of the woods.

"So did I hear all that right?" Freddie asked. "He's giving us the go-ahead?"

I nodded. "He wants to know who killed his father."

"Wow. That's just . . . so unlike some other sheriffs we know."

"Would you just go get the hoe?" I ordered sharply.

"Ha! *Ho* . . . it never gets old."

Chapter Thirty-eight

I wiped the back of my gloved hand across my brow, most likely leaving behind a pretty terrific smear of dirt. Despite the cold, damp air that had settled over us, I'd built up a sweat. "So," I said, tossing my shovel up onto the grass above, "I think that does it." I looked at the exposed coffin we had unearthed, feeling my already fast heart rate pick up. "You ready?"

It took us about half an hour to figure out how to work the backhoe properly. Then about another forty-five minutes to clear the bulk of the dirt out. There had been no sign of Matthew or his mother, which was good . . . but also a little creepy. A couple of times it felt like Freddie and I were the only people left in Otter Lake. After we shut the backhoe down, we spent more time than we probably needed to clearing off the coffin with our shovels. and digging a trench for us to be able to stand beside it. Probably because we both needed to work up the courage to do what needed to be done next.

"Ready? I've never been more ready for anything in my life," Freddie said, nodding and looking at the coffin. His voice sounded a little shaky, though.

I nodded in return. "Okay, well, go ahead."

"Right," Freddie said, stooping down half a second before jerking back up. "Do you think it's locked?" He turned and pointed up to the grass. "I could get my—"

"Why would it be locked?" I snapped. "How? Where would you even buy a lock for a coffin? Vampire hunter supply outlet?"

"Shush, shush, shush!" Freddie said, waving a frantic hand, ignoring me completely. "Did you hear that?"

"Hear what?"

"I think maybe it was an owl. A real one."

"What?" I stopped and listened. "No . . . well, maybe."

"It was. It was an owl hooting," Freddie said, face tight. "And we're standing in a grave. And look!"

"What now?"

"There's a cold fog coming in."

"What is your point, Freddie?"

"We're probably going to die."

"You need to pull it together, man," I said, shaking my fingers. Shoveling was hard work. "Okay, let's just do this together. I mean, there's no body in there . . . so, really, there's no problem." I noticed my head was shaking side-to-side a little too frantically. "I mean, we're really sure there's no body, right?"

"Right," Freddie said, leaning over to grip the lid. "It's fine. It's—Wah!" He jumped back, smacking at his arm with his free hand.

"What the—"

"Spider. I thought there was a spider," Freddie said, batting his arm one more time for good measure. "Okay, we seriously need to get this over with."

I nodded as we both bent over to grip the lid.

"On the count of three?" Freddie asked.

I nodded.

"One."

I closed my eyes.

"Two."

I inhaled deeply.

"Wait, wait, wait," Freddie said, stepping away.

"Oh my God!"

"I can't. I can't," he said quickly. "This here is bad, bad energy. You're the non-superstitious one. You need to do it."

"Fine," I said squinting my face up into an exaggerated *Whatever* expression. "This is so not a big deal." I bent over the coffin again, swallowed hard, and gripped the lid with my fingers. "In fact, I don't even need a countdown."

"Uh-huh."

I gave a little practice lift. Definitely not locked. Not even stiff.

"I'll just skip, one and two, and move right to thr—"

Then I screamed.

Chapter Thirty-nine

Freddie was screaming too. In fact it was hard to tell where my screams began and his ended.

"Freddie! Skeleton!" I yelled, finally making words. I jumped back and grabbed him.

"I know!"

"There wasn't supposed to be a body!"

"I know!"

I think I would have fallen down if Freddie and I hadn't been clutching each other so tightly.

"We are bad, bad people, Freddie."

"I know!"

I shook his arm. "Would you please say something other than *I know*!"

"This . . . is now a felony."

"Oh my God! Not that!" I brought one hand up to my face. I was feeling hot and cold and a little buzzy all over. "I'm so sorry, Mr. Ramsbottom," I said quietly, glancing back down to the skeleton's face. "Wherever you are, we are so sorry."

"We're going to need more lawyers," Freddie said. "A lot more lawyers. A team of lawyers."

"It's still dark," I mumbled. "Maybe we can get it all covered back up, put the sod back in place. Maybe it will rain. Or better yet snow. I—"

"Stop it! You're babbling," Freddie snapped. "You know that's not going to happen. Would you look at this hole?"

I shook my head. He was right. Our dig looked nothing like those dug-out graves in the movies. It was a big ugly gaping hole. "Matthew's never going to be able to hide this from his mom. I thought you knew how to work that thing." I flung a hand up at the backhoe.

"And so the blaming begins," Freddie said, nodding. "Why do I let you get me into—"

"You can't put this all on me, Mr. New Face of Security!"

"Fine," he said sharply. "But you can't deny that whenever you come back to town, things get crazy! I get crazy!" He shook his head some more. "This isn't me. I used to lead a quiet life, telling fortunes on the Internet."

"Don't you even—" I stopped myself and took a breath. "Okay, we need to focus here. We have to at least try to make things right. But first—" My eyes traveled against my will back down to the remains of Mr. Ramsbottom.

"Oh, don't look at me," Freddie said, backing himself up against the dirt wall.

"We've come this far," I said with a hard swallow. "If there's something to save the twins in this casket, I have to find it."

Freddie nodded. "Although I gotta tell ya, I'm starting to think our hundred-year-old source may have some of his details wrong."

I leaned toward the coffin, hands reaching ever-so-slowly toward the inside when I suddenly snatched them back. "Are you going to help me?"

"I can't, Erica," Freddie said, not able to meet my eyes.

"Skeletons are just . . . too much. I can't. What if I get, like, a piece of bone on me? I'll start screaming again."

"Well, that's just great," I said, jumping up to grab my flashlight before passing it to him. "Hold this. Point it at the . . . you know what."

Freddie twisted his face into a pained grimace, but he did what he was told.

"Okay, so," I said, not ready to look down yet at Mr. Ramsbottom, "if the lawyer just tossed it into the coffin, it should be easy to find. I'll just—" I reached down again with my hands, but I couldn't quite turn my face to look.

Freddie was shaking his head no. His lips curled in between his teeth.

I felt my fingertips brush against the satin lining of the coffin.

"Erica?" Freddie whispered.

"What?"

"Do you believe in ghosts?"

"Seriously?" I shouted, cranking my head to look up at him, but all I got was the glare of the flashlight. "You're asking me that now!"

"It's just I've had some weird experiences lately—whoa," he said. "You look freaky. We can talk about it later."

I moved my hands up and down the near side of the coffin, from shoes to shoulder . . . staying away from the skull. Then I leaned farther across the body to search the other side. Freddie moaned in the background.

"You know," I said, blowing a piece of hair from my eyes that had somehow managed to escape my cap. "If we don't end up in prison, I think we need to remember this moment. This is why we can't work togeth—Whoa!"

Suddenly Freddie hip-checked me to the side. "I see something."

I struggled to get back on my feet on the uneven ground as I watched Freddie reach into the coffin. A second later, his hand shot into the air clutching a letter.

"I don't believe it." I could barely hear my words over the pounding in my chest. "Open it! Open it!"

"Hold the flashlight," Freddie said, tossing it to me. It hit my knuckles and tumbled to the ground.

"Erica! Learn how to catch!"

"I'm sorry. I'm sorry," I said, scooping it up.

I heard the sound of the envelope opening.

"I got it," Freddie said, unfolding the letter. "Hold the light."

I directed the beam toward his hands. Freddie grabbed my wrist, adjusting the angle. He then ran his finger in a line across the paper. I could hear him reading under his breath.

"What does it say? What does it say?"

"Give me a second," Freddie hissed. "I'm still reading. Oh my . . ."

"What! What?"

Suddenly his finger stopped and he gasped.

"So help me—"

"No," he whispered.

"Freddie!"

He slowly looked up to meet my eyes. "Well, this just might change everything."

Chapter Forty

I snatched the letter from his hands. "Would you stop saying that."

"Careful," Freddie shouted. "You're going to tear it. I'll tell you. He wasn't planning on leaving the estate to Kit Kat."

My stomach sank. "No, that means Mrs. Masterson didn't have a motive to kill her father . . . or Mr. Clarke."

"He wasn't going leave the estate to Kit Kat," Freddie repeated, a smile spreading across his face, "but he wasn't going to leave it to his daughter either."

"What?" My eyes dropped back down to the letter, but I couldn't read the words and hold the flashlight. "Then who?"

"The town," Freddie said. "He was thinking of leaving everything to Otter Lake."

"What? Why would he—" I began. "You know what? It doesn't matter. This could be enough. We need to go to Grady."

"And tell him what? We accidentally dug up a grave with a backhoe and discovered Mrs. Masterson's father's will . . . along with, guess what? His body! I'm not going down for that. Not yet. We need to follow this lead."

I reached up to grab the grass at the lip of the hole, digging my foot into the dirt of the wall. "This is too important. We'll have to face the consequences . . . with your team of lawyers."

"You know I don't actually have a team of lawyers, right?" Freddie asked. "I mean, I could probably get one. I don't think my grandmother would let me go to jail. You, maybe."

I scrambled against the wall trying to find leverage, but the dirt kept tumbling away. I growled. Maybe this whole *what comes next* discussion was moot because Freddie and I were never getting out of this grave. "Would you give me a hand here?"

Freddie laced his fingers together to give me a boost. I reached up again and—

—a hand clamped around my wrist.

Freddie screamed . . .

. . . but I didn't.

Somewhere deep down I knew who it was. I just knew. "Erica."

I cast one last look back at Mr. Ramsbottom. Hanging out with him was looking better all the time.

I sighed before finally looking up.

"Hi, Grady."

Chapter Forty-one

"Rhonda, would you take Freddie inside?" Grady asked in an empty-sounding voice. "I'd like a minute alone with Erica."

Grady had given Freddie and me a lift back to the sheriff's station. At least I liked to think of it as a lift . . . but I couldn't help but notice we sat in the back, while Grady sat all by his lonesome up front. Not a one of us said a word on the drive back into town although Freddie kept elbowing me in the ribs while darting his eyes over to Grady. I got that he wanted me to say something to make the situation better, but I couldn't think of the words that would manage that feat.

"Sure, but—" Rhonda stopped and leaned in closer to the window. "You, uh, know what you're doing here, boss?"

Grady shot her a look. "I'm pretty sure I do."

"I just mean," she added, tilting her head from side to side, "it's been a crazy night. Tempers are high. I wouldn't want you saying anything to Erica—I mean, the suspect—here that you'll later regret."

"It's fine."

"But given the amount of time you've spent using the office computer to search for date ideas, I just thought—"

"Rhonda!"

"Right, sorry," she said with a tight nod. "There's just one more—"

Grady silenced her with a pretty ominous glare.

"No, it's not that. Where do you want me to put Freddie?" she asked quickly. "We're kind of out of holding cells."

Grady flexed his jaw. "Put him in that one in the basement."

"The basement!" Freddie yelled. "After what we were just doing?"

Grady didn't answer. Instead he scratched his hairline under the brow of his sheriff's hat, before just whipping it off and tossing it on the seat beside him. "But keep an eye on him, okay? And don't give him anything through the bars, and if he suddenly plays sick, don't open the gate."

"Dammit, Grady," Freddie said. "Get out of my head."

"Right." Rhonda opened Freddie's door. "Come with me, Ng. And you heard the man. No funny stuff."

"I wouldn't dream of it," Freddie said, heaving himself out. "But do you have a nail file I could borrow, I have this terrible rough edge that—"

"Freddie," Grady warned in a voice that somehow managed to suck all the air out the car.

"I'm playing," Freddie chuckled, right before shooting me some *uh-oh* eyes. He then leaned in and whispered, "I don't think this is going to be a fun conversation. Good luck. I'll be in the basement."

I nodded.

Freddie shut the door, and the silence he left behind was . . . unpleasant. I studied the back of Grady's head. He was staring out the window again. More than anything, I wanted to touch the back of his neck, maybe massage some of the tension out of his shoulders, but as always, there was something keeping us apart. In this case it was the cage separating the back of the cruiser.

"So," Grady said, taking a breath. "Grave robbing."

I shifted over to where Freddie had been sitting to try to get a look at his face. "We had it on good authority that there was no body."

Grady nodded.

"Mr. Carver swore—"

He waved a hand in the air. "It doesn't matter. I don't want to hear it. Rhonda will be questioning—" He cut himself off. "Wait, Mr. Carver? Hundred-and-two-year-old Mr. Carver?"

"That guy knows a lot about this town. And he wasn't wrong about everything. He—"

"No. Wait. Stop." He halfheartedly waved his hand in the air again before moving it back to his forehead. "I mean it. Save it for Rhonda."

"Grady," I said quietly. It was getting hard to talk over the lump in my throat. "I really am sorry."

"Not sorry enough to stop, though."

"It's the twins." Great, now my eyes were getting all watery. "They need me."

I watched him pull his bottom lip through his teeth. "And that right there is the problem, isn't it? Everybody needs Erica to save the day. Except nobody really thinks that except you and Freddie. The Dynamic Duo. Saving Otter Lake from—I don't even know what you guys tell yourselves you're doing."

"Okay, just hold on." I clenched my teeth, trying to consider my words instead of just snapping back. "Have you looked at what we found in Mr. Ramsbottom's grave?"

"What?" Grady asked with false lightness. "You mean this?" He held the letter up pinched between two fingers.

"Of course I mean that." Again, I wished I could touch him, grab his hand. "It changes everything, Grady."

"Really," he said, again with that slow nod. "Everything. Wow."

My cheeks flushed. "It's evidence of a motive for Mrs. Masterson killing her father." I got that Grady was beyond upset with me, but Tweety being falsely accused of murder—confessing to a crime she didn't commit for God knows what reason—still trumped everything else. You'd think he could see that.

"Oh, I see," he continued. "Evidence." He turned in his seat to meet my eye. For a second he dropped the cool demeanor. "But evidence for a . . . what again? A fifty-, sixty-year-old murder that we don't even know happened?" He nodded, then shook his head side-to-side, turning back to the windshield. "I'm not exactly sure how that helps us here."

"Grady, come on," I said, trying to keep control of my voice. "You know as well as I do, if Mrs. Masterson could kill her father, she could kill her husband. Maybe Mr. Masterson knew what that letter said—and Mr. Clarke! What about Mr. Clarke?"

"Oh, now I get it," Grady said, still nodding. It made me sad to see him this way—mad, sarcastic, almost bitter. It wasn't like him . . . and I had made him this way. "Okay, well, let's do a little role-playing here—"

"I'm guessing it's not the fun kind," I muttered.

"No, it's not," he replied. "But don't worry. You don't have to do anything. You just sit back and relax. I'll play both parts."

I slumped back in the seat, folding my arms across my chest.

"So, Sheriff Forrester, can you tell me how it is that you came across this letter, Exhibit A?" Grady asked the question in a really smarmy voice that didn't take a genius to realize was that of a lawyer.

He then turned his head to answer the question he had posed to himself. "It was found in the grave of Mr. Abraham Ramsbottom, the defendant's father."

He turned his head back the other way. "Found? Really? That sounds like an interesting story. Can you explain?"

"Erica Bloom and Freddie Ng dug up the grave and found the letter."

I rubbed the spot between my eyebrows. Nope. This definitely wasn't going to be the fun kind of role-play.

"My, that's quite serious. Grave digging is a felony in New Hampshire."

I threw my hands halfheartedly into the air. Guess that settled it.

Grady turned to look at me to make sure I was paying attention. "Oh yes, a felony."

I leaned back again against the seat.

"Sheriff Forrester," said the lawyer—the lawyer whom I was beginning to really dislike—"is it true that you were dating said Erica Bloom at the time she dug up the grave?"

My eyes flashed to Grady's, but he was facing front again. I couldn't help but notice the use of past tense in that question.

Grady shook his head. "I wouldn't say we were dating. Dating implies a certain amount of trust and respect and—"

"Hmm, but isn't it true that just days before Ms. Bloom was involved in the grave-digging incident that you had her over to your house for dinner?"

"That's true."

"Marinated salmon, was it?"

"It was."

"How long did you marinate that salmon for, Sheriff Forrester?"

"All right. All right," I said interrupting. "I get it, but I don't think the lawyer would really be interested in—"

"Overruled," Grady snapped, looking back at me before resuming his questioning of himself.

I blew some air out my lips.

"Eight hours."

"Wow. Eight hours. That certainly shows a certain amount of, what?" Lawyer Grady tapped his chin. "Care? Wouldn't you say, Sheriff Forrester?"

"Yes, I would. You see, I had been waiting for this opportunity with Erica for a long time. Since we were kids, one might say—"

"Grady, I—"

"But the timing was never right, and Erica had an unconventional upbringing that left her with some trust issues, and, well, I was always a dumb kid. I thought maybe Erica had finally reached a place in her life where she was ready for a relationship. I really felt I was."

My eyes filled up again. This trip had all gone so epically wrong. I couldn't help but wonder where we would be, what we would be doing right now, if Mr. Masterson were still alive.

"So, just so we're clear, Sheriff Forrester, you are asking this court to accept into evidence a letter dug up illegally from a grave—an act that has caused great emotional distress to my client—by someone you are romantically involved with."

"I wouldn't say we're romantically involved. Erica won't let that—"

"But you do have feelings for this person. Remember, Sheriff, you are under oath."

"Yes."

"Your Honor, I would like this letter to be withdrawn and stricken from the record as evidence."

"Granted, Mr. Lawyer sir," Grady said, suddenly

switching to a female voice. "I'm with you one hundred percent. What kind of rinky-dink operation do they have going on over there at Otter Lake?"

"I doubt she'd say rinky-dink," I replied sullenly.

Grady turned again to face me. "That's all you have to say?"

There was so much I wanted to say . . . but it wouldn't be enough.

I rubbed my face. What the hell was the matter with me? What was I doing? I could lose my job over this. I could go to jail. And then there was Grady. When I looked at him, I saw everything I ever wanted . . .

But then there was Tweety and Kit Kat.

"Grady, when I got into town a few days ago—" I took a moment to get ahold of my voice. It was cracking on me. "I didn't mean for this to happen. It wasn't at all how I wanted things to go down."

Grady closed his eyes and shook his head. "I know that. But what do you want me to do, Erica? Pretend that I don't know what you and Freddie are up to? Pretend that I don't know there's a good chance you're breaking the law?"

Suddenly something occurred to me. "How did you know we were there tonight? Were you following us?" I couldn't imagine we had gotten to a place where Grady would watch me and Freddie commit a felony, knowing he was going to arrest us when we were through, but—

"Wow," Grady said. "I have been busting my ass trying to keep you and Freddie out of jail and—" He held his hands up. "Erica, you and Freddie were off-roading a backhoe in the middle of the night. We got a call. A bunch of them actually. Mr. Connelly saw you from across the lake with his telescope."

I rubbed my face again. "We're idiots, Grady. I'm sorry. We went too far."

"I get it. Look, if I were you, I'd let Freddie drag me into these, what? Adventures? He's something else." He pointed a finger at me. "Don't tell him I said that. And you guys do have a way of . . . shaking evidence loose. But take that video from the fair, for example. Freddie making me get a subpoena? Really? I'm on your side." He shook his head. "But you're right. The truth is I'm not you. I'm not Freddie. And this isn't high school. I have rules to follow. Laws." He paused again. "You know what I was doing when I left you guys in the cruiser over at Hemlock Estate?"

"What?"

"I had to tell Mrs. Masterson what you two had done."

A sick heat flooded my cheeks.

"I know you guys think she's a murderer—hell, maybe she is—but hearing about her father?" He shook his head. "She broke down. And it wasn't the Mrs. Masterson we're all used to seeing around town." He sighed. "Not exactly how I wanted to spend my night, you know?"

I swore quietly under my breath. "Grady, it was my idea to dig up the grave. Freddie didn't want to."

Silence fell over us again.

Finally Grady said, "I gotta be done, Erica."

I looked out the window, not seeing anything. "I guess the grave digging was a bridge too far, huh?"

He pinched his lips together and nodded slowly.

"But Grady," I said, hating the sound of begging in my voice. "I know what we did was wrong, but . . . when I found Kit Kat lying in the grass, bleeding . . . I don't know. Things changed. I really didn't believe Mr. Ramsbottom was buried there, but even so, I never should have taken the chance. But . . . but, I don't know what I'm trying to say here." I took a moment to collect my thoughts. Finally I said, "You do know if you were in jail facing murder charges, Freddie and I would dig up a grave for you too. You know *that*, right?"

He let out a surprised bark of laughter. "I . . . suppose on some level I do."

I sighed. "But I guess that doesn't change where we're at right now."

"No . . . it doesn't."

I wiped at the tears in my eyes. "I also want to make sure that you know when it comes to how I feel . . . about you . . ." I stopped, unable to find the words.

"I know, Erica. It's okay." He threw me a half smile. "I guess the timing's still not right."

"I guess." I slapped at the metal cage separating us.

"Don't hit the grate," Grady said. "If Rhonda sees you do that, she might pull her gun."

"Really?" I asked, glancing over to the steps of the sheriff's department. "Because . . . I think she's bringing us ice cream."

Grady smiled at Rhonda, who was holding two bowls up in the air. "I do love this town."

Chapter Forty-two

After ice cream on the steps of the sheriff's department, Grady told Rhonda to take me to Tweety's cell. I could tell he didn't exactly want me rooming with her, but space was limited, and he probably felt she was the better option over Freddie.

We barely made it into the building before I heard Tweety shout, "What's going on? Is Kit Kat okay?"

"No change," Rhonda shouted back.

"She knows?" I asked.

Rhonda nodded.

"Erica, is that you?"

"It's me." I walked down the hallway.

"Oh for the love of—"

"I know." I held up a hand once I got into view. "Okay? You don't have to say it. I know."

"I told you to stay out of this."

"I know!"

"Well, come on in," Tweety said, stepping away from the bars. "But I get the bed."

I glanced over to the one cot against the wall then looked to Rhonda.

"I'll find you something," she said, turning her key in the lock. "At least a sleeping bag."

"Thanks."

"You want to shower? I mean I have to watch you and everything, but—"

I put up a hand. "Let's hold off on that for a bit. I just want to sit down."

"Rhonda, hon," Tweety said. "Get Erica and me some drinks, would you? Something with a bite. We've got things to discuss."

"Sure, I—wait," she said, wagging a finger. "Fool me once."

Tweety dropped herself heavily down onto the cot, making the springs groan. "Worth a shot."

I sat on the floor on the other side of the concrete room.

Tweety's watery blue eyes trailed over me. She looked tired. "What have you been doing? Wrestling pigs?"

"I wish," I mumbled. I looked over to the little table in the corner. Pretty sure that wasn't standard prison decoration. Neither were the cans of soda on it, the celebrity magazines, the half-eaten bag of chips, the prescription bottle—Tweety had *the* diabetes, go figure—or the box of takeout from the Dawg. "You got a pretty nice setup here."

"No chitchat," Tweety said, cutting the air with her hand. "Spill. Why are you here?"

"I—" I cut myself off and looked up at the ceiling, but that only made my eyes well up. The entire night suddenly seemed . . . nuts. "I . . . Freddie and I, we dug up Mr. Ramsbottom's grave, well, memorial site."

Tweety's face went slack. Then she blinked a few times.

"Again, I know, okay?" I said, looking out the bars to the blank wall of the hallway. "I don't need your judgment too."

Suddenly Tweety snorted. My eyes shot back to her. Yup, arms crossed over belly, body bouncing up and down—then the eruption of laughter. I shook my head and looked back out the bars.

"What the hell is the matter with you?" she said, wiping tears from her the folds of her eyes. "I mean, how did you even dig it up?"

"Backhoe," I said flatly, picking at a flaked bit of concrete on the floor. "Freddie owns a backhoe."

She laughed even harder at that.

After a few more minutes of hysterics, Tweety calmed down and said, "I wish Kit Kat had been here for that." She shook her head. "Jesus, Erica."

"I know." I let out a hiss after the flake of concrete I was picking jabbed me underneath my fingernail. I brought it to my mouth. "I know."

"What were you thinking?"

I rested my wrists on my knees and turned my palms to the ceiling. "Mr. Carver, Otter Lake's old librarian, told us there was a rumor that Mr. Ramsbottom left Hemlock Estate to Kit Kat. He said there might be evidence in the memorial coffin." I put air quotes around "coffin."

Tweety's face hardened. "I see. And what exactly did you find in the coffin?"

"Mr. Ramsbottom."

Her eyes widened again and she burst out into more laughter. "He's not supposed to be in there!"

"Yeah, thanks," I said, looking away. "We found a letter too. Turns out he didn't leave Hemlock Estate to Kit Kat."

"No kidding," Tweety said through the laughter. "I could have told you that."

My eyes snapped back to hers. "Except you haven't been telling me much of anything."

Tweety's laughter died pretty quickly, and it was her turn to look away.

"Nope," I said, dropping my hands between my knees.

"Mr. Ramsbottom didn't leave anything to Kit Kat." I inhaled deeply. "Didn't want to leave anything to his daughter either."

Tweety's eyes snapped back to mine.

"Turns out, this letter was to his lawyer. A letter saying he wanted to change his will," I said, studying Tweety's face.

"Well?" she asked.

"He wanted to leave Hemlock Estate to the town."

Tweety held my eyes for a moment then made a scoffing sound before looking away.

"I wonder why he'd do that?" I asked, picking some grave dirt off my wrist. "Must have been pretty upset with his daughter. I thought Hemlock Estate was meant to be a legacy thing."

Tweety flicked her eyes to mine but said nothing.

"I'm thinking maybe he didn't like her choice of fiancé?"

She didn't even look at me this time.

"I mean, from what I hear, Mr. Masterson, Mick, was a little rough around the edges back in the day." I tapped the air with a finger and squinted. "Not exactly the type of guy Mr. Ramsbottom would want for a son-in-law."

Tweety shook her head, face still turned.

"But I also heard that Mrs. Masterson, back then Olivia Ramsbottom, wasn't the type of girl to take no for an answer. What Olivia wants, Olivia gets."

Tweety huffed a dry laugh.

"Would have given her a pretty good motive to murder her father if that's what actually happened."

Tweety whipped her face back around. "It was a heart attack. Everyone knows it was a heart attack."

"Come on, Tweety." I shook my head. "I know that you didn't kill Mr. Ramsbottom. I know that you didn't kill

Mr. Masterson. You are not a murderer. But what did you do?"

She pinched her lips together a moment then said, "You sure about this letter? You read it yourself?"

"I'm sure. I did."

She ran a hand across her lips.

"What? Just tell me what you're thinking. What this means to you."

"Nothing," she said quietly. "It doesn't mean anything."

I sighed. "Really?"

Tweety shot me a withering look.

"Fine. At least tell me what Mr. Masterson wanted with you that day."

Tweety's face twisted into confusion then dropped. "You mean, at the fair?"

I nodded even though her reaction kind of begged the question of how many different days I needed to ask her about.

"Dumb old dog wanted to run away with me." She chuckled faintly. "Said his whole life had been a lie. That the money wasn't worth leaving me." She shook her head. "At least I think he said that. He was having trouble staying awake. I didn't realize . . ." Some emotion crossed her face, but it was too quick to read. "Can you believe that? After all these years?"

"What did you say to him?"

A devilish smile broke out across her face. "I told him to go f—"

"Whoa!" I shouted, holding my hands up.

She shrugged and then sighed through her nose. "I really did love him back then. Figured out pretty quick he wasn't who I thought he was, but it was hard to let go of the . . . dream. Guess it still bothers me a bit." She shook her head and looked off again. "Now that I think about it, despite all that stuff, what I said to him . . . well, they probably weren't the best last words to give to a man."

I raised my eyebrows and nodded. "Probably not."

"But in fairness, I didn't know he was dying."

"So why are you confessing?"

Her eyes flicked to mine. "I'm old, Erica," she said before taking a long pause. "And I made a promise a long, long time ago. I'm not about to break it now."

I threw my hands in the air. "You're killing me. What promise?"

She held up a finger for me to wait. "Rhonda?" she called out.

"Yeah?"

"You got this jail cell wired for sound?"

"What? You mean, bugged?" Rhonda called back from down the hall.

"Yeah."

"No. I mean . . . why?" A moment passed. "Maybe. I mean . . . shoot. No."

"Thanks, Rhonda," Tweety turned back to me. I watched her swallow then lick her lips. "I'm going to tell you this, Erica, because maybe then you'll see why you need to back off. But it doesn't leave this room."

I nodded.

"I made a vow to protect my sister." A small shudder ran over her. "My mother made me promise her on her deathbed."

"But what are you protecting Kit Kat from?"

She rolled her head back and forth against the concrete wall, looking up at the ceiling. "I don't know. Herself?"

"Tweety, what are you saying?"

"It was Kit Kat who killed Mr. Ramsbottom all those years ago." She stopped for a moment then added, "And I've been trying to cover it up ever since."

Chapter Forty-three

"No. Nope," I said, shaking my head. I had to pinch my lips together for a moment to hold back the emotion bubbling up in my chest. "I don't believe it. How?"

She shrugged. "Poison, I think. We had monkshood in the garden. Someone said he had vomited in the tent."

"Did she confess any of this to you?"

"No. She never did that."

"Then how do you know?"

"I knew there was something going on with her and Mr. Ramsbottom. I caught them talking once or twice, real passionate stuff." She shook her head again. "But after he died, she started acting really strangely, and—"

"That could be for a million different reasons," I near-shouted before I caught myself. I leaned over to attempt a peek around the wall to see if Rhonda was listening, but I couldn't get the angle. Tweety leaned and looked too then shook her head.

"As I was saying," I whispered. "Acting funny is not a confession. Half the people in this town—"

"Then there was the letter."

Everything suddenly felt very cold. "What letter?"

"Just a letter. Addressed to me."

I waited for her to keep going.

"It said, *I know what your sister did.*"

"Who sent it?"

"Don't know."

I stared at her a moment, dumbfounded. "Well, that doesn't mean anything. It could've been the real murderer trying to pin it on Kit Kat. It could have been Olivia Masterson! Maybe she was worried the rumors were true and her father had left Hemlock Estate to Kit Kat and she wanted to scare you off asking questions. Maybe—"

"Erica," Tweety said, closing her eyes and waving me off. "I know my sister. The way she was acting . . . she couldn't even look me in the eye afterward. I know."

"So what?" I tossed my hands in the air. "You just lived together all these years and never talked about it?"

"It got easier after a while. Barely even thought about it much after a few years. It's still Kit Kat," she said, leaning toward me. "I couldn't turn her in. And I knew she wasn't going to do anything like that again." She patted her chest. "I'd make sure of it. Well . . . at least I tried."

"So what? You think she killed Mr. Masterson too? Is that why you're confessing?"

She leaned farther away from me. "I don't know, okay? She might have. If she thought he was going to hurt me again. But that's neither here nor there. The letter said—"

"The letter from fifty years ago?" I asked.

"No. The new one."

"What new one? How new?"

"I got it yesterday. I was sleeping. When I woke up, it was on the floor."

"In the jail? Tweety, what the—" I growled. "Did you tell someone? What did it say?"

"Confess, or your sister will pay for her crime. I have proof."

"Tweety! Oh my God! Whoever wrote that note was the murderer! We have to find out who was here yesterday." I jumped to my feet. "Rh—"

A thin pillow smacked me in the face. Hard. "Ow!"

"Quiet," she ordered. "Don't you dare."

"We have to—"

"I already flushed the note," she said pointing to the toilet. "I'm not taking any chances with Kit Kat. What if she's got brain damage? How do you think a brain-damaged senior citizen's going to do in prison, Erica?"

I opened my mouth, but nothing came out.

"Not good," she said. "That's how."

"Tweety, I—" I couldn't figure out what to say to her to bring some sense to the situation. "I just can't. Nope. I don't believe it. This is crazy! Kit Kat is not a murderer!" I rubbed my hand over my mouth. "There's something more going on. And we are not going to let the person who is screwing with you just get away with it while you confess your way into prison."

"But I am guilty. I've been protecting Kit Kat all these years."

"She didn't need protecting. This is bull—"

"Erica," Tweety snapped, pointing at the floor. "My mother wanted me to protect Kit Kat because I think she always knew there was something a little wrong with her. She wasn't as strong as me. She never could control her emotions. I can take prison. Kit Kat can't. You make sure that doesn't happen."

"You know," I said, struggling to hang on to my emotions, "you can confess to killing about Mr. Masterson, and you can confess about Mr. Ramsbottom to protect your sister, but you can't confess about Mr. Clarke. They're already thinking Kit Kat may have murdered him last night." I pointed to the foyer. "That her injuries were from him, fighting back."

Tweety's face went white. She worked her lips a few times as though she wasn't quite sure what to say. "Nah, I don't buy it. She wouldn't. Mr. Ramsbottom was a long time ago, and they had something going on. As for Mick, I don't know. But not Peter Clarke. He was a good man. No."

"Tweety, I—"

She pointed a wicked finger at me. "If things go south, you make sure that lawyer uncle of yours gets her into one of those facilities. Not prison. Someplace nice. With a lawn . . . and crafts."

"Kit Kat hates crafts!"

"I don't want to talk about it anymore." Tweety lay back onto the cot and rolled over to face the wall. "I'm going to sleep."

"What? Well that's just great," I said to her back. "Perfect. You know, I think I'm going to get my uncle to look into a facility for *you* . . . with crafts. You need it," I mumbled. "And I still don't believe it, by the way. I'm going to get to the bottom of all this."

"Erica, honey. I mean this with love," she said before pausing a moment. I waited for the inevitable warning to leave it alone, but instead she said, "You smell like dirt. Go let Rhonda watch you shower."

After about half an hour of turning everything over in my mind, I decided a shower might not be a bad idea . . . but not because I smelled like dirt.

I called Rhonda, and she was more than happy to let me out. I think all this arresting of friends and neighbors was starting to get to her. As we walked down the hall to the employee bathroom, I asked, as subtly as I could, "Rhonda, do you guys keep track of everyone who comes into the building?"

"All visitors," she said. "The rest, I just keep note of up here." She tapped the side of her head.

"Anyone come to visit Tweety yesterday?"

"Nope. Not that I recall."

"I don't suppose you'd let me take a look at that list?" I asked, raising my eyebrows.

She smiled. "I don't suppose you'd tell me why?"

I stopped walking to meet Rhonda's eye. As eccentric as Rhonda could be, she did on occasion have a sort of canny insight into things. "I think maybe the real murderer came to visit Tweety yesterday. Maybe dropped something off to her? While she was sleeping?"

She furrowed her brow. "I wasn't on the desk all of yesterday," she said, letting the sentence trail before she added, "but I'll look into it."

"Thank you." I gave her wrist a squeeze with my cuffed hand. "Don't suppose we could look at the list together now?"

She squeezed me back. "Don't suppose you'd tell me why you think the murderer was here yesterday?"

I pinched my lips together. Part of me did want to tell Rhonda everything Tweety had said, but I couldn't stomach that big a betrayal. Besides, Rhonda might actually believe all this ridiculousness about Kit Kat killing Mr. Ramsbottom back in the day—and then this mess would get even uglier. "No . . . I don't suppose I could."

"Didn't think so," Rhonda said, leading me a few more steps. "You know, it's none of my business, but I'm still hoping the two of you make it work." She flicked her eyes over to Grady's office. The door was shut, but I could see him through the window, sitting behind his desk, face lit up from the glow of the computer screen.

"He's done, Rhonda," I said, feeling my chest tighten. "He told me so."

She scoffed. "He's not done. But would it kill you to make it a little easier for him?"

I sighed.

"You and Freddie breaking all these laws right under his nose? Grave digging? It's embarrassing. He's sheriff!"

"I know. I know." Just then Grady looked over to us. I could see his eyes soften with concern. It almost looked like he was going to get up . . . but as quickly as the moment came, it passed. He looked back at the computer. "It's not like I'm going out of my way to destroy our relationship. Despite what *he* may think." I waved my cuffed hands in his direction. "I'm just really worried about the twins."

"I get it," she said with a sigh. "I don't like how this all seems to be playing out myself. Tweety confessing? Doesn't make sense. Now Kit Kat in the hospital? And just so you know, we are working on it." She shook her head. "The fates do seem to be against you two. It would almost be romantic if you weren't so . . ."

"Old?" I offered. "Freddie says we're too old for this to be cute."

"I was going to go with stupid." She shrugged. "Sorry. All this is really frustrating for me to watch. I'm still rooting for you, though. He's a good guy. I want him to be happy. And when you're not acting like a complete loon, you seem to do that for him." Her eyes flashed to mine, worried. "And vice versa, of course."

I gave her a sad smile.

"I'll see if I can put in a good word for you," she said. "I think you'd have cute kids."

I laughed. "Well thanks, but I'm not sure it will do much good."

"You don't know that. Just think of me as your Fairy Godmother," she said. "Now let's get you cleaned up."

Rhonda trusted me enough to stand outside the door of the washroom, so at least I got to shower in private. She also lent me some things to wear while she washed my grave-digging clothes. But despite all her consideration, and the sleeping bag, I couldn't sleep. My mind was turning most of the night, and every time I did start to doze, I dreamed a skeleton was grabbing my arm.

"Rise and shine."

I blinked my eyes open.

"What's going on?" I asked, forcing the words through the thickness in my throat. "Why are you getting us up so early?"

"You're free," Rhonda said, putting the keys in the door. "I thought you'd want to get out of here asap."

"What?" I asked, pushing myself up. "I haven't even called my uncle Jack yet." I thought given the amount of pro bono work I was pushing in his direction, he at least deserved the night off.

"Just between you and me," she began, bringing a hand up to cover the side of her mouth, "Grady was up all night looking into records, trying to find a way to spring you."

I wiped the corner of my mouth. "He was?"

"Uh-huh," she said. "He's sleeping like a cute little puppy in his office now."

"How? I don't understand . . ."

"Olivia Masterson never got the proper permission from the town to bury her father on the property. It's an illegal grave site. So technically you and Freddie just dug up a box. Vandalism at best. It's her fault there's a dead body in it. Grady already talked to Matthew, and he's backing your story about him giving you permission to dig up the . . . box. I don't think Mrs. Masterson wants anyone knowing about this for obvious reasons." Rhonda swung the door open. "So for the moment, she's not pressing charges. You're free to go."

I hauled up my stiff body.

"You get going," Tweety said, slapping me on the hip. "Check in at the hospital. Make sure Kit Kat is okay."

"Got it."

"And Erica," Tweety said, voice full of warning. "I meant what I said last night. You need—"

"Yeah. Yeah. Stay out of it. I know," I said. "But I meant what I said last night too, and—"

"What was it you said last night?" Rhonda asked, non-chalantly scratching the back of her neck.

"I—" I tore my eyes away from her and back to Tweety. "I don't buy it. And I'm going to find out the truth."

Rhonda shut the barred door and turned the lock as I hurried down the hall.

I heard Tweety shout intentionally loud enough for me to hear, "Rhonda, you need to keep an eye on her. Lord only knows who she'll dig up next."

Just as I made it down the hallway, I saw Freddie heading out the front doors.

"Hey! Wait up!" I hurried my step, taking just one quick peek in on Grady. He was asleep on his couch. The fur-row in his brow I had been seeing a lot of lately still hadn't disappeared. I resisted the urge to go in there and rub it away. I'd probably get myself arrested for as-sault. "Freddie!" I pushed out the front doors after him. "Freddie?"

He stopped on the stairs but didn't turn.

"What's the matter?"

"What's the matter?" he asked, spinning on me. "What's the matter?"

My eyes scanned him. He did not look good. Face hag-gard. Eyes definitely bloodshot. "Sleep well?"

He didn't answer right away. Just gaped at me.

I took a step back in preparation for what I thought might be coming.

"I slept in the basement of a prison. After digging up a grave. No, I did not sleep well! I still have grave dirt down my pants!"

"Well, you could have showered—"

"I am not showering in front of Rhonda Cooke!"

"Freddie, what happened?" I asked. "You weren't this upset last night."

"That's because I was high on the adrenaline you were pushing. I wasn't thinking clearly. I'm still not." He clutched his head. "This is all happening so fast."

"No, no. Something's not right here," I said. "You love the adrenaline."

"Well, adrenaline has a cost, Erica, and I'm paying it."

"What does that even mean?" I asked, studying his face some more. "Seriously, did something happen?"

Freddie planted his hands on his hips then looked off to the side of the building shaking his head. "Fine. Yes."

"What?"

He sighed, but it came out more as a shudder. "Grady . . . called my parents."

I gasped. I suddenly found myself looking around for my mother. Most likely she would have chained herself to a tree to protest my imprisonment. Thankfully they were all bare. "He didn't!"

"He did," Freddie said in a shaky voice. "I'm in big trouble, Erica. I only talked to them briefly, but my dad said something about maybe selling my home."

"No!"

Freddie moved one hand to clutch his forehead. "Why did I have to make that pig sound? That's what this is really all about, you know . . . and *Lightning*." He dropped his eyes to mine. "Which I have to say makes me wonder about, you know, *compensation* issues. You should check that out before you buy the cow so to speak."

"You're the one who bought the boat!" I waved my hands in the air. "We're getting off track. What did Grady say to you?"

"He said, and I quote, *Freddie, you need to check yourself before you wreck yourself.*"

My face dropped. "He did not say that."

"Well, not exactly in those words, but that was the message." Freddie ran his hands over his eyes. "What am I going to do, Erica?"

"It's going to be okay. The charges have been dropped. We just carry on with the investigation and—"

"What? Carry on? No, no, no. Did you not hear me? I need to walk the straight and narrow."

I grabbed his shoulders. "No, that's the last thing you need to do. We need to solve this case. We need to help the twins. You won't believe what Tweety told me last night." His eyes flickered with curiosity. "And you need to show your parents the success you're going to make of Otter Lake Security."

Freddie studied my face for a moment. "Our relationship has been taking some strange turn as of late, Erica."

"You gotta trust me on this. I've got a lead . . . and it's a hot one."

He didn't say anything, but I could sense his interest growing.

"If it pans out, it could break this whole case wide open."

"You're talking like a gumshoe detective."

"Do you want me to stop?"

He shook his head no.

"This is just one minor setback on your journey, Freddie . . ."

His gaze tightened.

". . . your journey to greatness."

"You had better not be messing with me."

"Inside that building," I said, pointing back to the doors, "is a list. And on that list is a name . . . the name of a murderer."

"How could you possibly know that?"

I told him as quickly as I could all that Tweety had said.

"Wait, wait, wait! So Kit Kat did kill Mr. Ramsbottom?"

"No, well, Tweety thinks she might have after some sort of lovers' quarrel—"

"What!"

"Well, I don't believe it, but Tweety does, and she'll do anything to protect her sister."

"Oh my God," Freddie said, grabbing his head again. "That's so sweet. And messed up. This is all too much!"

"Look, we don't have time for you to process everything right now," I said, giving his shoulders another shake. "We need that name before Tweety signs that stupid confession. This situation needs a hero."

He didn't say anything, but I knew I was getting to him.

"What I need you to do is cause a distraction. Get Rhonda to come outside so I can sneak in to take a look at that list. Can you do that, Freddie? Can you cause a distraction?"

He held his straight face for a moment longer, but then he mumbled, "Can I cause a distraction? Can I cause a . . ." He trailed off as he pushed past me to walk up the stairs to the sheriff's department. He then shouted in a voice louder than I would have thought possible, "I will burn this place to the ground!"

Chapter Forty-four

I scurried over to the bushes that lined the stairs and ducked behind them. I hadn't expected Freddie to start off with such a bang, but there was nothing to do but go with it. I ground my feet into the dirt and crouched down between the bush and brick wall, pushing away the thin braches scratching at my neck.

"I demand justice!"

I peeked through the branches. Freddie had his arms spread wide and was turning in a slow circle. My eyes darted to the doors. No sign of Rhonda yet. Hopefully, Grady was a heavy sleeper.

"I say, I say," Freddie shouted, suddenly slipping into his southern accent—he really must be tired—"is this the United States of America? Or is this Communist Russia?"

I looked at the doors again. Still nothing.

Freddie turned to where I was hiding in the bushes and started to shrug but cut it off with a jolt when the doors swung open.

"Freddie! What are you doing?" Rhonda shout-whispered, speed-walking outside. "You just got out!"

"I don't know," he said putting his hand to his forehead.

"But I'm not feeling well. Maybe I didn't drink enough prison water. I feel f—" And just like that, Freddie hit the ground in what I hoped was a break fall. Rhonda rushed over and started to smack his cheeks. I half stood to make sure he was okay. His left hand shot me a thumbs-up.

Go time.

I frog-walked out of the bushes, then ran in a crouch to the front doors. I swung the door open just enough so that I could slide through, then dropped to my hands and knees. Hopefully Grady was still asleep, but I couldn't take any chances. I needed to stay below the bottom frame of his office window.

I scuttled toward the front desk, only stopping to take one quick look behind me. Rhonda was talking on her shoulder walkie-talkie thing, probably calling an ambulance, by the look of Freddie's protesting hand waves. Oh boy.

I peeked up over the desk. Okay, so Rhonda wasn't exactly a clean freak. I shuffled through the scattered papers, every now and then darting a glance over to Grady's office. No sign.

Come on. Come on.

I lifted my head again to look outside.

Was that a fire truck?

I reshuffled the papers. Seriously, where was the stupid—

Bingo! Sign-in ledger.

I ran my finger down the column of dates.

Dammit! Nothing for yesterday. Either the murderer snuck in—which seemed highly improbable, given that the only entrance to the hallway that led to Tweety's cell was from the front foyer—or it was someone who came to the prison so often that they weren't considered a visitor at all . . .

I brushed the grit from the floor off my hands before

planting them back down to get dirty all over again. I scurried back around the desk. I needed to get out of here
before—

Just then the front doors swung open. Rhonda stalked
in, muttering, "Freddie and his freaking jail water—Erica!"

Chapter Forty-five

"Hi, Rhonda," I whispered, waving at her . . . squatted right below Grady's office window.

"What are you—" She gasped so loudly I thought her lungs might collapse in on themselves. "You were looking for the list!" she whispered with a point back toward the desk. "I told you I'd look into it! You're not helping! Not with Tweety's case! Not with him!"

"I know. I just—"

Her point swung to Grady's office. "Are you trying to kill him! I told you he can't take much more!"

"I'm sorry," I whispered back. Then I had another thought. My brow furrowed. "But you know, it's not like he's some sort of endangered bird. I think—"

I stopped when I saw Rhonda's eyes roll up to the window.

"Everything all right?" I heard Grady's voice call out.

Rhonda nodded silently.

"You released Erica?"

Her eyes dropped back down to mine. "You're lucky I'm a romantic," she muttered.

"Sorry?" Grady asked.

"Nothing, boss. She's gone."

"Good." A moment later, he added, "She tell you anything we could use to help Tweety? It's certainly not like she'd tell me."

I rolled my eyes. That was so unfair. I wanted to tell him stuff, and I would . . . if he'd stop throwing me in jail.

"Well," Rhonda said, hooking her thumbs through her belt loops. "She seems to think the real killer made a visit to Tweety yesterday."

"What? Here?"

"But she pulled another *Erica* and wouldn't tell me why."

My jaw dropped, but Rhonda flashed me a clear *What are you going to do about it?* look.

"Okay, get me a list of everyone who has been in this building for the last forty-eight hours."

"Well, that's the thing," Rhonda said. "I've already looked at the ledger. Nobody's on the list."

I heard Grady growl—much closer to the window than he had been just moments before. I inched my way toward the exit just as his door opened. I froze.

"What do you mean nobody's on the list? I—never mind. Question the new kid, Amos. He was on the desk yesterday. I want to know everybody who came through that door. Office deliveries. UPS. Medical supplies. The server from the Dawg. And by the way, no more takeout for Tweety. She's going to have a coronary in that cell. Call my mom. She offered to make her a real meal."

Rhonda nodded. "So you think Erica and Freddie are onto something?"

"The crime-fighting duo usually is." His voice sounded quieter this time, like he had moved back farther into his office.

I slid again toward the doors, but Rhonda held up a fin-

ger for me to wait. "You know, boss, Erica seems to think
you meant it when you said you two were through."

"Rhonda," he said, voice full of exasperation. I could
just see his hands on his hips. "What does that have to do
with anything?"

"So . . . are you through?"

"No. I mean, I would love to . . . Erica and I, we . . . I
don't know! Just get me that list!"

The door slammed.

Rhonda shot me a self-satisfied smile and jerked a
thumb at the door.

Didn't have to ask me twice.

I crawled toward the exit. Big smile plastered across my
face. Not only was Grady not through, but their conversation had triggered something in my mind . . . something
that just might change everything.

Once outside, I jumped to my feet. "Freddie! Get out
of that fire truck! We have work to do!"

Chapter Forty-six

"So where are we going?"

"To check something out," I said, trying not to break out into a run. There were even more people crowded in the midway than usual, slowing us down. It made sense. It was Saturday, the second-to-last day of the fair. It didn't help anything that Freddie was still covered in mud. Lots of people were giving us double takes.

Thoughts bounced around in my brain as I replayed Grady's words, but the paths they were following weren't random anymore . . . broken trails were linking together . . . a pattern was coming through. Yes. *Yes!* It was all coming together. I just needed to go back and check one thing, but if I was right . . . oh ho ho, I was going to nail that—

"You know something. Did you see a name? Do you know who did it?"

"Not a name. Just follow me," I said, focusing on my path. "I've got a hunch, and if I'm right, it will all be clear in just a second."

"Oh God. I don't know if I can take it," Freddie said with a little skip. "Just tell me."

"Okay, so—"

"No! Don't!" he shouted. "Show me whatever it is that you're going to show me. I don't want to ruin it!"

"Fine," I said, cutting a path through the crowd.

"It's going to be good, though, right? Like a *Sixth Sense* moment?"

I slowed for a millisecond. "Well, that's a lot of pressure. I don't know if—just come on!"

There! I spotted the photo board by the entrance to the agricultural building.

"We're going there? To the photos?"

I ran the last couple of steps, Freddie at my heels. "Just be quiet for half a second." My eyes scanned the board. "I need to—there!"

I snatched a photo from its pin, tore off its cellophane wrapping, and whipped it around to show Freddie. He stepped back, squinting.

"What am I looking at here?" He leaned in closer again. "Wait . . . is that—?"

"It is" I said, nodding. "Now look at where he's looking."

"I can't tell," Freddie mumbled. "Oh my God! And is that . . . ?"

"It is," I said, trying to get ahold of the adrenaline pounding through my veins. "So, you get where I'm going with this?"

Freddie's eyes snapped up to mine. "Oh baby, I'm already there."

"He said it's the only picture he had of—"

"*Her* from that day," Freddie finished, shaking his head. "And we thought he meant the store, but he's really looking at . . . that . . . that . . . son of a pharmacist!"

Chapter Forty-seven

"I'm so angry," Freddie said, tapping the table. "And hungry. I'm skipping the pancakes. I feel like I need to order something bloody."

After our discovery, we decided to head over to the Dawg to talk about everything and get some breakfast. We were going to need our strength. There was so much we still needed to put together before we decided what we were going to do about it.

"I'm angry too," I said, tucking my foot under my leg.

"And imagine him watering those chrysanthemums like he's not some sort of psychopath?" Freddie huffed a breath. "But how did you know? What made you think of the picture?"

I bit my lower lip and looked up at the bar TV without really seeing what was on the screen. "Someone dropped that letter off to Tweety yesterday in the prison. Someone who wasn't on the guest list. So it had to be a person who just faded into the background. A cleaner. The delivery person for the Dawg. A—"

"A pharmacist."

I nodded. "I spotted Tweety's diabetes medication on her nightstand in the jail cell."

"Wait, Tweety got a nightstand? I didn't get a nightstand. And I still haven't showered. Though I made a pretty good mess in the washroom back there."

"Focus, Freddie," I said. "The meds were still in the bag, unopened. Brand new. And then I remembered the picture." I picked up the photograph we had taken from the fair. The grand opening of the pharmacy. It hadn't registered before—probably because at the time Freddie's *bow chicky bow bow* was still ringing in my ears—but Sully Junior wasn't looking at the pharmacy with love on his face. Oh no, he was looking at Olivia Ramsbottom. I didn't recognize her at the time. How could I? I didn't know what she looked like as a young woman . . . not until I saw all the photos at Hemlock Estate. But it still didn't click then. Nope, it wasn't until I thought of Mr. Sullivan as a suspect for the first time back at the sheriff's department that I remembered that look of intense love . . . and then it just dawned on me. What if the *her* he was talking about was a real person?

Freddie gestured to me to pass the picture to him. "That there is a boy in love. But if he is the murderer, it was a pretty big risk for him to take the letter to the prison like that."

"He got lucky with Tweety being asleep, and he knew that once she read the letter, she'd clam right up to protect her sister," I said. "You know what else? He also knew Mr. Masterson had a prescription for morphine. He could have easily slipped him an extra patch or two at the fair." I tapped the table. "Maybe that's what the ME found suspicious, though . . . maybe he stuck it on in a unusual location . . . the back of the neck or something. Or maybe he fiddled with the potency somehow."

"We have to fix that video," Freddie said. "You thought you saw a man. Stupid seagull. Wait! Didn't Marg say something about him being there?"

"Yeah," I said with a point. "I think you're right. She said, *Ask Sully. He was there.* But I thought she meant in the pharmacy that morning when she bought the cough drops."

"But what are we thinking here? Does Mrs. Masterson know? Were *they* having an affair? Maybe it was all her idea! Even Matthew said that his mother was really manipulative. Maybe she's been using this lovesick man to do all her dirty work. Oh my God!" Freddie leaned across the table to grab my arm and shake it. "She could have gotten him to kill her father all those years ago because she was worried about her inheritance!"

"Holy crap! You're right!" I said, struggling to keep my voice down. "I can't believe I didn't think of that sooner!" A rush of relief ran from my scalp to my toes. I knew Kit Kat hadn't killed anyone.

"I can't believe that Tweety thought Kit Kat did it all this time," Freddie said. "It's just so weird. Can you imagine living with someone you believed was a murderer for forty, fifty years? *Can you empty the dishwasher?* would always have to be followed up with *Please don't kill me!*" He threw his hands up in the air. "Where's Shelley? Is someone going to serve us or do I have to go to the bar?"

"I don't think it was like that," I said, twirling the fork on the table. "I think maybe Tweety just saw it as a terrible thing that happened once and would never happen again. It's like those two have some weird sibling thing going on where they're so close, they can't see each other clearly."

"Whoa . . . that's kind of deep," Freddie said slowly. Then he added, "But seriously, I'm starving." He got to his feet and shouted, "Steak! I want steak!"

"Keep your pants on, Freddie," Big Don, owner of the Dawg, shouted back from behind the bar. "We're short-staffed! Everybody's at the fair."

Freddie dropped back into the booth. "Oh my God. *I'm* going to kill someone soon if I don't get something to eat."

I pushed the bowl of peanuts in his direction. "Here, have some nuts."

"I don't want peanuts," Freddie said, picking up a handful and dropping them in his mouth. "Okay, let's focus now on the plan," he mumbled through his chewing.

"We have a plan?"

"No," he snapped. "But we obviously need one."

I nodded. Freddie was scary when he was hungry.

"Okay, so first, the picture and the prescription are circumstantial evidence at best. Especially considering Tweety's not about to tell Grady about the letters." He flicked the photo. "We need more proof."

"Agreed."

"So we have to go get more. And there's only one place more evidence might be."

"You don't mean," I leaned in and whispered, "breaking into the pharmacy?"

"Really?" Freddie asked dropping his chin to his chest. "You just dug up a grave and you have qualms about this?"

"Keep your voice down," I hissed before leaning back against the booth to really consider the idea.

"I need to solve this case, Erica. Now more than ever. You were right. I have to prove to my parents that I can make this work. I can't be homeless. I wouldn't do well on the streets," he said before quickly tagging on, "and the twins."

"You're right. We don't have any other choice. We need to do something," I said. "But breaking into the pharmacy isn't the way to go."

"Why not?"

"Grady performed a little legal role-play for me in the cruiser last night."

"I'm guessing it wasn't the fun kind."

"We are spending too much time together."

Freddie's brow furrowed in question.

"Never mind. The point is he can't use evidence that we obtain illegally."

"Well, that's just great. So, short of going after a confession again, where does that leave us?"

I shook my head. The last time Freddie and I had gone after a murderer, we had planned to record the conversation on his phone. We didn't actually end up needing it, which was good, seeing as how in hindsight I wasn't really sure about all the legalities. Suddenly my phone chimed. "I have to go. My uncle's almost at the retreat."

"Okay, call me later, and we'll figure this thing out. I'm sure I can come up with something by then if I EVER GET MY FOOD," he shouted across the restaurant.

"Got it." Just as I reached the door, I heard Freddie groan in . . . ecstasy? I turned to see Big Don plunking a plate with steak and fries down in front of him.

"I'm so sorry," Freddie said, looking up at him. "You know I love you, right?"

"I take it you're okay now?" I called out over my shoulder.

"Go," Freddie mumbled, piece of steak already in his mouth. "I'll be fine."

I sped past the red, gold, and still-green trees crowded against the shoreline of the lake with my new bestie, *Lightning*. The sight was heartbreakingly beautiful . . . heartbreaking because for a brief second it occurred to me that the twins might never see their home like this again.

I couldn't let that happen. I knew we were on the right track. We just needed to bring it home.

As I pulled closer into the dock, I spotted Red leaving in his pontoon. He raised his hand in a wave, which I returned. My uncle must have arrived.

I anchored the boat before jumping to the canoe and then the dock—a move I was getting better and better at— then hiked my way up to the retreat. I had just made it to the porch steps when the sound of a door slamming stopped me in my tracks.

"Really, Summer? Really? The silent treatment?"

A moment later my uncle barged through the front door onto the porch, jolting back when he spotted me. "Erica!"

"Hi," I said, shoving my hands into my grave-digging pants. I couldn't remember the last time I had seen him in person. Maybe when I was eight, nine? He had handled all of my previous legal troubles over the phone. I was surprised to see just how much he looked like my mother. They could have been twins.

"Hi," he said back, rolling down his shirtsleeves. "It's so nice to see you."

It was nice . . . and awkward. Very awkward.

"Things not good in there?" I asked, flashing my eyes to the door.

He sighed. "Not exactly. Your mother and I have our issues, but . . . she's not even talking to me."

"Oh." I laughed. "It's not you. She's taken a vow of silence."

His brow furrowed. "What?"

"A vow of silence. It's for the retreat. Silence of the Soul."

I could see the thought moving behind my uncle's eyes; then a smile spread across his face, taking about ten years off him. "Well," he said, stopping to chuckle, "that would explain some of what happened in there. Of course, there's no mistaking the bird she flipped me."

My eyes flew wide. "Really?"

"Ah . . . I'm used to it."

"Oh, okay," I said, moving to sit on one of the deck chairs. My uncle followed suit. "So what's going on with the confession?"

"I've delayed until Monday. The sheriff was quite accommodating." His eyes searched mine—which made me wonder if Grady had filled him in on the train wreck of our relationship. "Twyla, though, seems quite adamant to get it done. Says she'll do it without me if I'm not there first thing."

I nodded.

"They'll transfer her to the state prison after that to await sentencing."

"State?"

"Well," my uncle said, sounding somewhat surprised, "they can't keep her here forever."

I leaned back in the chair and shook my head. Given that it was Saturday, that really didn't give Freddie and me much time.

"Your mother really will never speak to me again if Twyla goes to jail." He paused a beat. "I was also sorry to hear about Twyla's sister. Kit Kat is it?"

I nodded.

"You know, Sheriff Forrester intimated that he's getting some pressure to charge Kit Kat—Katherine—with Peter Clarke's murder." He looked out toward the lake before turning back to face me. "He also mentioned something about you digging up a grave?"

I sucked some air through my teeth. "Yeah, it was something like that."

"What the heck is going on in Otter Lake, Erica?"

I shook my head. I wanted to tell my uncle all my theories, get his perspective, but that might lead to telling him about the plan to come up with more evidence against Mr. Sullivan . . . and that might lead to all sorts of legal warnings. Even worse, he might tell my mother. Or Grady. So instead I said, "So what caused the rift between you and Mom anyway?"

He shot me a near-incredulous look. "You don't know? She never told you?"

"No."

"Figures," he said with a chuckle.

I waited, but when he didn't answer, I prodded. "So?"

"Well, I guess you could say it was the inheritance," he answered. "As is so often the case with families."

"What inheritance?"

"From our parents," my uncle said, turning to look at me again. "The inheritance that allowed your mother to buy this island?"

"Oh," I said, frowning. I suppose I did know that. "Why would that be a problem between the two of you?"

He inhaled deeply and threw his hands into the air before letting them drop between his knees. "She didn't approve of how I spent my half."

Again, I waited for him to continue.

"You see, she used hers to buy the island then donated the other three million to charity. Because, you know, the island was fine in her mind. She was devoting her life to helping women. Whereas I—"

"I'm sorry?" I asked with a cough. "Did you say three million?"

"We each got about four point five," he said, looking out again across the lake. "But as I was saying, I was already articling, doing mostly pro bono work and—"

Four point five . . .

"—so I used the money to take things to the next level. I wanted to make a bigger impact on the world. Have some influence. And I'll have you know," he said with a point to nobody, "my firm donates—"

. . . million?

"Bah, it doesn't matter. But I am not the soulless monster she makes me out to be. She's just so rigid . . . and uncompromising."

"Four point five million . . . dollars?"

He looked back at me. "You really didn't know."

"I did not."

He studied me a moment then asked, "What *do* you know about our family, Erica?"

I shrugged. "Not much at all. I thought your father was into . . ." I stopped myself again. "Actually I don't know what he was into."

"Munitions. He ran a munitions factory."

"Oh," I said, letting that information sink in. "Yeah, Mom wouldn't approve of that at all."

"No . . . no she didn't." He laughed sadly. "One day we should sit down and have a talk about our family. You know, there was a time when we were inseparable, your mother and I. We were—" He cut himself off again, waving a hand. "Doesn't matter."

"I'm sorry."

"I want to win this case for her, though. I'd like my older sister to have a little esteem for me . . . you too for that matter," he said, giving me a smile. "You remind me of my mother."

I took a slow breath, not sure how I felt about asking the next question. "Um, Uncle Jack?"

"Hmm?"

"I don't suppose my mother"—I cringed—"ever told you who my father was?"

He turned again to study my face. "You mean . . ." He stopped himself and looked up at the sky. "Summer sometimes." He looked back down to me. "I don't know, Erica. She never said. But if you ever want my help finding out, I'll do what I can."

"Thanks." I paused a moment. "Can I ask you another question? A legal one this time?"

"Sure."

"When I do, though . . . can you maybe not read too much into it? Or tell anyone I asked?"

He considered me for a moment then nodded.

"Is it illegal to tape a conversation without one of the parties knowing?"

He caught my eye and held it before saying, "New Hampshire has very strict recording laws. It is one of only twelve states that require the consent of both parties."

"Right. Right," I said with a nod. "But what about loopholes?"

He narrowed his gaze. "I am becoming increasingly uncomfortable with this conversation."

"Oh," I said, reaching a hand toward him. "Don't worry I'd never implicate you—"

"No. I'm worried about your physical safety, and mine," he said, jerking a thumb back toward the lodge, "should your mother find out I was advising you."

"I hear ya," I said with a nod. "But just . . . aren't there expectation-of-privacy loopholes?"

He shook his head. "The law is pretty clear."

I sighed. "Thank you." Freddie and I would obviously have to think of something else.

Another moment passed.

A crow cawed in the distance.

"So four point five million?"

"Four point five."

"Do I want to know which charity she donated it to?"

"You do not."

I called Freddie after I had spoken with my uncle. He hadn't come up with any ideas yet on how to trap Mr. Sullivan, and I was starting to feel pretty desperate. I took a long walk around the island waiting for my Eureka moment, but it never came.

One day left. It wasn't enough time.

I grabbed some food from the fridge and went to bed early. I felt bad leaving Uncle Jack alone with my mom and the guests for a silent dinner, but I was just too worried to make polite non-conversation.

I spent a good three, four hours lying on my bed staring up at my ceiling trying to think of something, anything, that would help, but beyond going over to the mainland and trying to shake the truth out of Mr. Sullivan and/or Mrs. Masterson, I had nothing. Not to mention, Grady wouldn't be able to use those confessions in court either. Stupid law. I couldn't even entertain fantasies of busting Tweety out of jail. I'd seen Rhonda wrestle back in high school. She could take me. Besides, Tweety would never leave Kit Kat to take the blame.

At some point I must have dozed off because it was two a.m. when my phone buzzed.

I cracked an eye open and looked at the screen.

Text from Freddie.

I straightened up in bed. Maybe he had an idea.

Okay, I really have to ask you this now.

I rubbed my eyes. That didn't exactly sound like an idea. *What?*

Do you believe in ghosts?

I sighed. Definitely not an idea. *Why?*

A noise woke me up, and when I looked outside, there was a pumpkin person standing on the end of my dock.

I jerked up straighter and looked around my room. For what, I don't know. *Are you sure?*

It was foggy. But I think maybe it was Mr. Ramsbottom's ghost.

I sighed again and typed, *Go to sleep, Freddie.*

He obviously didn't take my suggestion seriously because my phone buzzed a second later. *Have you thought of a plan?*

No. You?

No. But all the terror has all my neurons firing. I'll have one soon. Promise.

I shook my head and smiled. *'Night, Freddie.*

Oh sure, yeah. I'll be getting lots of sleep now.

I tossed my phone on the bed and got up. I doubted I was going to be able to fall back asleep either. Maybe my mom had some of that tea Mrs. Masterson liked. I threw a heavy sweater over my shoulders and padded down the hall. The light in the kitchen was already on.

"Mom?"

She was seated at the table, hands wrapped around a mug. She looked up at me, face etched with concern. I guess everybody was up worrying tonight. She waved a hand for me to sit before getting up and moving to the cupboard.

"Can't sleep either, huh?"

She smiled sadly and passed me a mug of steaming liquid. Mm, chamomile. She then held up a finger and disappeared down the hallway. A moment later she returned with some delicate white fabric in her hands.

I raised an eyebrow in question. "What's that?"

She held it up for me.

"Is . . . is that a christening gown?"

She smiled and nodded.

"Um . . . my christening gown?" It felt strange even to say the words. My mother was not one for organized religion.

She set the fabric down on the table then began . . . folding back the air around it? Next she put her hands to her face in mock surprise.

"It was a gift," I said.

She nodded again and pointed in the direction of the twins' cottage.

"Oh." I picked up the dress and turned it over in my hands. Somehow the delicate material made me think about just how difficult it must have been raising a child—on an island no less—without a partner or family. My mom had always said she couldn't imagine how she would have gotten by without the twins. But she said it in her airy, flighty way. I didn't really give it much thought . . . until now.

Suddenly I looked up to see my mother's hands flailing about. Hmm, I guess while I had been looking at the dress, my mother had been miming something. I couldn't be sure, but given her exaggerated smile, the imaginary baby she was holding in her arms, and all the gesturing to the sky, I was willing to bet she was acting out the story of my baptism into nature. I just smiled at her and nodded when I thought she might be through. I really didn't see the need for her to repeat all that.

"So," I said a moment later, changing the subject. "I had a talk with Uncle Jack today."

My mom scowled and dropped her imaginary baby on the floor.

"He, uh, didn't quite come off as the—what did you used to call him? Soulless money maggot?—you've made him out to be."

She huffed some air through her nose, which, if we were going to get technical about it, kind of sounded like a noise to me, but I didn't want her to try to stop breathing to prove a point.

"He actually seemed really kind of eager to help." I leaned back into my chair. "And he mentioned he'd like to, uh, mend some fences with his big sister."

My mother shot me a dry look.

"I couldn't help but think, seeing as you're all about forgiveness and family reunification, that maybe you should hear him out, you know, without flipping him the bird." I shrugged. "Say something if you disagree."

The barest of smiles touched the corner of her mouth.

"I really would love the chance to say a few things, Summer."

I spun around in my chair to see my uncle standing in the threshold.

"Couldn't sleep," he offered.

My mother got to her feet, stood there a moment, then moved to the cupboard to get yet another mug.

"Well," I said, pushing my chair back. "I'll give you two some privacy."

"Erica," he said, following me into the hall. "Before you go . . . about our conversation earlier."

"Yes?"

"Well, not that I want to encourage you doing . . . anything, but . . ."

"But what?"

"If you were looking for a loophole, public cameras might be it."

I nodded, immediately thinking of the tapes. "Yeah, I've given that some thought, but there aren't exactly a lot of street cams in Otter Lake."

My uncle shook his head. "You'd be surprised how many cameras there are in public places these days. And when, as you mentioned, there is no expectation of privacy, well, the law becomes a little muddier. You would still need a subpoena to get the footage, but it's legal . . . ish."

I leaned my shoulder against the wall as I thought about it. "But you're still saying I can't set up a camera myself?"

"Not if you're planning to trap someone with it. No."

I sighed. "Well, thank you for giving it some thought." I took a step back then jerked a thumb toward the kitchen. "And good luck in there."

He chuckled. "Thanks. I'll need it."

When I got back to my room, I picked up my phone and texted,

Hey, I don't suppose you've got any other cameras set up around town?

A moment later, the reply came. *No. Why?*

I let out a long exhale. *Long shot.* I then typed the briefest version I could of what my uncle had said.

I waited for Freddie's reply, but when it didn't come right away, I got back into bed and pulled the cover over my shoulder, still holding my phone.

After a few more minutes, I figured Freddie had just gone back to sleep. It was almost three. My eyes drifted shut. Maybe something would come to me in a dr—

Suddenly my phone buzzed.

I cracked an eye and swiped the screen.

He said all public cameras were okay?

I pushed myself up onto one elbow. *Yeah, basically, with a subpoena, But we can't plant one.*

We don't have to.

I sat all the way up in bed. *Tell me this means you have a plan.*

Chills ran down my back as I waited for the reply.

I have a plan.

Before I could text back, he added, *And it involves a Taser!*

I could feel my brow furrowing.

I know how you feel about killing people.

Chapter Forty-eight

"In closing," Mrs. Masterson announced, voice booming out from the speakers on the stage, "I just wanted to add that you all have reminded me tonight of the importance of tradition and community."

She was finally wrapping things up. I shook my fingers in the air before shoving them back into my pockets. It was a cold night. Hadn't stopped the people from coming out, though. And that was good . . . witnesses were good. Made it seem less likely that I would, you know, die.

"As you all know, this has been an incredibly difficult time for me personally. But the overwhelming love and support I have received from all of you has allowed me to be here tonight, as I have been for nearly fifty years. Otter Lake is so much more than a mark on a map. It's even more than a community. We are a family."

A bunch of people nodded. A few murmured their agreement.

I was standing in the crowd gathered for Mrs. Masterson's speech, getting ready to launch phase one of *the plan*. Mr. Sullivan stood about thirty yards away. Front row and center. Just as we had anticipated. Guess that meant this was really happening . . . like really, really happening.

"Our town events knit us together with unbreakable bonds, but they would not be possible without all of your hard work. So thank you once again to all of the volunteers. Your efforts have not gone unnoticed. Good night."

The crowd applauded, then fell in and broke apart. The rides would go on for at least a few more hours, but that was it. The end of another Fall Festival. I needed to hurry.

My heart thudded in my chest as I popped into place the earbud Freddie had given me. "Hey? You there?"

"I'm here. All's a go."

"The speech is over," I whispered back. "I'm moving in."

"Acknowledged. I'll let Rex know."

My eyes darted over the crowd. Where did he go? For a second, I thought I had lost Mr. Sullivan, but then I spotted him trailing Mrs. Masterson . . . of course. She was walking with Matthew and another man holding a camera. I was pretty sure he worked for the town paper.

I blew out the breath I had been holding then hurried forward.

Go time.

Basically, the plan was for me to confront Mr. Sullivan with the photo from the fair, tell him I knew about the letters, and goad him into a confession. It was our go-to move. Our theory was that if we played it just right, he wouldn't be able to stop himself from talking about his undying love for Mrs. Masterson. Unfortunately there were a number of tricky parts to the plan.

Getting him alone was number one.

I sidestepped some couples and small groups of people. Man, it was a busy night. If I wasn't careful, I might lose this chance. I needed to get to him before he disappeared into the crowd.

"Mr. Sullivan!" I called out when I was just a few feet back. He didn't turn. "Mr. Sullivan!"

He shot an annoyed look over his shoulder. "Erica, hello," he said without breaking stride.

"Can I speak to you a moment?"

"No, I'm sorry. I need a word with—someone."

I quickened my pace.

"*Erica! I can see you*," Freddie hissed in my ear. "*You're letting him get away.*"

"I'm trying," I muttered, pushing through more of the crowd. "He's spritely."

"*Well, at least you're going in the right direction.*"

I looked up at the flashing Ferris wheel looming over me.

And there was tricky point number two.

Freddie's big realization had come when he remembered the Ride Cam at the fair. It was the perfect way to tape Mr. Sullivan legally . . . sort of. Freddie had talked to Rex, and apparently he had no problem moving the video equipment from the Dead Zone ride to the one of the carts on the Ferris wheel . . . for fifty bucks. Now I just had to get Mr. Sullivan on it.

"Mr. Sullivan, I really need to speak with you!"

"What is it?" he asked, turning on me. "I'm busy."

I exhaled hard. "I thought you might like to go for a ride with me? On the Ferris wheel?"

"*That sounded weird, Erica*," Freddie whispered in my earbud. "*I told you we should have practiced.*"

"That's lovely for you to offer." I could tell by his expression he thought it was weird too. "But as I've said, I'm busy."

"But I really need to talk to you."

"Not right now."

"*Erica? Are you getting on? I don't think he can hold*

the cart much longer." I spotted Rex standing on the platform at the base of the wheel. He had stopped the line.

"Mr. Sullivan, please," I begged, reaching for his arm. "It's a matter of life and death."

Suddenly someone stepped in front of me, forcing me to drop my arm . . . someone with a really large chest . . . and a badge.

"Life and death, huh? I'd love to hear all about it."

Say hello to tricky point number three.

I closed my eyes. "Grady."

"You know, there was a time," he said, scratching his brow, "not too long ago when you said my name with affection and not like it was a four-letter word."

"*Get rid of him!*" Freddie shouted.

"Grady, this really isn't—"

"A good time? I'm sure it's not." He planted his hands on his hips. "What's going on, Erica?"

I couldn't lie anymore . . . but I couldn't tell him either! I rose up on my toes and looked over his shoulder. Oh no. Mr. Sullivan had caught up to Matthew and his mother, and . . . she looked kind of uncomfortable. Not guilty uncomfortable. But the kind of uncomfortable that comes from having to stand too close to someone creepy. Frick.

"Okay," Grady said, taking a breath. "Why don't we start with an easier question. Where's Freddie?"

"*Don't look over here,*" Freddie said quickly. "*Don't look over—Gah! You looked over here.*"

Grady tracked my gaze then swore under his breath. "Tell me what you're planning."

"Grady, I would, but . . . you'll probably think you'll have to stop it for some legal reason, but you don't! Promise. And I swear to you this is our best, maybe only chance to clear the twins."

"Tell me."

I moaned, rising up on my toes again to look again over his shoulder at Sully.

"Listen," Grady snapped, grabbing my attention back. "I know you told Rhonda to look into who came by the prison. And it just so happens that one of those people was Mr. Sullivan. The same Mr. Sullivan that you are trying desperately to get on that Ferris wheel. I don't believe this is a coincidence, Erica."

I pulled my lips between my teeth.

"Nor do I believe," he said with a sharp point at the side of my head, "that that earbud you are wearing is a hearing aid."

I opened my mouth to say something, but nothing came out.

Grady inhaled slowly then said, "Did you ever stop to think, Erica, that maybe I wanted to help? That maybe I could help?"

"Grady, I—Matthew!" I lurched past Grady to one side to grab his arm. He was walking past us . . . without his mother. "Wait!"

I glanced back up at Grady. Crap. He looked . . . *something*, but there was no time to think about that.

"Where's your mother?"

"My mother?" Matthew asked with a smile. "She's taking a ride on the wheel with Mr. Sullivan. The paper wanted a picture."

"Mr. Sullivan?"

"*Uh-oh*," Freddie said in my ear. "*That wasn't the plan.*"

"Yeah, he practically knocked me over trying to get to—Hey! Erica! Where are you—"

I dodged past Matthew, launching into a sprint.

"Erica! We're not done here!" I heard Grady call.

I ran to the metal fence, planted a hand on the railing, and hopped over.

"Hey!" someone shouted. "Boobsie Bloom's cutting the line."

"Really?" I shouted over my shoulder. "Really?"

"*Erica! What are you doing?*" Freddie yelled.

I ran up the few platform steps to Rex.

"I tried to hold it for you—" I pushed past him and hopped into the next pod that was slowly pulling past the platform. "Hey! You can't get on when it's moving!"

"Too late!" Once inside, I gripped the sidewalls and craned my neck to see up to the cart above. *Shoot*! I couldn't see a thing. Damn these newfangled Ferris wheel carts with their high safety walls.

"*Um, Erica,*" Freddie said in my ear. "*I'm going to ask again. What are you doing?*"

"Mrs. Masterson got on the ride with Mr. Sullivan! She's in danger."

"*And you're what?*" Freddie asked. "*Chasing after them?*"

"I . . ." I suddenly stopped and looked around at my cart.

"*No, really,*" Freddie added. "*Good work. Keep going. You've almost got them.*"

"Oh, shut up," I said, collapsing into the seat. "I panicked. She shouldn't be up there with him!" I gestured to nobody.

"*Well, on the bright side, you might be interested to know that I've changed my opinion about you and Grady.*"

"You have?"

"*Yup, you're made for each other.*"

"Why? Why would you say that?"

"*Look down below.*"

I stood up, gripping the sides of the cart. I bent over to look down . . . and there was Grady, looking up at me in a cart all his own.

"*Watch out, Erica,*" Freddie said drily. "*I think he's gaining on you.*"

Chapter Forty-nine

"Erica!" Grady shouted up. "I told you we are not done talking!"

Well . . . at least I had finally gotten him on the Ferris wheel.

"Freddie?" I slumped down into the seat of the cart as the wheel took me higher. "Get Rex to stop the ride when Mrs. Masterson makes the next pass. It's off . . . the whole thing is off. It's too risky."

"No. No. No. Not yet. Don't you see, Erica? This is even better. I'm looking at them right now," Freddie said. *"Sully's about to burst. He's going to confess. I can see it on his face. We just need to hang on."*

"Really?"

"Swear to God."

"No, it's too dangerous, and you should have seen Mrs. Masterson's face when he came up to her. I don't think she was in on it."

"Erica, he's not going to hurt her. In his mind he must believe that everything he does is for her."

"Said every stalker ever."

"Well . . . point taken. But don't you see? It's like an act of God."

I shook my head. *Yeah, God*, I thought, darting a glance over to the evil jack-o'-lantern overlooking our town. I let out a shaky breath. This could be our only chance to exonerate the twins . . . but it was never the plan to put someone else in danger. "I don't kn—"

"Wait! Hush, they're talking!"

My eyes flashed up to the bottom of the cart. "What are they saying?"

"Okay. Okay. It's nice to see you, Martin. How have you been?" Freddie relayed quickly. *"Oh my*—Olivia, darling, you don't have to pretend. We're alone."*

I pinched my lips together, waiting for more. When it didn't come, I said, "Freddie! Keep going—"

"They're not saying anything! He's just looking at her like—Wait!" Another moment passed, then Freddie said in his Mrs. Masterson voice, "I'm afraid I don't understand."

"Everything we've always wanted, Olivia. Everything we have waited for. It's here. You're free of that man. That lying, cheating—" Freddie gasped.

"What! What!"

"She slapped him! Oh my God—You will not speak of my husband that way," Freddie finished back in the dignified feminine voice—which suddenly sounded a little southern.

"Oh Freddie," I moaned. We were coming to the ground again. "Tell Rex to stop the ride."

"He's almost there Erica! He's going to confess!"

"Freddie—"

"Listen! After all I've done for you. Mick. Your father . . ." Freddie said, then switched to Olivia's voice. "You . . . you killed them!" He switched again. "For you! It was all for you!"

"That's it, Freddie! That's enough! We've got to—"

"*Okay, you're right,*" Freddie said quickly. "*Rex, stop— Rex?*"

"Freddie?"

"*Rex is gone. He's gone!*"

"What do you mean, *gone*?" I slid to the side of my cart just as it was swooping past the platform. Freddie was alone in the little booth. "Where did he go?"

"*I don't know! Rex?*"

"Erica!" Grady called out. "What's going on?"

"Nothing good," I shouted back. "Freddie, what's happening with Mrs. Masterson?"

"*He's not happy, Erica. Not happy at all.* You lied to me. You led me to believe . . . *She's saying she has no idea what he's talking about.*" He switched to his female voice. "I never meant for you to think that we were anything more than friends." Freddie stopped talking a moment, then I heard, "*Hey . . . what are you doing in here?*"

"Freddie?" I shouted. "Who are you talking to?"

Then just as we were swooping back up to the top of the arch . . . the Ferris wheel jerked to a stop with a trailing *Peeeeuuuwww* sound, lights clicking off.

"Freddie?" I asked, clutching the sides of the cart.

"*Hey! What are—get back here!*"

I put my knees up on the hard seat of the cart and twisted over the backrest to see what was happening.

"Freddie? Talk to me."

"*Erica! It's the pumpkin people.*" Freddie's voice was all jumpy . . . and the sound was cracking up, like . . . like he was running! "*One of them took the key to the Ferris wheel!*"

"What! Well, get it back!"

"*I'm trying. I—*"

Suddenly my earbud crackled into static.

My eyes darted over the ground below. Nothing . . .

nothing . . . nothing. There! I spotted Freddie running after someone. A pumpkin person!

My eyes snapped back up to the cart above me. Dammit! I couldn't see anything!

"Grady!" I yelled, leaning over. "Call Rhonda. The fire department! Everybody! We got a situation up there!"

"What?"

"I think Mr. Sullivan—"

Just then Mrs. Masterson's scream pierced the air.

"Help! He's going to kill me!"

Chapter Fifty

Crap! Crap! *Crap!* I looked up. The entire cart was shaking.

He was going to kill her . . . and it was our fault. Maybe if we had just gone to Grady with our suspicions. Maybe if—

Mrs. Masterson screamed again, but the sound was cut short. I strained to listen. Was that . . . coughing? No! She was gagging.

Oh God! He was probably strangling her!

My eyes flashed back down to Grady. He was yelling into his walkie-talkie.

Help would never get here in time.

I took another look up, but I knew I was just delaying. It was pretty clear what I had to do.

I gripped the sidewalls of my cart before getting to my feet. I then turned and stepped up onto my seat, reaching up and pressing my hand against the underside of the canopy roof of my pod for balance as the cart dipped down with my weight. I slid my fingers to the edge of the roof, found a grip, and put one foot onto the top of the wall that formed the seats.

"Erica!" I heard Grady shout. "Tell me that is not your foot I'm seeing!"

I grunted and brought my other foot up—my pod swinging wildly beneath my feet. I gripped the roof tightly and waited for the cart to stop swinging, my eyes darting around.

Some strange part of my brain was thinking it was almost fitting that the last thing I would ever see was the town and lake all aglow with the carnival lights. And hey! I was finally living in the moment . . . and it was terrifying!

"Erica!" Grady's voice came again. "Get down!"

"She's in trouble," I shouted back. "He's going to kill her."

Mrs. Masterson screamed again just then as though to prove my point.

"I'm coming up after you!"

"No! Grady! Don't touch my cart! I'll fall!"

"Dammit, Erica!"

I stretched one hand farther across the top of the canopy roof, feeling around for anything I could use to pull myself up. Nothing. Crap! I flashed my eyes around at the other carts. It looked like there was a long metal rod that attached each pod to the wheel . . . but it ran right down the middle of the roof. I couldn't reach it. I looked around again. Maybe if I could somehow push myself up a little higher . . .

I reached my foot out to the scaffolding of the ride. If I planted my foot just right on the metal beam of the wheel and pushed off, I might be able to get enough leverage to heave myself up to the bar running across the roof of my cart.

I slowly side-shuffled along the top of the cart, then lifted my one foot off the ledge.

"Erica!" Grady shouted. "Don't you even think it!"

I planted my foot against a beam and tested my weight.

"Erica!"

I took a breath. *Okay, one . . . two . . . three!*

I pushed hard against the enormous spoke with my foot—hearing Grady shout—launching myself up and over.

Got it!

I scrambled on to the top of the roof.

Oh, thank God.

I lay flat on my belly for a moment with my eyes closed before I peeked up at the cart above me. The screaming had stopped, but the cart was still shaking.

"I'm coming, Mrs. Masterson!" I yelled, pushing myself up to all fours. "Hang on!"

I brought one foot up . . . then the other until I was resting in a low squat. Oooh, I did not like that feeling at all. Thankfully, because they were above me, they were farther out on the wheel, which meant if I stood up, right in the middle of my pod, where the balance was the best, I should be able to reach the back lip of theirs.

"Please, Erica! Stop!" Grady called out again, pleading in his voice. "Help is on its way! You don't have to do this!"

"I have to, Grady. I suspected it was him! And I didn't tell you!"

I pushed slowly up through the heels of my feet . . . one hand reaching up for balance . . .

Once I was standing, I looked over to the cart above me. Sully had Mrs. Masterson by the neck, her back pinned against the seat, the edge of their pod tilting toward me.

"I did everything!" he shouted. "Everything was for you!"

"Hey! Sully!" I shouted.

Mr. Sullivan snapped his face to mine, features twisted in manic rage.

"Let her go!"

Mr. Sullivan looked at me as though he couldn't believe what I was doing. Me! At least I wasn't killing someone!

"This ends now," he said. "I can't take anymore." He pushed Mrs. Masterson farther over the edge of the cart. Her arms flew back over the wall to the side.

I reached into my pocket and pulled out the Taser. The Taser that Freddie had insisted I bring . . . when we'd thought I'd be the one in the cart with Mr. Sullivan . . .

I flicked it on. The little machine hummed to life.

I could do this. Her hand was right there. I'd give it to her then drop back down. That's all. I could do this . . .

"Mrs. Masterson!" I screamed, reaching for her hand. "Taser!"

I felt her fingers close around the small weapon as Sully lunged forward—his hand landing on my shoulder—

"Erica! No!"

—pushing me back into nothingness.

Chapter Fifty-one

"So, did you see the cover of this morning's paper?" Freddie asked, pushing open the door to my hospital room.

"Where the hell have you been?"

"Whoa," he said stopping dead in his tracks. "That is one serious cast."

"It's not a cast." I looked down at the thick fabric contraption that was covering my arm, pinning it to my chest. "Nothing's broken. A couple of things are torn, though. It's just to keep my shoulder immobilized, so it doesn't pop out again."

"Ugh, that's terrible," Freddie said. "But we have much more important matters to discuss."

"Yeah we do," I said, pushing myself up with my good hand. "Like what the hell happened to you last night?"

"Not that," Freddie said. "This." He tossed the newspaper he was holding over to me. I instinctively moved my hurt right arm to pin it to my lap. Pain rocketed from my shoulder up to my neck. "Oh shoot! Frick! Nutballs!"

"What are you doing?" Freddie asked. "I thought you weren't supposed to move it!"

I gritted my teeth and shot him a glare.

"Sorry," he said, wrinkling his nose. "But look at it!"

I tilted the paper up with my left hand so I could see the headline.

"Holy crap . . . they got a picture. I mean . . . I saw the photographer but . . ."

I let the paper drop to my lap and looked up at the ceiling. "I think I'm going to be sick." My mind flashed back to that horrible, nauseating feeling of Mr. Sullivan pushing me back . . . back off the roof of the cart . . . back into the air . . .

"Sick?" Freddie shouted, snapping me out of the memory. "Why would you be sick? This is awesome! This changes everything!"

I tilted the paper up, trying to keep my eyes from the picture that showed my legs dangling in the air from Grady's cart. The headline ran, HERO SHERIFF SNATCHES FALLING WOMAN FROM FERRIS WHEEL.

"It's making the national news," Freddie added. "My parents saw it online! I told them you were one of my employees. They were suitably impressed, so I don't think I'll be moving anytime soon, and Rhonda told me that the morning talk shows are already calling." He was on a roll now. "I mean, we'll have to massage the narrative. A better headline would have been SHERIFF ASSISTS OTTER LAKE SECURITY EMPLOYEE IN STOPPING MURDER, or better yet OTTER LAKE SECURITY EMPLOYEE STOPS MURDER ASSISTED BY SHERIFF."

"Freddie." I put up a hand. "I get it."

"I think Grady will be pleased, though, now that he's got his small-town-hero slash quarterback slash Prince Charming card back." Freddie picked up the paper again and squinted at the photo. "He does kind of look like a brown-haired Thor."

I put my free hand over my face.

In the moment when I had lost my footing, I had been certain I was going to die. In hindsight, I couldn't help but think it would have been nice if my entire life had flashed before my eyes—well, at least the good parts—but it had all happened so fast. . Thankfully, some part of me knew to reach out as I fell . . . and I had caught the lip of Grady's cart right under my arm. It only slowed me for a fraction of a second, but it was long enough for Grady to grab my arm . . .

I've got you. Hang on, baby. I've got you.

"What?" Freddie asked, snapping me back into the moment. "The near-death thing getting to you?"

I nodded, closing my eyes.

I'm not letting you go. Not ever. Not anymore.

"I know what will cheer you up."

I peeked through my fingers.

"Kit Kat's awake."

"What?"

"And she's feeling *feisty*," he said. "She ordered a pizza to her room, but I hear she's not sharing until someone goes on a beer run."

"Really?"

Freddie nodded. "I already showed her the paper. You are in lots of trouble."

"That's wonderful," I said, feeling the tears come to my eyes. "And Tweety?"

"Already let her go."

"And Mrs. Masterson?" I asked. "Mr. Sullivan?"

"Recovering . . . and jailed," Freddie said, ticking off boxes in the air. "His heart stood up to the shock, so you're not a killer."

"I want to go see Kit Kat," I said moving to push myself up with my good hand. Pain gripped my chest. Apparently I had a cracked rib too.

"You can't." Freddie flopped into the chair by my bed. "The nurse is with her. She said she'd come get us when she's done."

I settled back against the pillow. "Okay, well, that will give us time to talk."

Freddie brought his thumb to his mouth and started chewing on the side of the nail. "Sure," he mumbled. "About what?"

I slapped the bed. "About what happened to you last night!"

He looked out the window.

"Freddie?"

He pinched his lips together and shook his head.

"Look, I nearly died last night—"

"I feel really bad about that. I do," he said. "Even if the publicity is awesome."

"Then tell me."

"I don't want to," he said quickly. "You won't believe me."

"This is ridiculous." I took a really good look at his face. He hadn't looked that pale a moment ago . . . or sweaty. "You look like you have seen a ghost."

His face dropped. "How did you—"

Just then the door to my room opened. "You can see her now."

Freddie and I whipped our heads around.

The nurse, standing in the doorway, repeated a little more uncertainly, "You can see her now?"

"We'll be right there," Freddie answered quickly.

I shot him a look. "This isn't over."

After getting lost a few times, we finally found Kit Kat's room. Tweety was already inside.

"Well, well, well, if it isn't Frick and Frack, Detective Edition," Kit Kat croaked from her bed. "Pizza?" She patted the box beside her.

I waved her off but returned her smile.

Tweety planted a hand on the armrest of her chair to turn and face us. "Rhonda tells me you worked pretty hard to get yourself killed last night, Erica."

"She the one who dropped you off?" I asked, sitting down on the edge of the bed.

She nodded. "Also told me we have you two to thank for getting ol' Sully to expose himself."

Her sister snorted.

"Not exactly," I muttered. "He beat us to the punch."

Freddie swatted me, but at least it was on the good arm. "Why do you always have to do that?"

"What?"

"Last time it was all *We didn't technically solve the murder.*"

I peered up at Freddie. "Is that my voice you're doing right now? 'Cause I don't think I sound like that."

"And now you're all *He beat us to the punch,*" Freddie said, waving his hands in the air then letting them drop with disgust. "I'm trying to run a business here."

"As I was saying," I said, turning back to the twins. "I'm just glad I was there for Mrs. Masterson. Then again, we probably should have told Grady our suspicions right away and maybe—"

"Quibbling!" Freddie shouted.

"So now that Sully's confessed to Mr. Masterson's, Mr. Clarke's, and Mr. Ramsbottom's murders, I guess—"

"Mr. Ramsbottom?" the twins asked in unison.

"Uh-huh," I said, glaring at Tweety. "You heard me. Confessed."

Tweety wasn't looking at me, though. She was looking at Kit Kat—and Kit Kat back at her, identical expressions on their faces.

"I thought you—"

"I thought you—"

"Wait . . ." Tweety said, pointing at her sister. "You thought *I* killed Mr. Ramsbottom?" She swung the finger around to point at her own chest. "Why would I kill him? You were the one sleeping with him!"

"Sleeping with him!" Kit Kat yelled. "That old goat?"

"You were always sneaking off with him! I thought you killed him in some sort of lovers' quarrel."

"What! Lovers' quarrel, my heinie. I've yet to meet the man worth killing for," she said, grimacing. She then sat up a little in the bed. "I was trying to help you save your relationship with Mick! I knew how much you loved him. I thought Mr. Ramsbottom was paying him to date his daughter."

"No," I corrected, jumping in. "Mr. Ramsbottom didn't want Olivia with Mick either."

"Huh," she said, furrowing her brow. "You know, I remember him being pretty ticked that day when I told him it was a cheap shot to buy Mick a new car. He didn't say much, but . . . he must have figured out Olivia had done it."

Tweety planted her hands on the arms of her chair and straightened herself up. "And what would make you think that I would want to be with a man who could be bought off anyway?"

"I don't know," Kit Kat shouted back. "I never understood what you saw in Mick in the first place, but it bugged me that they thought they could interfere with all their money. I was just trying to get to the bottom of everything that day when he died." She gasped . . . which made her cough for a moment. "You know, come to think of it, I remember little Sully sulking around that tent—"

"And wait a minute . . . why would you think I killed him?" Tweety yelled.

"Obviously because he was buying Mick off!"

"Well, I'll be," Tweety said, shaking her head. "And to think I spent all those years living with you, taking care of you, watching you . . . all because I didn't want you going off and killing someone else."

"Me?" Kit Kat shrieked. "I've been doing that for you!"

"Please," Tweety muttered.

"I had to!" Kit Kat yelled, flopping her hands on the bed. "Mother made me promise her on her deathbed to take care of you. It was always, *Take care of your sister, she's not like you . . . might be a little touched*," she said, eyes lost in memory but tapping the side of her head with her finger.

"She always said that to me!"

Freddie leaned over to me. "This is hilarious," he whispered. "Better than bingo."

"Why would she say that to you?" Kit Kat shot back. "I mean, between the two of us, I'm clearly the stable one."

"Stable one? Stable one! You thought you were living with a murderer all these years." Tweety scoffed. "That's hardly stable."

"So did you!"

Both women suddenly stopped yelling and just looked at each other for a moment . . . before their bellies started to shake. A moment later laughter erupted.

"You know I've never noticed it before," Freddie said, leaning down again to my ear, "but the twins . . . they can be kind of creepy."

I nodded.

"I'm glad I'm not living on an island with them."

I looked at him with big eyes. "Right?"

"Erica," Tweety said, grabbing my attention back. "I want you to know something. I mean, we want you to know something." She looked at her sister, who nodded. "I . . . I'm not good with words but . . . well, your mother's always saying you were the best thing that ever happened to her, and we want you to know . . ." She pinched her lips together and shook her head.

My throat suddenly felt tight.

Kit Kat squeezed her sister's hand. "What my sister is trying to say is that you and your mother . . . well, you two are the best things that have ever happened to us."

I took a shaky breath and nodded.

"You did a good job too, Ng," she said, looking at Freddie. "Thank you."

I heard him mumble something like, *Yeah, no problem*, but it had a definite sniff at the end.

"Okay," Tweety said, clapping her hands. "Enough of all that. Who's going to go on that beer run? I could really use a drink."

Chapter Fifty-two

I spent the rest of the day in the hospital and then the next back home at the retreat. My mother was officially done with her Silence of the Soul vow, and all of the guests had gone home. She kept up the silence, though, for the reporters who kept calling. They didn't know quite what to do with it, so they eventually gave up. My uncle Jack had left too. We promised to stay in touch. He invited me to come visit anytime I wanted, so I could learn more about our family. I told him I just might take him up on that.

I was planning on staying another day or two even though it might get me in more trouble at work. I just couldn't see managing the bus with all the pain. I had already missed more work than I had scheduled off, and given that I had received a message from my boss saying that we needed to talk when I got in, I was guessing I had some disciplinary action coming. At least the sling on my arm might buy me some sympathy.

The big issue holding me back, however, was Grady. Always Grady. We still hadn't talked . . . and I couldn't see leaving without saying good-bye. But I just couldn't seem to call him either. What had passed between us on that

Ferris wheel had been intense, but I also worried, in a strange way, that it might mean the end for us. Especially seeing as he hadn't called me either.

When I woke up the next morning, much to my delighted surprise, I found that my mother had bought coffee for me. Organic, free-trade coffee.

I peeked out the kitchen window while it was brewing. Frost had brushed the grass overnight, but it looked sunny enough. When it was ready, I poured myself a cup, threw on a jacket over my sling, and walked out onto the porch . . .

. . . only to find a man crouched there.

"Matthew?"

"Morning," he replied, looking up from where he had knelt to scratch Caesar's many chins. "Your mom's cat is awesome."

"Yeah," I said. "He's not that great."

Matthew looked up at me again.

"He's the favorite. We have issues."

He chuckled, brushed the fur from his hands, and rose to his feet. "How's your arm?"

"Getting better," I said, taking a sip of coffee. Mmm, social justice coffee did taste better than regular. "Do you want some?"

"No. No," he replied. "I just heard you might be leaving soon, and I wanted to come by."

"Right," I answered with a smile. A moment passed. "To say good-bye?"

"Yes," he said, stepping closer, "but I also wanted to say thank you."

"Really?"

"Well yeah, it probably sounds funny given everything that's happened—the grave digging in particular comes to mind—but you have really helped me since I got home."

"I have?"

He shoved his hands in his pockets and nodded. "I'm

still trying to process all my feelings about my father's death . . . but talking to you really helped."

He looked like he wanted to say more, so I waited.

"I meant it when I said that all of Freddie's and your antics . . . kind of left me feeling a little less crazy." He shook his head and squeezed his eyes shut. "That doesn't sound right."

"It sounds fine." I would have reached out to touch his arm, but my one hand was holding the coffee and the other was in the sling. "Really."

"I also wanted to let you know that I've let go of any hope for, well, you and me," Matthew said, squinting and looking out to the trees—just the slightest hint of flirtatiousness in his expression.

"Oh really?"

"Grady did save your life after all." He shrugged. "I mean really, it's not enough he looks like . . . who? Thor? He has to *be* a hero too?" Matthew sighed. "I can't compete with that." He flashed me a smile. "Not even with a castle . . . with a really big turret." He froze. "That sounded less weird in my head."

I smiled back at him. "Well, I appreciate you letting me know our status." I sighed, looking out at the lake. "But I don't know about Grady and me getting back together. You see, he has these serious issues with my breaking the law . . . and putting my life in danger. And I think maybe what happened on the Ferris wheel really drove those issues home."

"By the look on your face, though, I can see that you're not happy about it."

"What can I say? Those first loves—"

"—are a killer," Matthew finished. "You can be honest, though. You like the whole brooding-sheriff thing with all the complicated issues standing between you two being together. Although I could have him beat there, you know, with *our* issues," he said, moving his hand back and forth between us.

"Our issues?"

"You did nearly get my mother killed."

"About that. I am so sorry—"

"Could you imagine what Thanksgiving would be like?"

"Matthew!"

"My guess is awkward." He held my gaze for a moment then laughed. "I'm kidding. I'm thankful that you helped expose my father's killer. So is she. You nearly died saving her." He looked me in the eye as though to show me his sincerity, but then looked away when the emotion got to be too much. "It's funny. They let me watch the recording from the Ferris wheel . . . she still loves him. Despite the fact that he wanted to leave her to be with Tweety. She *still* loves him. Well, in her own way."

I nodded.

"I don't understand it," he said, crossing his arms over his chest, "but then again, I'm not sure I want to."

"Love can be complicated."

"That it can." He looked at me and gave me a sad smile. "Well, I guess on that note, I will take my leave."

"Oh, okay," I said, clutching my coffee, mainly because I was resisting the urge to put it down and give him a hug, which probably wasn't—Oh, what the hell? I put my coffee on the porch floor and reached out with my good arm to pull him in for a hug. He slipped his arms around me and pulled me in lightly, so as not to hurt me. Goose bumps ran wild over my body. Probably just the cold.

"You know," Matthew whispered in my ear. "You don't have to give me some big good-bye."

I pulled back—which meant my face was just inches from his. "I don't?"

We stayed in the closeness just a moment longer before

Matthew cleared his throat and stepped back. "Just say hello on your next visit."

"What?"

"My mom's moving down to Florida to live with her cousins. Too many memories here, I guess. So I'm moving into Hemlock Estate. Apparently it is still legally ours, seeing as my grandfather never actually changed his will."

"You are?"

"It needs some work," he said, stepping farther away from me and closer to the stairs. "And I've always loved the place." He dropped down onto the step. "I can work from anywhere really."

"Oh well," I said, bending to retrieve my coffee, "in that case, I guess I'll see you around."

He held his hand up in the air while his eyes trailed over my face. "See you around, Erica."

I watched Matthew walk the gravel path toward the steps that led down to lake, one hand in his pocket.

Wow. I just could not stop looking at that man's pants.

"So there I was on this glorious astral plane of existence, and I could feel Kit Kat's spirit calling me, so I floated in my ethereal form toward her energy, wrapping her in the love and vitality of all the guests who had devoted their time and energy to her healing, and—"

"She hasn't stopped talking for twenty minutes straight," Freddie muttered under his breath.

I nodded. "It's like this every time."

Freddie had decided to come over for dinner . . . which I was pretty grateful for. I couldn't listen to my mother all by myself. I didn't have enough ears. We had come out to sit on the porch after dinner to watch the sun go down. It was dropping pretty fast . . . probably to get a break from her too.

"Erica was there," my mother went on. "Pacing. And—"

"On the astral plane?" Freddie asked.

"Of course."

I closed my eyes. "No, I wasn't."

"Anyway, you were there," my mother continued. "But your bangs were back from your face, allowing your true beauty to shine through, and I know that's what saved Kit Kat's life. It's—"

"Wait, Erica's beauty saved Kit Kat's life?" Freddie asked, way too much shock in his voice.

"No," my mother laughed, "the beauty of us all. It was a truly miraculous experience. More than I have ever experienced before. I think I need to write it down. I've never actually penned a book before, but many guests have asked me to. I believe I do need to share this experience with others, so that they can—"

"Dessert?" Freddie asked, desperation tinging his voice. "Is there dessert?"

"Of course," my mother said, getting to her feet and moving to the door. "Let me see what I can rustle up. I know I have carob and rice flour. Perhaps some maple syrup, but I don't want to disrupt our systems too much with the sugar. I also have . . ." Her voice faded into the depths of the retreat.

Freddie mouthed the words, *Oh my God*, without turning to look at me.

"I tried to warn you."

We sat for a just moment in silence before I said, "So . . ." Freddie had been avoiding me too since the hospital. Well, at least avoiding being alone with me. Probably because he knew I was going to ask, "Feel like telling me a ghost story?"

He sighed and took a long sip from his bottle.

"Come on. You need to tell me what happened before

my mother comes back and talks us into another astral plane."

He tapped the mouth of his bottle against the armrest of his chair while biting his lip.

"You need to tell someone."

He shook his head.

"Freddie, you know you can trust m—"

"Fine!" he shouted, sending some startled birds into the air. He then inhaled a breath, held it a moment, and let it go. "But so help me, if you make fun of this . . ."

"I won't. I swear to God." I put my swearing hand in the air . . . along with my beer.

"All right, so how much did you see from the Ferris wheel?"

"Well, I saw you chase the kids into the maze after Rex disappeared."

"Yeah, turns out one of them—I'm thinking Bret Michaels, don't even get me started on his parents naming him that—paid Rex twenty bucks to leave me in the booth. Which, I guess, means it's true what they say . . ."

I raised an eyebrow.

"Carnie friends aren't forever friends."

"Nobody says that," I said, watching the sun dip into the lake. "So what happened after that?"

"Well, you would have been proud of me," Freddie said. "Even though I was surrounded by pumpkin people, I wasn't freaked out. I knew it was the kids because really only teenage boys wear that much body spray."

"Okay."

"But after a minute or two in there . . . things started to get weird."

"Weird how?" I asked, pulling up the blanket I had draped over my knees. The temperature was really dropping with the setting sun.

"They were all shouting and running. They were so fast. They'd zoom past an entrance . . . brush right by me!" Freddie flashed his beer hand in front of his face, spilling a few drops. "Then they were gone! I got disoriented, lost . . . it was all so confusing."

A crow cawed just then, making me jump.

"Then this cold mist settled in . . . and everything got quiet. I felt like I had slipped into another realm . . . an alternate reality . . . filled with nightmares."

I chuckled. "Freddie, I—"

"Zip it!" he hissed. "You're going to miss the good part." He took another breath then continued, "So suddenly I found myself in the middle of the maze, and everything went quiet. The boys had disappeared. I was all alone. Actually, no . . . it wasn't completely quiet. There was a scream in the distance."

"Yeah, that was probably me."

"But I was all alone—" He paused, letting his eyes drift with the memory before shooting them back to me. "—and then I wasn't!"

"What are you talking about?"

Freddie held up a hand, wiggling his fingers. "I felt something . . . someone at my back."

"Come on," I said, ignoring the chills suddenly running up my arms.

"I'm serious, Erica," Freddie said. "Part of me knew I had to turn around. I had to face it, but I was frozen— paralyzed with fear! Do you know what that feels like, Erica?"

"Yeah, Freddie, I kind of do. Remember the Ferris wheel—"

"Shush! My story," he said with a point. "So I waited . . . hoping the feeling would disappear . . . but it didn't. I knew the *presence* was still there. I could feel its breath on my neck."

"What! Freddie . . ."

"But it was cold breath . . . the breath of the dead."

I leaned a little away from him. "So what happened?"

"Well, I don't know how long I stood there. I couldn't move . . . yet somehow I also knew that if I didn't move, do something, I was going to die."

"So what did you do?"

"Nothing," Freddie said, turning his body completely around to look at me, "until it touched me."

I felt my eyes go wide.

"Fingers Erica . . . icy-cold fingers crept over my shoulder and—"

"And what?"

"I spun around, and—POW!" Freddie said, punching his own palm.

"You did what? Freddie!" I yelled, scooting up in my seat. "It was probably just a kid!"

"Okay, maybe it wasn't *pow*. I just kind of lashed out . . . a flail really. Seriously, what would you have done if you turned to see a pumpkin person staring you in the face?"

"Still, Freddie—"

"Let me finish, you who are suddenly so concerned for the youth of this town," he muttered.

"Well, you can't go around flailing out at teenagers."

"This was not a teenager," Freddie said. "Or at least, no mortal one."

I swallowed and waited for him to continue.

"So when I felt that hand on my shoulder, I whipped around and my hand shot out before I even knew what I was doing—right into the rotten folds of that huge pumpkin face!"

My hand flew to my mouth. "Oh my God."

"And when those wet pumpkin pieces settled . . ." he said, stopping to take a sip of beer.

"When the pumpkin pieces settled what?"

"There was nothing there . . ."

"What do you mean, *nothing*?"

"I mean, the body fell to the ground, but there was no head. It wasn't a person in a mask, Erica. It was a ghost," he said huskily, "and I killed it."

My jaw dropped a moment . . . it snapped it back up . . . then dropped again.

"That's right, Erica. It was already dead . . . or maybe it was never even alive." Freddie took another sip. "Kind of like your relationship with Grady."

I hurled a splash of beer in Freddie's direction.

"Hey!" he said, flinging his arms out. "Okay, well, I might have deserved that."

"I've got brownies!" my mother called out.

"Oh God," Freddie murmured. "Please let them be the special kind."

Chapter Fifty-three

The next morning, I got up early and went into town to look for Grady. I thought about calling him again for the thousandth time, but an apology only seemed right in person. I hadn't trusted him . . . and I should have. That mistake had almost cost Mrs. Masterson her life. It had almost cost me mine. I didn't think I could say the words without seeing him . . . without being able to look him in the eye. I went to his house, and then the station, but I couldn't find him.

I pushed leaving back as long as I could, but it was time to go. I had to stop by the retreat to say good-bye to my mother before Freddie dropped me off at the closest dock to the bus stop on the other side of the lake. I'd just call Grady from Chicago. He was obviously trying to avoid me . . . which didn't surprise me all that much. What had happened at the Ferris wheel had been harrowing, and I was willing to bet once all the adrenaline had died down, he had remembered that I was the one who had put myself in all that danger. We both probably needed some time to think about what we wanted to say.

I climbed into Freddie's boat docked at the marina and

sat in the passenger's seat. I brought my fingers to my mouth to blow some warm air on them. Man, it was getting cold. Freddie was supposed to meet me here any minute. I looked around the boat to see if maybe he had left his jacket when I heard, "Erica!"

I froze. I knew that *Erica*.

My head snapped up.

And there he was . . . Grady, trotting across the marina parking lot, hand in the air.

I jumped to my feet and eased out of the boat using my good hand for balance. I walked back down the long dock, shaking the nerves out of my fingers. My heart was beating so loudly I could barely hear.

When I got closer to the end, I had to sidestep two men I recognized but couldn't quite remember the names of. They nodded before heading off on one of the dock's branches. Just before they got out of range, I heard one of the men say, "Yeah, someone tore apart my wife's scarecrow in the corn maze if you can believe it."

"Really?"

"Looked like it had been punched in the face," the first man said. "She worked on that thing for two weeks."

I stopped and looked back at them, catching, "Kids. You should tell Sheriff Forrester. He'll get to the bottom of it."

I chuckled, shaking my head as I approached Grady.

"What's that smile for?"

"Oh," I said. "I was just eavesdropping." I tilted my head in the direction of the two men. "They were just talking about what a great sheriff this town has."

Grady smiled and looked down to his feet.

"Must feel good."

He peered up at me from under his hat. "Doesn't feel bad." He took a step closer. "I'm so glad I found you. How's the arm?" he asked, reaching out his fingertips to brush the fabric of the brace.

"Better," I said. "You know, a dislocated shoulder's a small price to pay."

"I keep going over and over it in my head. I wish I had caught you around the waist or—"

"Grady," I said, reaching out to touch his arm. "You saved my life."

He sighed. "I wanted to talk to you. I've been doing a lot of thinking and—"

"I wanted to talk to you, Grady. I need to apologize. You were right. I've got trust issues, and—"

Before I realized what was happening, Grady stepped forward, closing the distance between us, and slid both hands behind the back of my neck. His fingertips ran up into my hair as he pulled me in for a kiss.

A few glorious moments later, he pulled away.

If he hadn't been there to steady me, I would have fallen into the water.

"Now, that is a much better first kiss," Grady said quietly. "Let's just forget the last one."

I blinked a few times then mumbled, "What was that for?"

"Stay."

"I'm sorry?" I asked, trying to catch a rhythm with my breath.

"Stay."

"I have to—" I looked behind me back at *Lightning*, trying to remember what it was I had to do. "—the bus. I'm going to miss it."

"No, you don't."

I blew out some air. "Okay, I don't know what's going on right now, but the way you keep saying that . . . with that look in your eye . . . it's making it really hard for me to think straight. What exactly do you mean—"

"I mean *stay*."

"I know we should talk," I said, shaking my head. "But

Freddie's going to be here any minute to take me to the bus stop. I have to get back to work—"

"No, I don't mean for just right now. I mean, stay," he said, pointing to the ground. "Here. In Otter Lake."

"What?"

"Erica," he said, pushing his hat up on his head. "What happened on that Ferris wheel. I nearly lost you . . . and it brought a lot of things into really clear focus."

"Grady, we can't. You can't . . ." I grabbed my forehead, like that would help me think. This was all happening so fast.

"I want to be with you Erica. All the time."

"No," I said. "No, you don't mean that. You're just saying that because—" I snapped my fingers. "It's just like what they say in that movie about couples getting together because of intense experiences. It never works."

"Erica, I don't care what the movie says."

I pointed at him. "You gotta stop looking at me like that."

"Why?"

I threw my hands in the air. "What about all you said about my trust issues . . . and not believing in you?"

"We can talk about all that. I might have been blowing those things out of proportion. We just really need to have a decent conversation—"

I gasped and pointed at him again. "Rhonda told you that."

He shrugged. "I had a talk with her this morning. It turns out Rhonda has some pretty good insight into relationships. She also said she'd kick my ass if I didn't fix this."

"But Grady . . ." I scrambled to try to put my thoughts together. "My life is in Chicago."

He stepped toward me again. I stepped back . . . but he just stepped forward again! "You've been telling me that

Chicago's not your home. That you feel disconnected there."

That was true. I had said that. "But where would I live? The retreat? With my mom?"

"There are other options . . ." he began with a shrug.

"No, don't even say it." I pointed at him again sharply. "We are not there . . . yet."

"We'll figure it out," he said, reaching for my good hand. "I don't care what it takes."

I snatched my hand away. "My job! What would I do here?"

Grady inhaled deeply. "You . . . you could work with Freddie."

"What!"

"I know what the town's paying him." He shook his head. "And Honey Cove has even expressed some interest in Otter Lake Security, but . . . never mind that right now. That point is he can afford to take you on. Or partner with you. He needs a partner. Too much power isn't good for him."

"Did you hit your head on the Ferris wheel?" I asked, tipping up his hat. "I can't believe you're saying this."

"It would have to be different, though. One of you needs to work toward getting a private investigator license or something . . . and you need to work with Rhonda and me, not against us."

"This is nuts."

"No. What's nuts is you leaving again." He reached out to touch my face.

"Grady, I—"

"Erica!" a voice screamed. "Stop them!"

Both Grady and I turned to see who had yelled just as three teenage boys zoomed by us on the dock, nearly knocking us to the water.

Three boys wearing pumpkin heads.

"Erica!"

I looked past Grady to see Freddie running toward us.

"Stop them! They've got my keys!"

My head whipped back around to *Lightning*. Yup, all three boys had jumped in. A moment later the boat roared to life, *Miami Vice* theme song blaring.

Freddie slowed his run to a stop as he reached us. "*Lightning!*"

Grady stepped back toward the parking lot, bringing his shoulder walkie-talkie to his mouth. "I'll get Rhonda on it."

"Don't pretend like you're not happy about this, Forrester!" Freddie shouted with a wicked point.

Grady put his hands up as he continued to back away, the tiniest gleam of *something* in his eyes.

Freddie and I turned back to the water, eyes on the fading trail of yellow zipping across the lake.

Freddie's eyes turned to mine. "Do you think they'll hurt her?"

"No, no," I said, tearing my eyes away to pat him on the shoulder. "It's probably just a joyride."

His shoulders dropped a little. "Okay. You're right. But . . . but is it just me . . . or are they getting too close to the shore?"

My head whipped back around. Oh . . . oh, no. They were getting a little close.

"Erica? Erica! They're going too fast!"

"They're losing control! Bail!" I shouted across the lake, hands by the sides of my mouth. "Bail!"

Just then the three boys jumped off the boat right before a god-awful crack ripped across the lake.

"Oh my God!" I yelled, clutching Freddie's arm. "Are they okay?"

Grady ran up beside us. "One . . . two . . . and there's

three," he said, pointing out the heads bobbing in the water. "I . . . I think they're good, but I'll let Rhonda know. She's almost there." I saw the police boat coming from across the lake.

Freddie's eyes slowly turned to mine. "Tell me that did not just happen."

I looked back at the scene. Yup, *Lightning* had run right up on the shore. It looked . . . as though she might have even landed in a tree.

Grady turned away again to talk into his radio again.

"It never could have lasted," I tried. "Not really."

Freddie didn't move.

"She was too good for this lake. For all of us."

"Oh, just stop it!" Freddie yelled. "You never loved her!"

"I . . . I liked her! We were working our way toward something like lo—"

"Stop it. Just stop—" He snapped his mouth shut, eyes darting over my shoulder.

I turned. Grady had his arms out to Freddie . . . open for a hug?

"It's not her fault, Freddie. She just doesn't understand," he said, waving him in with his fingers. "To her she was just a machine."

"That's not—" I stopped myself. "Actually that's a pretty accurate statement."

Freddie froze for a moment then shuffled over to Grady's embrace. Grady patted him on the back . . . a little awkwardly . . . but patted nonetheless. Freddie, on the other hand, had his arms wrapped tightly around Grady, head against his chest.

A moment later, he looked over to me and mumbled, "You're going to have to find another ride to the bus stop. I can't even . . ."

"It's okay," I said, flashing my eyes back to Grady.

He was looking at me from over Freddie's head, smile on his face.

"I don't know that I'm in that much of a hurry after all."

Coming soon. . .

Don't miss the next novel in the delightful
Otter Lake mystery series

Snowed IN *With* MURDER

Available in February 2017
from St. Martin's Paperbacks